FIGHTING BACK

SCARLETT FINN

Also by Scarlett Finn

GO NOVELS
GO WITH IT
GO IT ALONE
GO ALL OUT
GO ALL IN
GO FULL CIRCLE

MCDADE BROTHERS NOVELS
ALL. ONLY.
ONLY YOURS

WRECK & RUIN
RUIN ME
RUIN HIM

THE BRANDED SERIES
BRANDED
SCARRED
MARKED

EXILE
HIDE & SEEK
KISS CHASE

TO DIE FOR...
TO DIE FOR TRUTH
TO DIE FOR HONOR
TO DIE FOR VIRTUE
TO DIE FOR DUTY
TO DIE FOR LOVE

LOVE AGAINST THE ODDS STANDALONE COLLECTION
SWEET SEAS
HEIR'S AFFAIR
RESCUED
MAESTRO'S MUSE
GETTING TRICKY
THIRTEEN
REMEMBER WHEN...
RELUCTANT SUSPICION
XY FACTOR

NOTHING TO...
NOTHING TO HIDE
NOTHING TO LOSE
NOTHING TO DECLARE
NOTHING TO US
NOTHING TO SAY
NOTHING TO YOU

KINDRED SERIES
RAVEN
SWALLOW
CUCKOO
SWIFT
FALCON
FINCH

THE EXPLICIT SERIES
EXPLICIT INSTRUCTION
EXPLICIT DETAIL
EXPLICIT MEMORY

MISTAKE DUET
MISTAKE ME NOT
SLEIGHT MISTAKE

RISQUÉ & HARROW INTERTWINED
TAKE A RISK
FIGHTING FATE
RISK IT ALL
FIGHTING BACK
GAME OF RISK

LOST & FOUND
LOST
FOUND

THE FORBIDDEN NOVELS
FORBIDDEN DESIRE
FORBIDDEN WANT
FORBIDDEN WISH
FORBIDDEN NEED

ONE

FOR WEEKS, the Stark family and everyone else from Dax's former life were in his rearview. That changed fast. Standing in the parking lot of the apartment building he and Ivy lived in, he'd been talking to Blaser, his new friend and boss, when Ivy's hand landed on his abs. His wife could cop a feel any time she wanted, but pleasure wasn't her motivation, she wasn't even looking at him.

Following her line of sight to find what had her transfixed, he was stunned to see a long black limo on the perimeter. Everyone else in the parking lot fixated on the mystery vehicle too. Except it wasn't a mystery. Not to him. That car was there for him. Such a show of opulence meant only one thing: the Starks had come to town.

His assumption was proven correct when the driver got out and rounded the vehicle to open the back door. Brad Stark emerged, buttoning his suit jacket, Dax in his sights. Did he have to make such a fucking show? Despising being any part of a spectacle, he crossed the parking lot to put an end to it.

Still shielded by the open limo door, Brad stood with his head held high, proud of the garish display. Yeah, he loved it while Dax hated it, but he wouldn't let that show. Why give him the satisfaction? Sauntering up, Dax paid no attention to the chauffeur standing at the head of the open door and came to a stop. With the car door in between them, he waited for Brad to explain himself.

"Care to take a ride?" Brad asked, without removing his sunglasses.

Since tracking Ivy down at the garage out back around a month ago, they'd lived in the building managed by the same guy who owned the garage. The gathering of residents outside were Brad's weapon. Making a scene wasn't part of his agenda, Brad knew that so had his request granted with a single nod. The driver moved aside to let him follow Brad into the car, then closed the door behind them.

Dax chose the seat opposite Brad, his back to the screen covered driver's area. Neither of them spoke until the car got moving.

"You need to come home," Brad said.

"If that's why you're here, save your breath and your gas," Dax said. "The answer is no."

"I didn't ask. I told you, you're coming home."

"What are you going to do? Drive me to the airport? Sorry, no ID."

"Brought a jet, it's waiting on a private airstrip."

His first thought was for Ivy. If he got on a jet with Brad, California would be their destination. If he didn't get on the jet, Brad would keep coming until he got his way. His wife could get caught in the crossfire. Just because he would end up complying with the request didn't mean he would give up without a fight.

"You have to give me something, a reason," Dax said. "You and Tryst miss me so bad that you had to chase me down?"

Brad and Trystan Stark were Maurice Stark's sons. They had been sort of surrogate brothers to him through the years. Sort of. There was more sibling rivalry than love or support.

"Mauri wants to see you, it's important."

"Sure it is," Dax said. "I told you I didn't give a fuck and that hasn't changed. I'm not interested in Maurice Stark, or you and your brother anymore."

"Still with Dune?"

"It's Harrow," Dax said, correcting Brad's use of Ivy's maiden name.

"Oh, that's right, you married the woman you were supposed to be training for Trystan… You're lucky he didn't kill you for that stunt."

In a different environment, Dax might have laughed. "If he wants to start something, he obviously knows where I am. Tell him to come visit. Ivy might even cook."

The little prick's balls on a skillet. Still counted, right?

"You are still with her," Brad said. "Serg said you were, but I've got to say, I didn't believe it."

Serg was one of Mauri's henchmen and a one-time close associate of his. "We're married," Dax said. "You think I'd have fucked around on the family if I wasn't sure she was the only female I wanted?"

"Do you want us to pick her up? She can join us on the trip."

"I haven't said I'm going anywhere yet," he said, clenching his jaw.

Maurice Stark exuded arrogance, he was a superior sonofabitch who taught his sons to be the same way. Brad managed it with eminence and authority, Dax did it with aloof indifference, and the youngest, Trystan, used overt ostentatious glitz to show the world he was better than everyone in it.

Truth be told, Dax wasn't like the other two, he was an unofficially adopted Stark. When he was a kid, he'd been caught in the act of picking Mauri's pocket. Instead of punishing him, Mauri took him home to be raised by the household staff.

At least that was the story Dax had been raised to believe for all of his thirty-three years, until Ivy Dune came in and turned his life on its head. After her, he started to ask questions of himself, he rebelled against who the Starks had conditioned him to be. In the process, Mauri revealed some truths he'd rather not know.

"Bruno bet money you wouldn't come," Brad said. "I took the bet. I knew as soon as you heard he'd bet on you being a coward, you'd leap onto a plane."

Finding out that Bruno, Mauri's contemporary and right-hand man, was his real father and the real reason that Mauri had taken pity on him as a kid, made him sick to his stomach. Grinding his teeth, he sought distraction in the world sweeping past the window.

"Why'd they send you?" Dax asked, still not tempted to return to the Golden State.

"Can't trust Tryst to do anything," Brad said. "The kid flipped out after you left and went on a binge. Mauri got Serg to track him down and drag him back to the mansion. He's been pretty much locked up since."

"He'll be loving that," Dax muttered.

Despite there only being a few months age difference between him and Trystan, he referred to Trystan as a child. The little prick still acted like a kid in a candy store as soon as drugs and sex were on offer.

"Mauri wants you back. Serg's been watching you, we sent him ahead, so he could give us the skinny on what you've been doing. Working security at that strip joint, Risqué? Got your wife answering phones at an auto garage? Come on, you know you're worth more than this. Come home."

"Why? To jump back into enforcing? You want me running the operation again?"

"No one did it better."

"I have a life here, a wife."

"We're not asking you to leave her behind, bring her. You can stay in the mansion together or move into your old place, I know you haven't sold it yet."

"Been a little busy."

"Then it all works out," Brad said, opening his arms. "If you're planning on living here, you'll need to come back home to sell your apartment. You'll need to pack up and move, right? You can stay in the mansion while you do that."

Sitting forward, Dax propped his elbows on his knees and looked Brad square in his eyes. "If you think that I'm going to trust you cock-sucking perverts anywhere near my wife—"

"Ivy's safe," Brad said and sighed in his typical condescending way.

Brad retrieved a bottle of water from the fridge like the objections bored him. Dax snatched the bottle and tossed it to the floor. Disrespect was the greatest enemy. The men stared each other down until Brad relented and spoke to reinforce his declaration.

"Mauri has told everyone to accept her as your wife. All the guys know it, so she's safe."

Mauri's word was absolute, but Dax didn't trust Brad any more than the motherfucker trusted him. "Like when you tried to take her from me at the beach house?" Dax asked, Brad's bottom lip twitched. "You came to that party and tried to get her to leave with you. What was that about?"

"Good old-fashioned double cross," Brad said. "Trystan wanted her, you had her, I was curious what all the fuss was about… I also had to test her obedience, to see how dependent on you she had become."

"And were you surprised?"

"That she refused? No," Brad said. "But I didn't see the love. I didn't see how dependent you'd become on her. You two played a good game."

Dax wasn't interested in impressing Brad. "Why now? Why should I come back when—"

"He's sick, Mauri is sick… We should've figured it out when he pulled that trick about Tryst marrying Ivy, he's known for months. It's cancer, stage four, inoperable, he's got about four months."

Wiping a hand over his mouth, he sat back. Much as Mauri pissed him off during the Ivy situation, he was the closest thing Dax had to a father. No one wanted to receive news like this about family.

His hand slid off his thigh to seek out its mate, its partner, except it wasn't there because his wife wasn't present.

Ivy had become his support. Without her here, he was lost as to the appropriate way to react.

"He wants to say goodbye?" Dax asked.

Mauri wasn't exactly the sentimental type, but Dax had grown up listening to the man talk. Mauri counselled him on everything from girls to his fighting technique. The world wouldn't be any worse off with one less crime boss in it, but he would be worse off without his mentor.

"He wants to settle old debts," Brad said. "Least that's what I think, he wouldn't give me details... Since you left, he hasn't been the same. I know he's not happy with the way things ended. Come back, hear him out. Say goodbye to the man who made you who you are."

He could refuse, but then he'd never know what Mauri wanted. "Okay," Dax conceded. "Take me back to the apartments, we'll leave in the morning."

"We can go right now. We'll get you on a plane and Serg can pick up—"

"Ivy won't go anywhere with anyone except me. She's a clever girl and my responsibility. She doesn't trust you bastards any more than I do, which is why she won't leave my side for a second. Take me home and come back in the morning."

"If you're just picking her up then why—"

"She doesn't jump at anyone's command. She'll need time to warm up to the idea of going back to the family who tried to take over her life."

That was an understatement. Ivy's love for him was real. If he made a big enough deal of it, she would support him in anything. But going back to California, back to the family who had nearly torn them apart... that would take some persuasion.

TWO

IVY PUT THE LAST PLATE in the kitchen cabinet and glanced at the clock on the wall. Brad Stark coming back into their lives spelled trouble, no two ways about it. He'd crossed the width of the country to seek Dax out. The Starks were serious about wanting him back. It couldn't be anything else, there was no other reason for Brad to be there.

If Trystan showed up, he'd have been hellbent on revenge. Brad wasn't so shallow; he did his father's bidding not his dirty work. If Maurice Stark wanted harm to come to her or Dax, minions would do it for him.

The image of Dax entering that car without looking back was imprinted on the inside of her eyelids, which was why she'd kept herself busy cleaning up their apartment.

Their new life was good, they were making friends, adjusting to life in their fresh environment. Dax had even found himself a couple of fights. Much as she didn't like to see him come home bloodied, his love of the underground circuit was a part of who he was.

With Brad back and Dax willing to hear him out, their lives could be disrupted. If their new friends asked questions, answers wouldn't be easy to give.

Wiping down the kitchen counters, she reminded herself how far Dax had come. Maybe he'd tell Brad to go to hell. If he did, there would be a major reward in it for him.

The living-kitchen area of their home ran the width the apartment, windows flanked the door. A narrow corridor at the rear led to the bathroom and bedroom. There wasn't much left to clean up, keeping her mind off Dax was growing harder by the second.

The front door opened. Oh thank God. It was so difficult not to yelp in response to the relief that overcame her. Coming home so soon, when she'd half expected him to be gone for days, was a good sign. Going to the fridge to retrieve the dinner steaks, she'd be happy to forget ever casting her eyes on Brad again.

"I got these from a place Bri recommended," she said of their female neighbor who she'd become friends with.

"That's it?" Dax asked.

He came up behind her and slid a hand over her hip while the other scooped her hair out of his way. His warm lips touched the artery pulsing in her neck. Ignoring him, she carried on seasoning the steaks.

"The butcher is supposed to be amazing. The guys at the garage were jealous when I said I'd picked them up, and for what they cost…"

The hand on her hip carried on around to her belly, his other skimmed down her arm, and he pried her fingers away from the knife she'd just picked up.

"Dax," she whined. When he unbuttoned her shorts, she smiled. "You have to be at the club in an hour, and I have to feed you before—"

"I stopped at Blaser's before I came up, he's giving us some time off."

"For a belated honeymoon?" she asked, coiling her arm around her body to slip his belt from its restraining loops. "Somewhere hot and far away from these shores?"

"Actually, yeah, that's one way to look at it. How does California sound?"

"Like my idea of hell," she said, withdrawing her hand before it got to the good stuff. "You're not much of a comedian, tough guy."

"I'm not kidding. We're going to California tomorrow."

"Oh no we're not," she said.

"We are."

With her hands on the counter, she used all of her weight to push her body back into his, giving her space to escape. After shoving him aside, she went to the sink and washed her hands, fighting to subdue the strength of her reaction.

Tossing the towel aside, she turned to face him. "You're going back to them?"

"We," he said, trying to encroach on her, but she removed herself from his path and headed into the living room.

"I am not going back to Maurice Stark. What about Trystan?"

"What about him?" Dax asked, his face set in a frown. "You're not afraid of him, you're not fucking afraid of anyone."

"It's the fucking part that I stick on. You didn't tell me about what happened the night you walked away. At that midnight meeting. I can guarantee no one floated their congratulations, did they?"

"Maurice has taken care of it," Dax said. "Brad told me that Maurice has told everyone about us and told them to keep their hands off you."

"Oh well if Brad told you, I guess it's okay."

"Why would he lie?"

"Why would he tell the truth?" she demanded. "And Bruno, what about him?"

His eyes went one way, his chin went up and his tongue darted out to moisten half of his top lip. She didn't like that tell, not one little bit.

"Forget about him." Dax spoke in his company voice, in that blunt, intimidating tone, then stalked over to the living room window. None of his actions encouraged reassurance.

"There's too much going on that you haven't told me about," she said. "I can't go back there."

"I can't leave you here. If they want to divide us, me going to California leaves you wide open."

"I thought you just said Maurice had taken care of things for us. Either you trust the guy, or you don't."

"Fine, if you want to stay here, stay here," he said.

Whipping around, he began to march toward the bedroom, but she hurried over to block the head of the hallway. "You do still trust him? How can you—"

Grabbing her arm, he tried to wrench her aside. "Maurice never lied to me," Dax said.

She got hold of him to keep herself in his way. "Maurice didn't tell you that he took care of it, Brad told you he did. Do you trust him?"

"Brad? No. I don't trust that bastard."

"Then why should we get on a plane with him?" she asked, reaching up to cup his cheek. "He's manipulating you. Whatever he wants you to do, it can't be worth the risk, can it?"

"He doesn't want me to do anything, Maurice wants to see me."

"Then he can get his ass on a plane and come here," she said, not wild about having Maurice Stark sniffing around in their new life.

"He can't get on a plane."

"Why not? Is immigration looking for him?" Her joke fell on deaf ears. He tried to look away again, so she slapped her other palm onto his other cheek. "What aren't you telling me? How did Brad upset you like this?"

"He's sick."

"Brad?"

Dax shook his head. "Mauri is sick, he's only got a few months."

Lowering from her tiptoes, her hands fell away. In the same moment they lost eye contact, he put a hand on her elbow to move her aside. She let him walk away from her. If

Maurice Stark was sick, it was understandable that Dax wanted to go see him. He had acted as a father to Dax, and Dax had always respected him.

Letting go of his relationship with Mauri was the hardest part of Dax's decision to be with her. Something had happened at the midnight meeting on the night he left the Stark mansion for good. He had never told her about it, but she suspected more had been exchanged than her husband wanted to confess.

Mauri had thoroughly trained Dax to follow his orders without question. For twenty years, that was exactly what Dax did… until he got entangled with her.

Heading for the bedroom, she found him packing things into an open suitcase that lay on the bed. "Devil's advocate," she said, "what if this is all a ruse just to get you back there?"

"You're not playing devil's anything," he replied. "You're your own advocate."

"Do you blame me? The last time I was with them—"

"Nothing evil happened, I kept you safe."

"Yeah, the days I spent in the beach house basement were a ball, and Bruno—"

"You don't have to worry about him," Dax said, zipping the partially filled case. "And I promised you wouldn't spend a night in that basement again, didn't I? We're going to my apartment in the city, you don't have to go anywhere near the Starks."

"You know it won't work out that way," she said. "I want to support you. We can't show them weakness, we have to be united, or they'll jump all over it and use it to their advantage."

"So what's your problem?" he asked. "You don't trust me? You think I'll hand you over to them if they ask?"

"You tried that before," she said.

"I didn't do it."

"No, you let me walk out of your apartment and we were separated for seven weeks."

"I stood up to them, that's what happened at the midnight meeting. I told them to go to hell, that I wanted nothing to do with them."

"They obviously didn't believe you," she said. "Otherwise, why are they here?"

"Mauri knew he was sick, he's known for a while, but he didn't tell anyone. It's part of the reason he wanted to see Trystan settled before he…"

Dax wouldn't break down; he wouldn't reveal how losing Mauri would affect him. Mauri had been the only consistent man in his life. Mauri was the man that Dax respected above all others. She couldn't ask him not to go. She could only hope it was true and that it wasn't some elaborate plan to hurt them again.

"Did Bruno know?"

"I don't know."

Fixated on the case, he balled his fists at his sides, which was the closest Dax would get to telling her he was upset. Crossing the room, she rubbed his back and pressed her lips to the dragon tattooed on his arm.

"If you want to go, we'll go," she said. "But don't forget what I said to you at the garage."

"This is my last chance," he said, bringing his eyes to hers. "If I fuck this up, you'll leave me?"

"I'm getting used to you being the only man allowed to touch me. If Bruno or Trystan lay their hands on me again—"

"Listen to me," he said. Twisting the quarter turn to face her, he took hold of her upper arms. "I know you won't admit to being scared; you won't give an inch. That stubborn, willful front of yours—"

"Uh, Kettle? Pot is calling."

"I am not going to let them hurt you."

"And how do I make you the same promise?" she asked. "They're hurting you already and most of them are still a continent away."

"I've been dealing with the Starks and their crew for twenty years, I can handle them now."

"You dealt with them while you were working with them, you were all on the same side. Neither is true anymore. What if they set you up with Rita or Fifi or—"

"Other women? You have nothing to worry about, and you know it. I won't bow to their pressure. We're solid, babygirl. We've been together almost five months, and the way I feel about you hasn't changed. In that garage I told you I wouldn't let you escape again; you made your choice my prison or theirs."

"Did you really think you were holding me against my will? Did you doubt how I felt about you?"

"I was used to Mauri being the one to tell me how it was. When he told me you were using me, it was easier to believe that and maintain the status quo than it was to believe you."

"Because I wanted to wreck your entire world."

With his index fingers, he touched her temples and traced down to move her hair back over her shoulders. "Which I don't think I ever thanked you for," he said.

"Thanked me?" she asked. "You're pleased that I…"

"That we got together, yeah, I'm damn pleased about that."

"Good, maybe you won't fuck it up this time," she said. "If we get to a point where you have to make a choice, I'd appreciate it if you let me know if that choice involves dropping me."

"Not gonna happen," he said, pulling her body into his to hold her in his arms.

"I should just ask you for a divorce now," she said, her lips squashed into his torso.

"That's not gonna happen either… You want me to pack for you?"

"No," she said, pushing out of his arms and bending to unzip the case. "If I let you pack for me, all I'll end up with is lingerie and flip-flops."

"I trust you to handle it," he said, smacking her ass. "I'll get the steaks on."

He left the room, and she flipped open the case, staring down at his strewn clothes. Going back to California and the Starks was going to test them as individuals and a couple. Passing that test wasn't guaranteed.

THREE

DAX RELEASED THE CALIFORNIA apartment door, and it dropped back into the frame. A few feet in front of him, Ivy expelled a breath that made her body sag. Coming back to California might be a huge mistake. Maybe. Mauri knew everything there was to know about Dax's past. If he ever wanted to find out who his mother was or how she ended up with Bruno, Mauri was his only hope to get that information.

Bruno couldn't stand him, and the animosity was mutual. If Dax tried to open communication, Bruno would use the opportunity to taunt him. The information wouldn't be trustworthy either, so what would be the point?

Ivy didn't go further into the apartment, she just stood in the entryway. Putting down the suitcase, he curled his hands around her shoulders and squeezed. During the flight, she hadn't said a word and he'd done his best not to talk to Brad either. Serg was on the flight as well. During the whole surreal experience, pretending to be buddies or happy in each other's company was more than any of them could fake.

Serg used to be his number two, so he used that lingering façade of authority to question his former colleague on the other men and the state of the operation. Ivy kept her attention out of the window, her scowl fixed on the clouds outside the aircraft. He caught Serg glancing at her with either confusion or concern throughout the journey. The sentiment couldn't reach too deep. After all, Serg had been sent to spy on them and report back to Brad. Serg's loyalty went as deep as his master's pockets.

Alone in his California apartment, he could put her at ease. Kissing her head, he bent his knees and traced his lips down her neck to her shoulder. Nudging the strap of her dress away with his chin, he insinuated his hand around to peel back her dress to expose one breast, which he quickly took into his palm.

The weight in his groin increased but when he tried to turn her toward the bedroom, she wouldn't move. Was this some other marital tradition he didn't know? He bent intending to scoop her up, but she pushed him off and walked away. Goddamn woman.

"I can get rid of that scowl if you loosen up," he said.

Being short with her probably wasn't fair. Her nerves were expected, but he was sick of seeing her spitting fury.

She went into the living room, so he followed. When she got into the middle of the space, she spun around, opening her arms. From that distance it was tough to tell, but he was sure her lower lashes were barricading a line of unshed tears. Shit. Crying was so unlike her that his own eyes widened, and he took a step back. How the hell did he…? Quelling his urge to retreat, he swallowed his discomfort and told himself to stay put, don't run like a pussy, it was just a few lousy tears.

"The last time we were here… I walked away, Dax. You wanted me to walk away from you."

He had refused the invite to the Stark mansion because he thought that coming back to the apartment would be better for her. Safe from the Starks. He hadn't taken account of their past. This place was safe from others, but not safe from their demons.

"You want to check into a hotel?"

Tipping her chin toward the ceiling, she sighed. "Forget it."

"No," he said. "What do you want me to do? If you don't want to be here, we'll go somewhere else."

"You don't give a fuck?" she asked. "You really don't think about what happened between us here?"

"I think about what happened in the bedroom," he said.

"No, you don't," she said, shaking her head. "Because when we had sex in there you thought it was the last time we'd ever be intimate. You were going to turn me over to them."

"But I didn't, did I?"

"No, you didn't," she said, going to the window. "I'm sorry, I know… I know, I need to get over this." Pulling the band out of her hair, she flicked it around her wrist in an expert move and ran her hands through her long, luxurious locks. "Okay."

"Okay, what?" he asked.

Ivy was an incredible woman, the best he'd met, but she was still a woman. One that often left him at a loss about what was going on in her head.

"Okay," she said, turning away from the window. "Just okay." Hooking her thumbs under the straps of her dress, she pulled it down, wiggling out of her panties in the same maneuver. "Come over here and fuck me."

If that was a power play, it worked. He didn't care she'd refused him in the hallway, not now she stood in his living room completely naked asking for action.

Shirking out of his clothes on his walk to her, he swooped down to pick her up. She coiled her legs around his waist and welcomed his mouth.

He started to take her to the couch, she broke their kiss and patted his shoulders. "No, there," she said, pointing at the window she'd been looking out of a moment before.

Glancing at that spot and then back at her, he arched a brow. "You want me to fuck you against the window when it's broad daylight outside?"

"There's a curtain over it," she said.

The flimsy gauze wouldn't endure the experience or conceal it either.

Still, he didn't care. Whatever her reasoning, he'd still get his.

She squealed and arched her body into his when her back touched the cold glass separated from her flesh by only the sheer material of the curtain. The investment in heat reflecting glass and the expensive air-conditioning in the apartment had been worth it, she couldn't get any closer unless she crawled inside his skin.

"You want to put on a show, Minx?" he asked, avoiding her mouth when she tried to kiss him again.

Now that he had her propped on the glass, he could free his hand and curled it around her chin to push her head as far back as it could go. The strained column of her throat brought heat to the weight hanging in his groin. Damn, his wife was fucking how. Licking the length of her gullet, he kissed his way back down, boosting her weight higher. Her knees closed on his ribs, her chest level with his mouth.

Closing his lips around her nipple, he hummed his approval. The vibration brought an exhale of want from her lips. He knew that sound. Damn, he loved that sound. That wasn't the only pleasure she had to give. The well of her moisture building on his torso between her legs proved, as always, it didn't take much to get her going. Keeping her chin up, he kissed the dark peaks of her breasts and rubbed his face between them.

His wife's cans could get a guy hard from twenty feet away, he'd caught glimpses of it happening. Only he was allowed this close. Possessing her was more of a turn on than the actual taste of her. This was his, she was his, and he wouldn't let any guy threaten that again.

"Dax," she whispered, tightening her legs, wriggling against him.

With his hands under her thighs, he backed off enough to let her body slide down the glass, straining the flimsy curtain at her back.

"You want something, Minx?"

"Only you."

This time, she kissed him. The plunge of her tongue on his gave him the impetus to ease his hips away. With a guiding hand, he surged forward, pushing his cock into her. Her kiss froze to release a breathy squeak, curling his lips.

Taking over the kiss, he fucked his way into her. Grabbing her hips, he tilted them to slam himself in deeper, working her clit at the same time. Her nails, her arms, her need to cling betrayed her want. The circle of her arms around his neck got tighter, crushing her breasts into him. Fuck, yeah.

When he withdrew, she eased back but the head of his cock never left her. She pitched forward matching his fervor with her own. Ivy Harrow didn't fuck around when it came to fulfilling herself.

The closer to orgasm she got, the faster and shorter her breathing became. Her head thumped back against the window, the kiss forgotten, her lips only moved to utter words of impending bliss. Fuck, she did things to him no other woman ever did before.

Driving on, he sped up, locking her pelvis on the glass, anchoring her for deeper penetration.

Pounding into the slippery passageway only open to him, he drove in, smacking the head of his dick deep. That sweet meeting spot where their bodies dovetailed together gave his life purpose. He'd never wanted a woman as much as he did her. Every time he slid into her was a gift, one he wouldn't give up.

Gasping his name, she cursed and began to quake around him, squeezing his dick so tight he couldn't move. To prevent himself from calling out, he locked his jaw while she milked the burst of his seed for every last drop, wringing him dry.

This was the first of many. He planned to continue fucking her for the rest of the day, into the night until she'd forgotten all about what happened the last time they occupied this apartment.

With her open palms, she lifted his head from where it rested on hers to look him in the eye. "Stranger," she said, still panting.

"What?"

She smoothed his hair away from his forehead. "I won't let them have you. I won't let them take you away from this, I promise."

There he was worried about her feeling like she was losing control of their relationship. All the time, she was formulating ways to hold onto him.

"I'm going nowhere, babygirl."

Sliding out of her body, he carried her to the couch and laid her down then stood up to examine her flushed skin. Her neck was reddened where his stubble burned her. The rest of her was still in the midst of a fever from their union.

Her hand rested on her abdomen; his eye caught on the diamond. Kneeling beside her, he picked up her hand and kissed the stone. He'd never considered marriage before Ivy. The women in his past were never around long enough for him to develop any kind of feelings. Back then, his dedication was to the Starks and that had been enough for him.

"You're not with me," she said, sitting up to run her fingers into his hair again. "You get that glare on your face, and I know that you're thinking about Mauri. Are you worried about losing him?"

"I worry about what he'll take with him," Dax said, sticking an arm under her legs, he lifted them to sit on the couch underneath. Dropping onto his side, he laid his spine along the back of the couch and kept Ivy angled against him. "And about what will happen to the organization when he's not around."

"You still care about that? About the Stark name?"

"Sure," he said. "It's instinct I guess."

"What will happen? Brad is going to take over, right?"

"He should, least that's what Brad's always thought," he said, fondling her breast.

"You don't think he will?"

Dax shrugged and slid lower to suck her nipple into a tight pebble. "Bruno won't just roll over; Brad won't give him the same respect that Mauri does."

"What about Trystan?"

"He's already pissed," Dax said. "After we left, he apparently went off on a crazy bender. Mauri's had him locked up in the mansion."

"Do you think they've…? Is there another woman for him? Has someone been abducted to take my place?"

"Maybe," Dax said, having not considered that. "It's a possibility, but…"

"But?"

"It didn't work with you. Maybe Mauri re-thought their approach. I don't know. I'll find out when I go over there."

"Which will be when?" she asked.

In time with her question, his cellphone rang.

The post-coital intimacy was shattered, and her expression cooled.

"It could be nothing," he said.

Extricating himself from their snug position, he climbed off the couch to snag his jeans from the middle of the room.

Retrieving the phone from his pocket, he recognized the number and answered. "Hello?"

"Come over to the house," Brad said down the phone line. "Mauri wants you to join him for dinner."

"I'm having dinner with my wife, thanks."

"Bring her," Brad said. "Mauri's invited you both."

"No, I'm not bringing her over there. Sitting around the table as a happy family is a crock of shit. If Mauri wants to see me, I'll come over, just me, for a sit down with him. I think we have a lot to talk about and we don't need you bastards listening in."

"Okay," Brad said.

He hadn't gone away to check anything with Mauri. The old man wasn't dead yet and wouldn't like Brad speaking for him. That meant either Dax was on speakerphone and Mauri was right there, or Mauri knew Dax would tell him where to stick his dinner invitation. He'd put money on the latter, Mauri wasn't the type to skulk.

"I'll be over in less than an hour."

"You're eager," Brad said. "For a guy who didn't want to come at all."

"Eager to get it over with," Dax said. "Tell Mauri to be ready."

Hanging up, he put his phone on the dining table, between they door and the open plan kitchen.

Ivy sat up on the couch. "You're going over there?"

"Yeah. Mauri wants to talk."

"I have to shower," she said, rising from the couch to head for the bedroom.

"You're not coming," he said, getting between her and the living room door.

"Why did I come all this way? I won't sit here cowering. I remember exactly what happened the last time you left me here and went over to that house."

She expected this to play out as it had before. He'd been a dick to her then. He'd departed the apartment secure in their relationship, in a playful mood after leaving her aroused and unsated. By the time he'd gotten back, to find her asleep in his bed, he'd been convinced she had played him just to ensure her freedom.

"Babygirl, things are different now. They're not going to convince me you don't love me now, are they?"

"I'm not afraid of them," she said, her defiant eyes narrowing on his. "If they want a fight—"

"You go in there looking for a fight and you'll create one. You need to be cool."

"Act natural?"

"Yeah," he said.

"After all they've done?" she asked. "I don't think so."

"If they hadn't caught you in Vegas, this wouldn't have happened. We wouldn't have happened," he said, dropping an arm around her shoulders and pulling her in close to kiss her.

"I know," she exhaled onto him when he lifted his lips. "That doesn't mean they should get away with their bullshit, does it?"

Her anger was understandable; the Starks hadn't treated her well.

The vehemence in her tone concerned him so much he backed off. "Payback? Is that why you came? You're gonna go on some crazy vengeance spree?"

"Why would vengeance be crazy?" she asked. "You told me it's what Trystan thrives on."

"Yeah, and look how that turned out for him," Dax said, clutching her forearm when she tried to back off. "You listen to me, Mrs. Harrow, I take care of the lowlifes, okay? If there's a score to settle that's my damn job. You keep your sexy ass right here at home. You cook, you clean, you suck my cock, that's your job."

"Don't," she said, twisting her arm out of his grip. "I know you like to think reminding me of that chauvinistic misogynist you played in the beach house will calm me down—"

"That's too many big words for a simple guy like me, Minx."

"Stop it," she said.

This depth of anger from her hadn't reared its head for a while, not since the last time they were there.

Grabbing her wrists, he thrust them behind her back as he rushed her against the wall. Switching both wrists into one hand, he used the other to snatch her jaw and hold her head up.

"Do you prefer the alternative?" he asked, giving her a shake when she tried to wrestle away.

Eventually she surrendered to his grip, she had no chance of physically overpowering him, they both knew it. Ideas of revenge contorted her expression. Why the fuck hadn't he seen it before?

"Let go of me," she growled.

"If you don't want to play, I have no choice, I've got to be serious. You prefer this? You're not going to miss my point now."

Squeezing her jaw, Dax forced her lips to part. His goal was to prevent her clenching her jaw in response to the fury that scalded her veins. But the temptation his action presented was too much to resist. He dipped his tongue into her mouth, pushing his kiss onto her. When he withdrew, he dragged his teeth over her bottom lip.

"Get your filthy fucking hands off me," she mumbled.

Damn if she didn't get his dick hard all over again. "You're mine to touch," he said. "You belong to me."

"I'm your partner, not your possession, and you are not leaving me here alone."

"I am. If I have to lash you to the wall, I will," he said. "I can't trust you now. When you get it in your head you want to start something, I'm the one who has to finish it. You see my dilemma?"

"You don't trust me," she said, trying again to writhe free of his control.

Consuming her mouth again, he kept going until she returned his kiss with the energy of the hatred she wanted to rain down on the Starks. In his opinion, this was a far healthier way to get rid of that venom.

Pulling her away from the wall, neither broke the kiss on their spinning journey toward the dining table. Anything they came into contact with clattered to the floor, but he didn't care about objects. He cared about the pain this woman had suffered. His woman. The pain had thrust her into a frenzy of unhealthy anger that could get her hurt if he let her release it elsewhere.

Shoving her face down onto the table, he pressed her skull with the weight of his own. Her hair covered her face and fluttered out with each huffing breath she took. One of her cheeks was squashed into the table, he kissed the other through her hair, then her temple, and kissed above her ear before he spoke, resting his forehead on her soft hair, pinning her so she couldn't squirm away from him.

"I own you, babygirl. You're still my goddamn prisoner, and I will punish anyone who hurts you."

"No," she said, trying to look at him, but his weight locked her down. "I fight my own battles."

"I told you," he said, tightening his grip on her wrists, her chest was crushed to the table, but he kept her arms there too, opposite the way she faced. Forcing her legs further apart with his own, he pushed a finger into her still wet center and began to work it in circles. "You'll never have to fear enemies while you're under my claim."

"You haven't claimed anything, tough guy," she spat out, working her hips against his invading digit.

When he snagged her earlobe in his teeth, she whimpered out her arousal and consent.

"I claim this body. Your mind and your fire are mine too," he whispered, then slammed his dick into her again.

This time, she screamed through her gritted teeth and the primal roar made him smile. This would release her frustration. If she wanted him to plan an attack on those who wronged her, he'd do that for her too.

FOUR

THE STARK MANSION was the same as he remembered it. On arrival, he hadn't been shown into the usual office they worked from, he was taken to Maurice's suite. That was unusual to the point of concerning.

Serg was on guard and told him to go straight in. No one was inside. The furniture was opulent, classic in its style. The focal point of the room was the large fireplace, almost taller than him. He'd never seen an actual fire burning there, then again, it had been a few years since he'd been in the usually private space.

The side door opened, and Mauri came in from the bedroom. The patriarch had lost weight, that was immediately obvious, but other than appearing slightly gaunt, there were no other indications of illness.

They stood for a few seconds, looking at each other, nothing threatening in the exchange. On an inhale, Mauri went to the Waterford in the corner to pour two fingers for each of them, neat.

"Brad said you were reluctant to come home," Mauri said, taking the glasses to the table between the two burgundy wingback chairs to the left of the fireplace. After putting them down, he sat. "Sit down with me, have a drink."

"I'm driving," Dax lied.

He wouldn't sit and drink like they were buddies and wanted to keep his wits about him. Given the skills Mauri knew he had, he wouldn't set just one guy on him if things got heated. Within seconds of pissing off Mauri he'd be surrounded by a dozen guys. At least.

"One won't hurt," Mauri said. "And we can get you a driver if—"

"This isn't a catch-up," Dax said, marching over to sit down. "I came here because Brad said you were sick. Why didn't you tell us?"

Mauri took a sip of the liquor. "Why do you think? If men like us show weakness, the vultures close in, don't they?"

"Men like us…? I'm nothing like you."

"That might be a convenient thing to say now," Mauri said. "But a few months ago, you were exactly like me, and proud of it too."

"Things have changed. I told you that—"

"How is Ms. Dune?"

"It's Harrow," Dax said. These fuckers deliberately used Ivy's maiden name. To piss him off? Power play? Could be a bunch of things. Did they want to belittle the marriage or maybe they wanted to remind him she would never be a part of him? "And I didn't come here to talk about her."

"Are you having trouble?" he asked, settling himself back in the chair. "Marriage is a big commitment. If you are struggling—"

"We're just fine," he said. "Marriage is easy."

"Either you truly have found your soulmate, or things between you and your other half are more strained than you want to confess to me."

"I wouldn't have walked away if I hadn't been sure about her."

"You gave up a lot for her. Your whole life. Is she appreciative?"

"Every damn day," he said with innuendo and sarcasm. "Now you want to tell me why the fuck I'm here?"

"I don't know. You chose to come. Why did you do that?"

Because Mauri meant a lot to him and had always looked after him. He wasn't ignorant to what Mauri had done for him as a child. Much as he didn't want to admit it, the way things had ended, the way he walked away for Ivy, still didn't sit right with him. Not because of her. No, he was sure of his marriage, he just didn't like how the situation came to a head.

"Brad said you were sick, said you wanted to talk to me, so I came."

"Just like old times," Mauri said and smiled.

The grooves on his cheeks were more prominent and on taking a closer look, his exhaustion was obvious. Could be the illness or may just be that business was busy.

"Had any shipment issues?" Dax asked, curious if the man was overworking himself. "Is everything running smoothly?"

"We've had nothing but problems," Mauri said, putting his glass down and rubbing his fingers across his forehead. "Since you left, no one else has been able to keep the men together. There has been tension in the ranks."

"Serg was respected—"

"And the men seemed happy to take his orders," Mauri said. "But he is not as efficient as you. Things have been missed. We almost got fucking busted because Serg gave one of the courier's directions that ended in a police precinct parking lot."

Laughing was easy for him, not being involved anymore. Mauri's frustration was obvious.

"That's Cecil's run," Dax said. "You miss the third turn and you're right there at police headquarters."

"Yes," Mauri said, leaning closer. "See, you know it all so well, you just… it's second nature to you."

"I did it for a long time," Dax said. He'd been working for Mauri since he was old enough to see over the steering wheel. "Cecil is one of our oldest contacts, and he's a real prick to get on the phone."

"We need you to come back, we need you at the helm."

"No," Dax said, already shaking his head. "Not a chance."

"Why not? I don't see why there would be a problem," Mauri said. "I have taken care of the men. They know you are married now. Ivy will be safe. She'll be safer here than wherever you've been holed up. She'll have full protection of the family."

"For how long?" Dax asked. "Word is that with you on your way out, the hyenas are circling. When you're gone, the venture will be picked apart. Brad isn't strong enough to hold it together on his own. He doesn't have the respect of the men, and he's sure not feared in the community. You ever seen him get blood on those fancy-ass Italian loafers?"

"You have their respect and you're feared. No one would cross you."

"Yeah, 'cause I know better than to turn my back on them," Dax said. "I'm not interested in taking over."

"You could," Mauri said, locking their eyes, sitting back slowly. "Would you be interested?"

"In taking over…? You're offering me the business?"

"Something could be worked out."

"No, Brad wouldn't… He's had his eyes on the prize for years."

"He can still run things as the legitimate face of the Starks."

"Legitimate?" Dax asked. "The haulage and dry-cleaning firms are fronts, they clean the money, there's nothing legitimate about that." Although they did have big haulage rigs and a few legitimate contracts meant to distract from the other cargo in the back of those trucks.

"You and Brad are not enemies," Mauri said. "You always got along."

"We never had to deal with each other. It's easy to be civil with the guy who's just another cog in the machine."

"You understand that machine. You have an affinity for this industry, Dax. Don't throw that away for a piece of ass."

"My wife is not a piece of ass. If you don't show her some goddamn respect—"

"Respect? I have nothing but respect for the woman who turned your head. I wasn't sure you would ever lower your defenses for long enough to let love in… Your choice caused difficulties in the family, yes, but you showed your commitment to her when you walked away from us. I have to say, I was… almost proud of you for standing up for her like you did."

He didn't want to be gratified, didn't want his own humble feelings to diminish his ego until he was under Mauri's boot again.

Sitting straighter, Dax snatched up the Scotch and took a mouthful. "Ivy is the best thing I have, and I am not going to disappoint her again."

"Ivy is a clever girl; you shouldn't refuse my offer before you have spoken to her. If she is as smart as you believe, she won't pass up a good thing, a secure future. She would walk into a position of power and that is very seductive. To be by your side when you take over this empire—"

"What does Trystan say about this? Have you told him Ivy and me are back in town? I don't think he'll be happy with your proposals."

"Trystan will be happy as long as there is money to spend."

"He hasn't straightened himself out? Your plan didn't work."

"We haven't given up on it yet," Mauri said. "I still believe finding the right woman will change him. It worked wonders for you. Tell me, does love clear your perspective?"

"It changes it," he said. "It changes a man's priorities. But you're not going to get Trystan to fall in love by beating a woman into submission."

"We realize what we did with Ivy was… unsuitable."

"She'd agree with you," Dax said.

Their tactics were harsh and ineffective, but as he'd said to his wife, he couldn't regret their actions, they brought her into his life, brought them together.

"I would love to see her," Maurice said. "To see you together."

Something the Starks hadn't witnessed. Interesting. Mauri and Ivy had met, but she had played the old man, telling him exactly what he wanted to hear. She led him believe their brainwashing worked.

"Why?"

"The woman got into your head; something not even I can boast."

"You were in my head," Dax said, slugging the last of the whisky and sliding the glass onto the table. "You've been in my head since I was thirteen."

"Obviously not, or my words would have worked when I asked you to bring Ivy to us."

"Protecting her is my number one priority."

"As it should be, you're her husband, and a formidable force. She's lucky to have you in her corner."

"I won't bring her here," Dax said. "Not until I see Trystan for myself. If I can't trust the bastard to keep his hands off—"

"You can trust him," Mauri said. "He's been in his suite for weeks. We've kept him entertained."

Which meant the booze and hookers to were shipped in. Trystan would only put up with being incarcerated at the mansion if the party came to him on a regular basis.

"And Bruno?" Dax asked, pissed off just to utter his name.

"What about him? He's around."

"He doesn't want to take over the operation?"

"He and I have… we've struggled to see eye-to-eye about this whole affair. Things between us are strained at the moment."

"What affair?" Dax asked. "Ivy and me or what you're suggesting for the company?"

"Both. Mostly he blames me for confessing the truth about your lineage."

"Lineage," he scoffed. "I don't give a fuck what you say that man is not my father."

"Not in any traditional sense, no. But biologically, there is no refuting—"

"I can refute it," Dax said.

He hadn't told Ivy and didn't want to face the idea it could be true. One of the country's most notorious gangsters couldn't be his father. Bruno's legend was filled with dark spots of torture and murder.

Bruno had a sadistic urge Ivy met during her last experience with him. Bruno had beaten her, caged her, fondled her at will, and turned her into his personal slave. All the while he'd steered clear, turning a blind eye to her torment and enjoying her in the nights when she came to him for sanctuary.

Maybe that was how she'd gotten into his heart. He'd never given it much thought, how she wormed her way into his affections. Seeing her endure humiliating experiences, and showing up each day with fresh bruises, he was amazed she didn't simper or withdraw. Through all that, she stayed strong. Breaking her was impossible.

How she held on to her strength was a mystery. The respect he had for that strength wouldn't allow him to lose her. She was a woman to be admired and revered. Every day he existed in awe of her.

"We can do blood tests if—"

"Why would I want proof?" Dax asked, springing out of his seat to storm to the fireplace. "I don't want to think that my biological father has…"

He couldn't bring himself to say the words.

"Felt up your wife?" Mauri asked. Dax whipped around, baring his teeth at the idea of any man touching Ivy. "I know what happened at the beach house. No one knew at that stage what was happening between you and Ivy. Tell me, when did you know you loved her?"

"You think I'm going to tell you?"

That realization hadn't smacked him in the face until he lost her. He had known something was going on, something inside of him was changing. Back then, love was a foreign concept. Ivy had known. The woman was too smart for her own good sometimes.

"I'm interested," Mauri said. "I always considered you to be my son and now that you're happily settled—"

"You want to come in and fuck it up for me?"

"No. I want to offer you more. As I understand it you've been working security at a strip club," Mauri said, smirking until he actually laughed. "That's beneath you. You're a weapon in your own right. Your skills are lethal in the ring and outside it when you are enforcing. If there's one thing you know how to do, it's how to take a man out. How do you subdue yourself when you throw out a sleazy customer?"

"I know how to restrain myself," he growled, scowling at Mauri's amusement.

"Did Ivy work there? I can't imagine how you would have reacted if a patron tried to take liberties with—"

"I would never let her work in a place like that," he said.

"You shouldn't have been working there either. Neither of you will have to worry about descending into those kinds of positions if you consider my offer. All I am suggesting is that you consider it."

"Does Brad know you're making this offer? Does Bruno?"

"Brad is happy for you to come back and join us."

"I'm not coming back just because you can't control your operation."

"You can control it, and we can offer you more. I am offering you a position here, a position of authority. You and Ivy can live right here at the mansion, and you can keep your place in the family."

"Until you're gone and then—"

"I think you can hold your own," Mauri said. "Once you're back, and they know there's nothing they can do about it, you will accept each other. Then when I am gone, you'll already have a foothold."

"I'm supposed to be grateful? No." Dax shook his head. "I'm not considering anything until I know you've laid it out to everyone. I'm not coming back to start a war with anyone. Truth is, I don't care enough to fight for the sanctity of your enterprise."

"I think you do." Mauri smiled. "Why else would you be here?"

"I came because Brad said you had something to say."

Mauri rose to his feet and came to stand in front of him. "Here's what I have to say: I want you here. I want you running things. I'm willing to do whatever it takes to make that happen."

"Whatever it takes?"

"What's your biggest problem? What's the biggest barrier to you coming home and taking your place at my side where you belong? Is it Ivy's objections? Or are you worried about Brad, Trystan, and Bruno?"

"I don't know."

"When you do, tell me, and I'll take care of the problem for you."

Mauri started to retreat, but Dax grabbed his shoulder, something he'd never done in the past. Both of them looked at the point of contact, stunned it had even happened. He didn't release his hold. Reminding himself he was no longer a lackey, that he was stronger and faster than Mauri, he had nothing to fear.

"Don't touch a hair on my wife's head."

"There are other ways to take care of problems," Mauri said. "I want to show you my commitment to this proposal. If talking about it with the others will alleviate your concerns, I'll take care of it. I have already set in motion a plan to persuade you."

"What plan?"

"When it comes together, I will clue you in. For now, I'd like it to remain a surprise."

Mauri backed away and went to drink the rest of his Scotch.

"It's not going to happen," Dax said though he lacked the conviction he'd held when he first came in.

"I want you to take my proposal back to Ivy, she will have to approve, I understand that. You must remind her of what luxury we can provide," Mauri said, holding his hands up to the mansion around them. "She can have anything that she wants; money will never be a barrier for her again. That kind of lure can be powerful for a woman of her background."

"What do you know about her background?"

Mauri didn't respond to the question. "Next Saturday I am having a party downstairs. I want you and Ivy to be my guests. You will be safe at a party; you've attended them here before. Until then, consider what I've said, talk it over, and we'll find a minute during the party to talk alone." Mauri went to the door he'd emerged from and turned back to smile. "Thank you for coming, son. You look strong and healthy. Ivy is good for you, I can tell. Send her my regards."

He went back into the side bedroom. A breath after that door closed, the double ones behind him opened to reveal Serg. Lost in thoughts of the discussion, he got out of there as fast as he could. He'd been away from Ivy for too long. The pull of Maurice Stark was strong, and that was a riptide he wasn't immune to.

FIVE

"A PARTY?" Ivy asked.

Dax just finished recounting the story of his meeting with Mauri at the mansion. They lay naked together in the pure white sheets of his bed, the night locked outside. When he'd got back, she'd been in bed already. As soon as he joined her, she'd sensed his frustration so let him vent some of that energy on her body.

After some physical exertion, he was calmer. She put him on his side of the bed and lay on her own side, putting some space between them to allow words to take the place of actions. Facing him, she stayed quiet while he relayed the story of his encounter with Mauri.

"It's next Saturday," he said. That day was Friday, giving them a week to think about the invitation. "He wants us both there."

"You told him what he could do with his party, right? You told him we weren't interested in anything he had to offer… didn't you?" His silence was conspicuous. Her suspicions were heightened when he rolled to his back and scrubbed his hands over his face.

"I'm going next door," he said and kicked the sheet away from his body.

Snatching his arm, Ivy bounded closer. Using all her strength, she subdued him, keeping him in bed. If he went next door into the second bedroom, she wouldn't see him for a couple of hours. His punch bag and weight bench were in there. Sweating was his favorite way to alleviate internal conflicts.

"Are you considering his offer?" His lack of a response was all the response she needed. "Oh my God, Dax." Sitting up in the center of the bed, she crossed her legs and gaped down at him. "You want to do it? You want to move back here, to California? You want to work with Brad? Sorry, you want to work under him?"

"I don't know," he said, leaping from the mattress. "I'm not going to say no without considering it. We owe Mauri—"

"What?" she asked, unable to prevent a frown from seizing her expression. "What do we owe him? Please, tell me, what is it you think you owe the man who asked you to give up the only woman you've ever loved for the sake of his playboy son? What do you think you owe him?"

"Don't you get it?" he asked, coming back to stand by the bed. "This could be an amazing chance for us." Crouching down, he rested his chest on the mattress and leaned over to snatch both of her hands. "We could run things; I could do things my way and—"

"Drugs," she said. "You want to deal drugs? You want to be responsible on an industrial scale for the lives and deaths of users across the continent?"

"People are going to use drugs whether we provide them or someone else does, recreational drugs aren't going anywhere. Why should we beg off and let someone else rake in the green? We could be rich and—"

"Money?" she asked, tugging her hands out of his. "If I wanted a mansion and a fancy car, I'd send you into the ring every night. I don't do that because I love you too much to see you hurt."

"I wouldn't have to be hurt doing this. I can stay in the background, send the other guys out to do the dangerous jobs."

"There will still be plenty of guys desperate to poach your territory, your employees, your customers. There's a reason that most drug kingpins don't see forty! I don't want to see you getting yourself in deep and being the fall guy when Brad can't handle what he's taken on. You said yourself Brad takes orders well, but he's not street smart. He doesn't know what he's doing."

"Which is why Mauri wants me in on the deal."

"Which might work out great while Mauri is alive and looking out for you. How long will it last when Brad decides he doesn't need you anymore? I don't trust any of them."

"I know," he said.

Moving away from the bed, he went into the bathroom, leaving her alone in their sheets.

"If you want to talk to Mauri again, we can go to the party," she called toward the bathroom. "But there's no way I want to move into that mansion! I would never... No, I can't!"

A minute or so later, he came back out and propped himself on the doorframe. "I want to see Trystan."

"At the party? Or before that?"

"Either," he said. "But it can wait for now."

"He's at the mansion?"

"Sounds like Mauri's had him locked up there for a while. I suppose when he found out Mauri was sick, he had an excuse to go even more off the rails."

"Do you think he's a threat?" she asked.

"To you?" He shook his head. "I'd like to see him try getting near you now. Mauri knows I'd walk if you were threatened."

"That doesn't make me feel better," she said, tangling her fingers in the bedsheet.

"You've fought him off once, you could do it again if you had to."

"I guess," she said, collapsing to her back. "I know he's responsible for us getting together, for us meeting, but…"

Swooping onto the bed with barely a sound, he ambushed her, covering her body with his, holding her in the submissive position. "But…?"

"I'd really like to stick a fork in his eye," she said, drawing her fingertip over the ivy tattooed on his arm.

"I'll remember that when I get him alone," he said and kissed her. Just when she was pliable enough to part her legs and arch up, he took his lips away. "I'm going next door for a while."

"He got you thinking, didn't he?" she said, running a hand into his hair. "Or is it being back here, in your old life, that's got you thinking? Do you miss it?"

"I miss kicking the shit out of scumbags," he said.

"Plenty of them around I guess," she said. "If you want to go back to enforcing, I can't stop you. But being here, around the Starks again, it feels wrong, Dax. They don't want us to be together."

"They don't care about us anymore," Dax said. "At least Mauri doesn't."

"Is that why you want to see Trystan? You want to be sure we can be safe here? To check he doesn't have some other agenda that could damage us."

"Trystan isn't a planner, he comes up with ideas and expects everyone else to figure out how to implement them," Dax said. "He doesn't think through his actions either, he just does whatever the hell he wants. I know 'cause I used to be the one picking up the pieces after he blew them all to shit."

Dax got a far off look in his eye that made her think there was something else on his mind. Something that was nothing to do with them or Trystan and their past. Something else was in his head, something he wasn't sharing with her. She'd give him some time to offer it to her. Then if he didn't spit it out in the next day or two, she would wheedle it out of him.

"Go next door and hit your bag," she said, dropping her arms and giving him a shove. "I'll be right here if you need another way to process."

Being physical, between the sheets, in the gym, or in the ring, was Dax's way of figuring the world out. He liked to have a goal and when he reached it, he felt he'd achieved something.

That night, she didn't pose enough of a challenge, so she'd let him go work up a sweat next door. When he came back, maybe he'd have figured out what to do next.

She had her own ideas of what would happen over the next few days. Those would keep. Her mess wasn't connected to Dax, a few doors needed to be closed before she could embrace whatever they were going to face with the Starks.

SIX

HAVING HAD THE NIGHT to think about it, Ivy was stuck on one thing: taking over the empire. That's what it came down to. Maurice wanted Dax to take over when he passed away. Brad would be the sophisticated front while Dax headed up the dirty work division.

The previous night, her first instinct had been to tell Dax no and demand they go home, but they'd argued enough over the last few days. When he did eventually come back to bed after beating up his punch bag, he hadn't woken her. By the time she was out of her morning shower, he gone for a run. Conversation over breakfast was stunted. Despite his excess of exercise, he was still torn about their future.

He'd gone out to pick up lunch. Takeout was his way of contributing to meals, he could cook steak and mix a mouth-watering salsa, but that was as far as his cookery talents extended.

Standing in the bedroom closet, scrutinizing the space filled with Dax's clothes and possessions, isolation crept in. The apartment was full of his things. All she had were the items she'd thrown together back east.

Dax had made something of himself, he had money, and a way to support himself. He could be cast out, penniless, and he would still be able to earn a living through his fighting. On top of that, he'd been offered a chance at owning part of a multi-million-dollar criminal empire.

She made their bed with fresh sheets and returned to the closet. Ignoring Dax's things, she sought out a sports bag, something smaller than the suitcase they'd brought on their trip.

The bag she located was the one they'd had in Vegas when they got married. Taking the bag out, she laid it on the bed, and unzipped it to check that it was empty. It wasn't. Inside lay a pile of zip ties bound by an elastic band.

Removing them, she thought of their wedding night. The night she'd first discovered the zip ties. Fingering the plastic, she was reminded of the night she tried to escape from the beach house. The first night Dax introduced her to the restraints. Now she would never consider sneaking out of her husband's bed to escape from him.

Tossing them aside, she pushed out the sides to give the bag its shape and went into the closet to retrieve some of her folded clothes. Those went into the bad first, then she returned to the closet for underwear.

The front door opened.

Digging out the last of her lacies, she grabbed a pair of Dax's socks, and closed the drawer with her elbow.

Quickly dropping the apparel into the bag on the bed, she hurried through to the kitchen intent on talking to Dax about her trip during lunch. But when she got there, her husband plating up lunch wasn't her focus, no, that landed on the giant standing at his side.

"Ivy," Dax said. "You remember Serg?"

Her forced smile couldn't be confused for genuine, but Dax carried on pulling containers from the brown bag on the kitchen counter behind the hutch that concealed the specifics of the food.

Serg rose from the stool on the living room side of the hutch and came toward her, hand extended.

Ivy took a step back. "Don't come over here."

Serg stopped.

Dax looked at her, cast his eyes to Serg, then brought them back to her. "You don't have to worry about Serg."

She wasn't worried or an idiot. The guy was nearly seven feet tall. His ice blonde hair and narrow eyes set people on edge. People being her.

"Who is worried?" she said without taking her eyes from Serg. "What are you doing here?"

"Catching up," Dax answered for Serg and brought three plates around to the dining table.

If Ivy had superpowers, she'd be reading Dax the riot act telepathically. To say she was pissed was the biggest understatement ever made. The apartment was supposed to be a safe space.

Despite not doing her direct harm, she didn't trust him.

Dax sat at the head of the table to tuck into his food. Serg picked up a bag from his feet, sat in a chair next to Dax and pulled out a pile of ledgers to push them over to the host. After tossing the bag aside, he began to eat.

"This is everything?" Dax asked, Serg nodded. "Where's the little green—"

"In the front," Serg said, leaning down to pull a small dark green, leather-bound book from the front pocket of the bag on the floor.

He handed it over. Dax pushed the larger books aside to focus on the little green one. he opened it next to his plate, read some and took another mouthful of food. Her attention remained on Serg. The thug glanced up at her and their gazes locked. Somehow, her husband felt the connection. He stopped reading to look at her too.

"Are you gonna stand there all day?" he asked. "Want me to get you a knife from the kitchen? Will that make you feel safer?"

She didn't appreciate his sarcasm. Hence the glare he landed on her.

"You married a lethal weapon," Serg said. "I might be a big guy, but size doesn't matter to Dax. I've seen him take down guys bigger than me."

She trusted Dax to protect her if he had to. But he and Serg were friends and potential future colleagues, her husband wouldn't be pissing off Serg any time soon.

"What is that?" she asked, nodding to the book under Dax's hand.

"The unofficial operations log," Dax said. "Where we keep track of who owes us what and how long they have to pay it."

We. Us. She couldn't help except to read into his words. He didn't speak of his life with the Starks in the past tense; he was in the present and very much a part of what Serg was showing him. His eyes returned to the book, and she crept around the table to where her lunch, in the place opposite Serg's.

With an intruder in their home, she wasn't in the slightest bit hungry. Her thoughts jarred; it wasn't her home. Dax lived there, but her time in his California apartment was limited.

"I'll leave you to it," she said, lowering her hand to pick up her plate.

Dax snatched her wrist. The anger in his eyes was unexpected. "Sit down," he said, squeezing her wrist to lower her into the chair perpendicular to his. When she was down, he turned to Serg without letting go of her. "This is a fucking mess."

"Yeah, things have gone to shit since you've been gone," Serg said, still eating his lunch. "I don't mind admitting I've struggled to keep it together. We've lost three guys since you left."

"Who?"

Serg gave three names, and she forked some salad leaves into her mouth. Dax still held her wrist, pinning her arm down, rendering it useless, meaning she had to eat her lunch and drink her water with only one hand.

Not that either of the men noticed her discomfort, they kept talking while eating. Dax was interested in what Serg was saying about who owed them money. Some of the names Serg relayed peeved Dax to the point of raising his voice.

Apparently, it was some big affront when particular guys tried to take advantage with Dax out of the picture.

"Got a few places to hit this afternoon," Serg said. "Wouldn't mind company."

Raising her chin, she held her breath in anticipation of Dax's response. Still, neither man paid her any attention.

Dax pushed his plate away and nodded. "Sure," he said. Her mouth dropped open. "I could use the exercise." The men rose from the table and because her husband had a hold of her, she was forced to stand up too. "Take care of this mess, will you, Minx?"

When he let her go, she immediately took her turn to snatch hold of him. Her action drew the focus of both men and her words slipped back into her throat. She couldn't chastise Dax in front of Serg. The last thing they needed was for the Starks to think there was tension in their relationship. She wouldn't give Mauri the satisfaction knowing he had the power to cause conflict.

If the Starks took it upon themselves to use a wedge to pry the couple apart, they might be successful, she'd seen it before. Instead of speaking, she rounded the corner of the table and slid her hands up his chest to guide his mouth down to hers.

"Be back by bedtime," she murmured, touching his lips with her fingertips.

"Start without me," Dax said. "Creeping up on these guys in the dark is sometimes the best approach."

He wouldn't be back all night? If the men were going to do their enforcing under the cloak of night, there was no need for Dax to leave at lunchtime. Something else was on the cards for the afternoon. Business or pleasure? Maybe she didn't want to know. Though that wouldn't stop her asking when her husband got home.

Smiling, even if it was plastic, was her only response to Dax smacking her ass. Serg grabbed the bag and books, and she remained stuck to the spot while the men vacated. Lowering her attention to the lunch mess, the last thing she felt like doing was playing the dutiful housewife.

If he was sliding back into his old life, revisiting hers became more urgent. Leaving the lunch plates untouched, she went into the bedroom and finished her packing. If Dax had no intention of coming back that night, she had no intention of sitting around waiting for him.

Grabbing her purse, she checked for her passport and credit cards. Dax had made sure she was covered which included getting her a cellphone. If he wanted to chase her, he was welcome to. But if she could get to the airport fast, he might never notice she was gone.

SEVEN

COINCIDENCE DIDN'T EXIST. Serg appearing at Dax's favorite lunch restaurant was not accidental. It had been a setup. Mauri probably ordered Serg to stay on his tail, it was the only explanation for the serendipitous meeting.

Playing along when Serg offered him a look at the books, Dax had declined Serg's invitation to take a table and eat in the restaurant. He'd told Ivy he wouldn't be out for long. If he just disappeared, she might have worried or been pissed off at him for ditching her. Inviting Serg back to the apartment made sense.

Ivy wasn't happy. Throughout the meal, he'd sensed her spitting fire. She'd kick his ass when he got home. When she'd tried to walk away from the dining table, he couldn't allow it, he just couldn't let her leave. She was his life. Whatever his business ventures in the future, she was going to be a part of them.

He had nothing to hide from her and wanted it to stay that way. If they did choose to stay and work with the Starks again, his wife would be a big part of the operation. Tagging her as a trophy wife, like most of the Stark women, wouldn't fly with her. They were a team. She'd sign off on everything.

If she didn't, it wouldn't happen. For him, it was as simple as that.

Holding her wrist during the lunch was for him, she kept him anchored. Needing something as much as he needed contact with her throughout that meal shook his bearings. Talking business with Serg, was supposed to be part of his past. Dealing with it all again was disconcerting because damn, he was good at it.

However, that woman, his wife, there at his side, in his grip, she was his future. She made it okay; she made everything okay. He could play the game so long as she remained at his side.

In the meantime, letting Serg and the Starks believe he was still a force to be reckoned with was essential to their survival. Showing them weakness or letting them think he was subordinate to Ivy, would put her in peril. He wouldn't allow them to use her against him. They had to believe he still had control of her, or they could hurt her to get to him. The truth? He would never act in a way to deliberately upset his wife. Not again.

Going around the work sites that afternoon was just like old times. As though he'd just returned from one of his minder trips with Trystan on another of his ridiculous party binges. When the rounds were done, he and Serg went to the bar. The guys welcomed him home without much surprise at seeing him.

After dark, they started to hit known locations of the men owing money to their people to scare them into submission. The first three visits were routine. Everything was routine. Like Ivy never was.

The clock on the dash read midnight. They still had half a dozen of these to do. Sometimes it could take hours to track down a specific person. His wife would hand him his balls when he got home.

Elevating his hips, he took his cellphone from his back pocket and punched in the apartment phone number then held the device to his ear.

"Checking in with the wife?" Serg asked from the driver's seat.

"Yeah," Dax said.

The phone rang out, no one was picked up. When the answering machine clicked in, he hung up with no intention of leaving a message.

"No one home?"

"She's probably in bed," he said, except that wasn't their deal.

Ivy waited up for him when he was working late. That had been the deal when he worked nightshift security in Risqué. Often wasn't home until three in the morning. Ivy always picked up when he called, no matter the hour.

"You did tell her to start without you," Serg said with a smile he wanted to wipe off his colleague's face. "Maybe she's busy."

If Ivy was pleasuring herself, she'd have picked up for sure. To rub his face in what he was missing. Wouldn't be beyond her to use her breathy play-by-play as an incentive to bring him home. Either she was way more pissed off than he realized, or she wasn't home at all.

Sitting straighter, alarm moved his thumb to the number of the cellphone he'd given her. The chill on his skin was the same adrenaline making his jaw tense. If she wasn't in the fucking apartment, he' go direct to wherever the hell she was and give her hell. He'd drag her back to the apartment by her hair if necessary.

Being out on the streets of LA wasn't safe at night. A woman like her, with her figure and face, would be in more danger. He couldn't believe she'd think to go anywhere without him by her side. She wasn't from LA; she'd never lived there and didn't know anyone. Without knowing the neighborhoods, she could wander into trouble without realizing the area's potential for it.

The ringing stopped. "Hello?"

Noise echoing in the background raised his chin. That wasn't his apartment. From the music and chatter, his guess would be nightclub. How dumb could she be? He wanted to yell at her, to drum into her how crazy it was for her to be out without him in what could be a threatening environment.

"Where are you?" he growled.

"Where are you?" she asked him right back.

Glancing at Serg, who was fixated on the windshield, Dax turned to his side window. "Give me the goddamn address, I'm coming to get you."

"You're not home," she said. "You would have called me from the landline if you were. You're still out with him, aren't you?"

"You're gonna be like this?"

"Yeah," she said. "You walked out on me, tough guy. You can't be pissed off I did the same thing back to you."

"Give me the address and we'll talk about this at home after I pick you up," he said.

Cooling his anger, his chest tightened with the sheer weight of his compulsion to snatch hold of his woman and shake some sense into her. He wanted to grab her and pin her to the nearest wall. Since being married, he'd been so busy trying to make sure she was happy that he hadn't attempted to force her into a submissive position. Though that was a joke, Ivy would never surrender her will to anyone, he knew because he and Bruno had tried it.

"I'm in a club," she said.

"I can tell."

"I can't hear you properly."

She heard him just fine. The tinge of antagonism in her tone betrayed how she didn't want to be talking, or rather answering, to him.

"I'll check every damn nightclub in LA if I have to," he said, forgetting for a moment that Serg was listening in.

"Won't help you much," she said.

"Why's that?"

"I'm not in California anymore."

His brakes jarred. "What the fuck—"

"You deal with your shit, Dax. I'll be back when I've dealt with mine." And she hung up the phone.

Lowering the phone from his ear, he blinked at the offending device. "Is there a problem?" Serg asked.

"No," he said, stuffing the phone back into his pocket.

God help the next scumbag they came across. Beating any little shit to a pulp would vent some of his tension. Maybe. He'd chased Ivy across the country once. If he had to do it again, nothing would stop him.

Tracking her down wouldn't take him too long. If she'd taken the cellphone he gave her, she'd have his credit cards too. In the information technology age, his wife couldn't get too far away from him.

Retrieving his phone again, he went online and logged into his credit card account to check the latest transactions. He and Serg were nearly at their destination, there wasn't much time for him to pin down her location.

Vegas. There was a transaction for a hotel in Las Vegas. Gritting his teeth, he put the phone back in his pocket. What in the fuck business did she have in Vegas? In her old stomping ground?

His wife knew he could track the credit cards, this wasn't her leaving him or ending their marriage. When she wanted him to follow, she made a habit of making herself easy to locate. Breadcrumbs. Just like the last time. The day she chose not to leave those breadcrumbs was the day he would start to worry.

With no one waiting at home, there was no hurry to get back. After his shift with Serg taking out his frustrations on local lowlifes, dealing with Ivy would be his number one priority.

EIGHT

SHE WASN'T IN A VEGAS NIGHTCLUB looking for a good time. No, she had checked into her hotel and gone on the hunt. Getting back to Vegas didn't feel like coming home. Almost as soon as the plane landed, she wanted to leave again. There was no familiar apartment, just another hotel.

Choosing to check into the hotel where she and Dax shared their wedding night gave him an obvious place to look, if he wanted to find her. During dinner, a plan started to come together.

Vegas was a city that came alive at night. After dinner, she headed for her old neighborhood and started to ask around for Trudi to see if she still worked the streets in the area. No one clammed up, as she expected they might.

Word was Trudi worked one of the call girl agencies. One of probably hundreds in the city. Office blocks were escort premises pimps dealt from. Girls answered phones and promised johns their requested piece of ass would come direct to their hotel room, or wherever else they requested the girls go to. Escorts came into the office, got the address then went off to do their thing. When they were done, they came back to the office or called in to get a new address, sometimes seeing several men in one night.

Giving the agency a bullshit story, it didn't take much to find out Trudi had been requested by a customer to come to a certain nightclub. Interrupting Trudi with a customer might be the only way her ex-roommate would talk to her.

So far, the trip hadn't been fruitful. Dax's call was the cherry on her sundae. After taking the call in a quieter corridor, she stowed her phone and found herself reluctant to go back into the crush of bodies. What was she doing there? Searching for a woman who was no doubt squirreled away in a darkened corner with a john? Great plan.

If surprising Trudi on a date wasn't going to work, her next option was more direct.

Getting out of the club was a relief. If she had to stomach one more guy assuming they could put their hands on her or slobber all over her, she might have turned to Dax's method of conflict resolution and brained one of them with the nearest solid object. Her hotel wasn't too far, so she went outside and started her walk back.

Dax was angry. That much was obvious. Guy had some nerve. When exactly was she supposed to tell him her plan? He hadn't given her much of a chance to share why she needed to be there. If he was happy running around with Serg, damaging people, he could have at it. As unhappy as he might be with her for taking off, he wouldn't worry about their relationship. Better not. She was pissed about his landing Serg on her at lunch, but not pissed enough to leave him.

Damn her for missing him. No man would've touched her if her husband was there, none of them would've dared approach. On buying her drink and seating herself at the bar to scan the club for Trudi, less than a minute passed before the first guy approached her.

After the third tried to hit on her, she got up to weave around. A moving target was harder to hit. It wasn't like the male interest was even a testament to her attractiveness. It was Vegas. Men came there wanting to get lucky—one way or another. And with enough liquor in them to drown an elephant, their confidence soared, and they'd hit on anything with a pair of breasts, believing themselves irresistible.

At the hotel, she missed Dax more. Fighting with him was so counterproductive. Hadn't they proved they could overcome adversity? They were going to be together. Nothing would prevent them from finding a future together.

When he had chosen the Starks over her before, they ended up apart with him chasing her across the continent. Prioritizing each other was the only way their marriage would survive.

Stripping out of her clothes, she took a shower and slid into her empty hotel room bed. Dax was her husband. Even when he was a jerk, he loved her. Pulling up the sheet, she turned off the lamp and fished her phone from her purse to write a text.

I'm safe, back at the hotel,
tucked up in bed alone.
I love you, you arrogant jerk.

She wouldn't hesitate to show him her wrath when they were back in the same room again. But while Stark stuff was going on, the threat of him losing himself was great. Reminding him they were together, and that he wasn't that person anymore, might be the only way to ensure they came out the other side together. Her phone made a noise, so she rolled over to grab it from the bedside.

You're not going to be able
to sit for a week by the time
I'm through with you, Minx.
You better damn well be
alone.

Well, it wasn't a declaration of undying love, but it gave her some reassurance he was alright. Being back out there, enforcing, was dangerous. Yes, okay, he'd done it for years, but all it took was one mistake, one prick with a weapon, and she could lose her only purpose.

Being pissed in the same house as each other was very different to being pissed at each other in different states. So, with a sigh, she closed her eyes and tried her best to sleep. They would fix them.

Serg distracting Dax had given her the opportunity to take care of her past without awkward explanations. She would have to explain eventually. Doing it after the fact would be easier than doing it before when he might want to be a part of the resolution.

This was something she had to do herself, except her husband knew her location. The clock was running. He could show up at any second, so she had to get this done and fast.

NINE

APPARENTLY, DAX WASN'T THE ONLY person who knew where she was. Knocking on her hotel room door brought her out of the bathroom still dripping from the shower. Because he could get the name of the hotel from his credit card statement, and because the timing was right depending on whether he finished with Serg before driving or flying to her, she was convinced her husband was that only possible visitor on the other side of the door.

Wrapped in only her towel, she opened the hotel room door, hair still dripping from the shower, prepared herself to face her husband's anger. But it wasn't Dax. The six-foot tall visitor had light brown hair and a smile that could melt the panties right off a woman. His brown eyes didn't captivate like Dax's did, and that smile was only skin deep. Its disarming nature would make a woman believe this man was harmless, she knew different.

"Saul," she said.

"Hey, baby," he said, ducking to kiss her cheek. "Why didn't you tell me you were in town?"

Backing off, she tucked in her towel and let him enter the room. "How did you find out?"

"I heard you were in the old neighborhood," he said, sauntering in and scrutinizing the details of the room. "Where's the hubby?"

"California," she said.

Saul spun around to land her in his sights. "It's finished already?"

"It's not finished, he's working," she said. "I came here to tie up my loose ends."

"Am I on that list?" he asked, sinking down to sit on the end of the bed. He stretched his legs out and relaxed back on his hands.

"Actually, yes," she said. "I hadn't gotten to you yet."

"Now I'm here," he said, leaning forward to tug on the flap of her towel. "Just in time to show you a good time."

Her smile flared. "No fun," she said, stepping over his legs to head back toward the bathroom. "You wait out here, I'll talk to you in a minute."

She hadn't locked a bathroom door in months, but did then, proving how little she trusted Saul Haynes. Saul was a great friend to everyone he met, a guy who knew how to get things. Networking was one of his strengths. Him knowing she was there was no big surprise. Or it shouldn't have been. The bigger question was why he'd come looking for her.

After drying her hair and pulling on the clothes she'd selected for the day, she went into the bedroom to find Saul standing in front of the window with her wallet in hand. Her purse was on the small round table beside him, next to the proud lamp also located there. Without an ounce of shame, he slid her credit card out of its slot.

"Harrow," he read.

"That's right," she said, crossing the room to take both wallet and credit card away from him.

"Don't know him."

Putting her purse back together, a smile tilted her lips. "I thought you knew everyone."

"Everyone in Vegas," he said.

"You used to say that you knew everyone on the West Coast."

"Does he have siblings? Who does he work for?"

"You don't know him," she said, unwilling to reveal too much.

"I might, maybe I'd know him if I saw him."

Placing her purse back on the table, she squinted up. "Does it upset you there's a stranger out there? Someone you don't know?"

He shrugged and sat down in the tub chair angled in the corner near the table. "Not really, I know him now, don't I? You can introduce us."

"He's in California," she said. "Did you not hear me say that a few minutes ago?"

"Yeah, but we'll cross paths eventually. You're not planning to cut me out of your life. We've shared a lot… is he the jealous type? Possessive? If he's controlling—"

"No man can beat you on that score, can they?" she said, leaning away when he snagged her skirt.

"You loved being my girlfriend," he said. "We had a lot of good times."

"Yeah, but not exclusively," she said.

"That why you ran off and married Harrow? Payback?"

"I left you, Saul, don't re-write history, and I did it months ago."

Ivy met Saul on one of her few nights out in Las Vegas, and he'd pursued her with zeal. After six months together, the sheen had definitely faded. By the time she encountered Trystan Stark in his GoldSpring suite, she and Saul had been broken up for around five months.

Breaking up with Saul had been a relief. For a time, she'd worried he wouldn't let her go. His short attention span was her savior. When he moved on to another busty brunette, she was quickly forgotten.

One thing Saul was never short of was female attention, or any kind of attention. Once he got bored, he didn't just drop people, they got shifted onto his periphery. Expected to hang around in case he had use for them again.

Saul liked to be adored, he liked to do people favors and be seen as a good guy, and he could keep a secret too. Somewhere along the way he'd learned a good way of winning people's confidence involved having a reputation for being discreet.

"Do you want to go to a casino?" he asked. "Your choice. We could take in a show if you want, I made dinner reservations for—"

"You're that eager to impress me all over again?" she quipped, folding her arms. "What were you doing in my purse? You've never been short a few bucks."

"Your phone made a noise," he said, "and I was curious."

He would never have offered that information without her prompt. Sometimes he enjoyed keeping secrets a little bit too much. Taking her phone from her bag to see why it had made a noise, she read a message from Dax, one Saul would've read too.

> *Just got in. Going for a nap,*
> *then we're gonna talk.*

"Sounds like there might be trouble," Saul said, he slid down in the seat and patted his thigh. "Come sit down and tell Daddy all about it."

"Yeah, right," she smiled at his tease, then responded to Dax's message.

> *Going to breakfast with my*
> *ex-boyfriend. Call me when*
> *you wake up.*

Devices weren't a priority when making ends meet was tough, so she was still getting used to texting. Being unreachable was one of the things Saul hated about her. When Saul bought her a cellphone, she'd thrown it right back at him. Any tool intended to increase his control over her, and her social calendar, was unwelcome. Her husband got her one out of concern and knew better than to manipulate her with it.

Texting Dax had become a habit while they were both working on the East Coast. He would text her when he was bored at work, or when he was at home waiting for her to come home from the garage. Because they worked opposing shifts, texting each other when they woke up, got home, or were about to go to sleep, was part of their routine.

One thing they never did was ignore each other's calls or texts. Nothing to do with rudeness, a lack of response would cause the other to be concerned, which was justified given their history.

When there was no immediate reply to her text message, she put the phone away. Dax would be asleep. He'd get back to her when he woke up… her mention of an ex guaranteed that. Hey, sometimes honesty was brutal.

"Dinner is out," she said. "I won't go on a date with you, Saul. But you can take me to breakfast."

"It's a start," he said, leaping out of the chair to go open the bedroom door for her.

It was almost eleven a.m., so it was closer to lunchtime, but Saul had done her a favor without any hesitation. The least she could do was share a meal with him. In public. While waiting for her husband's response to her text. Bets weren't his kneejerk response wouldn't be positive.

TEN

HAVING SAUL BACK in her life turned out to be fortuitous. He jumped right on board with her plan to get hold of Trudi. A male voice would be more convincing than a female one, so they arranged to meet in her hotel room that night to put the plan into motion.

Eager as she was to have Trudi where she wanted her, Dax was on her mind. He hadn't called. She knew better than most how much Dax loved his sleep. The man could sleep like the dead, and he could do it indefinitely. He'd had a long night talking to Mauri and making love to her, then met up with Serg and had another long night of enforcing. That added up to a lot of sleep debt to catch up on.

"When is she coming?" Ivy asked when Saul hung up the phone.

"She'll be here in an hour," he said, his triumphant smile brought him to his feet. "Where's the mini-bar?"

"You're not getting drunk in here," she said.

"Come on, it's on your old man's dime, right?"

"You can leave," she said. "You've done your bit."

"Oh," he whined. "You're not going to let me stay and watch the show?"

"No, I'm not. I'm not hanging out in a hotel room with you to wait for a hooker."

"We're not using the hooker; we're luring the hooker."

"I am luring her; I could've done this without you. You were the one who decided calling from the hotel room was more convincing. Trudi probably heard I was looking for her, and she won't be desperate to see me."

"No," he said, standing up from the bed where he'd been sitting to make the call. "Probably not. Were all the stories true? That you were kidnapped and—"

"We can talk about that tomorrow," she said. Grabbing his arm, she pulled him towards the hotel room door. "You need to get out of here because if Trudi sees you, she'll assume I'm not far behind."

He grinned. "Just like the old days."

With her palms planted on his back, she pushed him forward and reached around to open the hotel room door. "Get out of here, Saul." Except when she opened the door, there was a man right there on the other side of it. A man with an expression the devil would envy. "Dax…"

Still half tucked behind Saul, she came around him to stand between the two men.

Her husband swept her aside and grabbed Saul to haul him out and pin him to the corridor wall. "Who the fuck do you think you are?"

"No, no," Ivy said, trying to pry Dax away. "You can't do this here, Dax. Come on, baby, let him go."

"I do know you," Saul said, his face reddened as recognition grasped him. "Oh shit."

"That's right, buddy," Dax said, pleased he'd been identified.

How the hell could they know each other? Right then, she didn't care.

"Please let go of him, baby," she said, pulling on Dax's arm. "Nothing happened, he didn't touch me."

"Oh, God, no, no," Saul said, surprising her by being such a pussy. From his shallow breathing and the distressed panic in his eyes, it was obvious he knew Dax shouldn't be messed with. Saul's focus fled Dax's to land on her. "You married the goddamn Ravager? Why the fuck didn't you tell me that?"

"You disrespecting my wife?" Dax asked, pulling him forward to slam him back against the wall again.

"No! No, no, no I'm Ivy's friend. I was just helping her out, I—"

"Yeah," Dax said, yanking him forward to toss him away down the hotel corridor. "Get the fuck outta here and don't come back."

Snatching hold of her, he pulled her tight against him, pinning her under his arm to lead her back into the hotel room. As soon as they were inside, he slammed the door and shoved her out of his embrace.

"What the fuck are you doing?" he asked, looking around the place, probably for any signs of an indiscretion.

"What the fuck are you doing?" she asked, setting her hands on his chest to shove him, though he didn't budge. "You can't treat people that way!"

"Guys who come to my wife's hotel room while I'm not here? You're goddamn right I can!"

"No," she said, putting her hands to her hips. "He came here to call for a hooker."

His anger flickered to confusion before it rocketed to rage.

"A hooker? He came here to get laid?" Dax whipped around. "I'll break every one of his fucking fingers and—"

She got between him and the door. "No, he called and asked for Trudi to visit this hotel room. I needed a male voice. I tried to track her down myself last night, but I couldn't find her."

"Trudi?"

"My old roommate, the one that set me up."

"Set you up?"

"Trudi recommended the job that got me nabbed by the Starks," Ivy said. "She was my friend, and I want to talk to her. I want to know why she would do that."

"Money, babygirl."

That he used her pet name was a good sign. "I know she got paid, but I have a feeling it was Carlos, her pimp, who put her up to it. I want to know why. I want to make her look me in the eye and… I just have to see her."

"You plan to hurt her? Is that what he was for?" Dax asked. "You called your ex to enforce for you?"

"No! I didn't call Saul at all. He just showed up here this morning, just before I texted you, which I did, by the way, to prove to you I am being completely open and honest. I figured you'd want to know ahead of time, or while it was happening, rather than find it out later."

"You still care about him?"

"No," she said and sighed. "Will you please stand down red alert? Go sit on the bed."

"You didn't fuck him?"

Scowling at him, she poked his ribs. "No, I did not, and you're forgiven for asking me such an insulting question."

Dax went over to sit on the end of the bed and bent forward to unlace his boots. There was still a lot to talk about, and she trusted him to know that, but she suspected sex was in his mind's horizon.

"Trudi is on her way here," she said. "You can't be here when she arrives."

"Damn right I'm going to be here," he said, kicking off his boots and sliding himself up to sit at the top of the bed against the headboard. "I'm going to watch the whole fucking show. You're never leaving my sight again."

"You're overreacting."

"What the hell were you thinking leaving the apartment and coming here?" he asked, sitting upright. "I am so fucking pissed at you for—"

"You're pissed? How dare you say that to me! You were the one who brought his old buddy home to lunch and restrained me through the whole damn meal! Were you out all night? Did you think I was just going to sit in the apartment and wait for you? I'd have gone out of my mind with worry!"

"That what you wanted me to do! What do you think coming home to an empty apartment would've done for me? Huh?"

He bounded off the bed, her in his crosshairs, but she rushed to the window. Pulling the table in front of her as a barrier, the lamp on it wobbled side to side, walking on its base until she steadied it.

Dax stopped, wearing a frown. "What the fuck did you do that for?"

"Don't come over here," she said with intent. "I mean it, Dax Harrow, do not come any closer to me."

Confusion overcame him again. "Did that jerkoff hurt you? That why you're suddenly so worried?"

It hadn't occurred to her that her actions looked like an attempt to shield herself from physical harm. "No! I'm concerned for my virtue."

"I'm not gonna fuck you while I'm this pissed."

That wasn't a statement she could put in the bank. "I can't deal with this now. Trudi will be here soon. I have to think about what I'm going to say. I have to be together enough to deal with her. Why don't you go to the casino? We can argue later."

"You know it's not unusual for a hooker to show up with a pimp, did you think about that?"

"There are dozens of women who work for this agency, they would never have enough men to—"

"Sometimes there's a guy in the parking lot, or in the bar. Sometimes they stand in the room or right outside, have you thought about any of that?"

"If Trudi shows up with a guy, I'll call the cops."

"Do you think you're high priority for the cops? It could take them an hour to get here. Takes a fraction of that time to kill you."

Sure, he didn't want her hurt, but his aloof questions were meant to rile, not soothe.

Damn him for knowing she hadn't considered any of those things. "Okay," she conceded. "Maybe you can stay."

"Oh no," he said, shifting to sit on the end of the bed again. "You told me to leave." Sticking his feet in his boots, he tugged the laces to tighten them but didn't tie them. "I'll leave you to your righteous confrontation with your old friend who may or may not come with her personal bodyguard."

"You do that then," she said, edging out from behind the table. There was no way he'd let anyone hurt her, no matter how mad he was. He was calling her bluff, so she called his right back. "Mauri would be disappointed."

That statement stopped him in his tracks to peer closer. "Why's that?"

"You told me once that he always taught you not to bluff in life."

"Who's bluffing?"

With slow strides, she sashayed across to his location. "So you're going to let some big, mean man put his hands on me? Let him hit me and hurt me, take what he wants from me and soil your babygirl?"

When he inhaled through his nose, his lips all but disappeared because he compressed them so tight. "You're still a fucking minx."

"If you want to leave then go," she said, opening her hands on his pecs. "But I know you don't want to leave me."

She didn't mind playing dirty whenever it was required. Was it possible to be more grateful for her man? Grateful he was hers, that he'd come to her, and was willing to protect her, which he'd do with his life if necessary.

Unbuckling his belt, she glanced at the clock, then locked her eyes on his while pushing his jeans and underwear from his hips to sink to her knees. The point of the argument wasn't to win, she never wanted to belittle him. So licking her lips, she opened her mouth wide and took him into her throat. She could be a bitch, but she would always be his bitch.

Lifting her tongue, she pressed it to the underside of his shaft as she moved her head back. Still watching him, she circled her tongue around his head then pushed it into her cheek, using her hand to squeeze it from the outside. Pulling back again, she sucked him deep and withdrew. Repeating the motion with her mouth, she used her fingers to squeeze his base then closed them one by one around his engorged dick. Forcing her mouth away from him, she worked him with her hand and smiled, letting the head of his cock bounce against her lips.

"I love you, Master," she murmured, exhaling a long breath to coat him with her heated breath, her hand still pumping. "You came all this way for me, dropped everything and came right here."

"Yeah, I'm about to come right here," he said. "So quit talking."

Gripping her hair, he pushed her mouth to his penis and began to work her just as he wanted her to move. The quick rhythmic motion of her mouth and hand sped up until she brought him to the brink, and when he shot his semen into her throat, he held her right there to swallow it down. Even after he was done, he didn't let her move away, keeping her mouth full of his cock.

"You never get on a plane or leave the state I'm in without talking to me first," he said. She tried to nod, but he compelled her to stay still. "I'm gonna punish you later, after your friend is gone. But for now, you better understand, I have to know where you are at all times. All times, Minx, no exceptions. I protect my property, and you are prime real estate I plan to inhabit for a long time. Nothing takes you away from me, nothing, not even you."

Her only response to his speech was to blink her innocent eyes. She still couldn't speak, which she could tell he enjoyed from the way his cock hardened in her mouth. His hips surged forward, blocking her windpipe for a moment, then he let her go and bent to pull up his jeans.

Giving him pleasure, being owned by him awakened her sexual need. Wriggling on the floor, she parted her legs to let her damp core meet the carpet.

She grinned up at him. "I love being married."

He obviously hadn't expected her to be so happy after what he'd said, but she couldn't help it. Dax might be a jerk, but he was her jerk, and he knew how to push every one of her buttons.

ELEVEN

WAITING FOR TRUDI was agonizing. For her. Dax seemed to have all the patience in the world. He flicked on the TV and sat beside her on the bed, watching some mind-numbing sports results and replays that went round and round.

Ivy was getting twitchier as the seconds passed. "Could you keep a hard-on for this long?" she asked, glancing at his groin.

"How long?" he mumbled, still occupied by the television.

"An hour, do you think you could stay hard for a whole hour?"

"Do I win a prize at the end or…?"

"No, I'm saying if you were a guy who had called up for female company, would you be satisfied that it took this long for her to get here?"

"You didn't just call up looking for female company, you wanted a specific girl. If she was already occupied, you have to wait. Did they offer you other girls instead?"

"I don't know. I didn't make the call, Saul did."

"If it was an urgent situation, a guy wouldn't care which girl came over."

"So when your cock is hard it doesn't matter who rides it, is that what you're saying?"

"Yeah."

"Dax," she cried and snatched the remote control from his hand to switch off the TV.

"What?"

Clambering to her knees, she tilted her head to glare. "Think about what you just said, then think about why your wife might be mad about it."

He actually did take a few seconds to replay the conversation. "We weren't talking about my cock; we were talking about an imaginary cock. The cock of some loser who'd call up a service to have a random tramp come suck it for him. I don't need a random tramp," he said, stroking her arm. "I have my own specific one."

"You don't think I'm a tramp."

"No, I don't, but you like it when I talk dirty," he said. Plucking the remote from her hand, he put an arm around her to move her away from blocking his view of the TV. He pulled her down to lie on his chest, but the embrace wasn't one of love, he just wanted a clear view of the screen. "You were the one locked up in a bedroom with another guy less than an hour ago."

"Saul was here for ten minutes," she mumbled. "Check the hotel security tapes if you want to."

If Dax wanted to do that, he would find a way to get hold of them.

"You're way too addicted to my spunk to go tasting someone else's," he said, turning on the TV. "And now I know he knows who I am, I'm not worried."

"I had no idea that Saul went to watch underground fights. He must have known you before I did."

"I don't know him," Dax said. "I couldn't pick him out of a line-up, but yeah, he's clearly a fan of the circuit. Guys don't advertise that, keeping it quiet is one of the ways it stays underground and keeps guys like me outta jail."

The knock on the door killed her questions. She sprang up out of his arms.

"Answer the door," she whispered, taking the remote control from him.

"Okay," he said. Had he taken that as a request for protection? She turned off the TV and started toward the bathroom. "Where are you going?"

"Invite her in, you know," Ivy said, eying him and gesturing at the bed.

"Whoa," he said, rounding the bed to get hold of her. "I'm not fucking around with her. I don't even know this girl."

"If I answer the door, she'll get spooked and run. Invite her in. Once we know it's her and she's alone, I'll come out and you can wait in the bathroom."

"How much does she charge for the hour?" he muttered.

"I don't know. What does that matter?"

"I didn't stop at an ATM," he snarked. "They always want to be paid first."

Glaring, she didn't appreciate him being snide, but there wasn't time to argue. She kissed him and spun away to dash into the bathroom. Without closing the bathroom door all the way, she plastered herself to the wall beside it to eavesdrop on Dax and Trudi's exchange.

After listening to his footsteps on the carpet, she heard the room door open.

Trudi's voice rang out. "I… oh my God, hell-oh."

"Hey," Dax grumbled. "Trudi?"

"Even if I wasn't I would say hell yeah right now, wow, you walked right out of every woman's sex fantasy."

Dax would be a hooker's dream client. His sculpted body and skill in the bedroom would delight every female, if Ivy ever chose to share him, which she never would.

"I'll do you for free," Trudi said.

On top of everything Dax had done for her since they'd gotten together, this humiliation was a new low. She'd be generous with her gratitude later.

"Thanks," Dax said. "Come in."

"Any time you need a ride, you can call me direct. I can't believe you waited. You requested me personally, but I've never worked you before," Trudi said. "I would remember that for sure. How do you know me?"

The room door closed.

Only two voices. That meant Trudi was alone.

"You were recommended," Dax mumbled. "You work alone?"

"I can call a friend," Trudi flirted. "How many of us do you want? After they hear how hot you are, I guarantee there will be a waiting list."

Before this could get any more irritating mortifying, she came out of the bathroom. Trudi's arms were around Dax, hanging off his neck. He, on the other hand, was motionless with his head tipped back to avoid Trudi's kiss.

"I think you know my wife," he said when he saw her.

Trudi turned, giving Dax the opportunity to duck out of her embrace.

"Ivy," Trudi said, and her desire cleared. "What are you doing here?"

"I'm here to see you," Ivy said. "You heard I got married, right? This is Dax."

"That's your husband?" Trudi said, taking another good look at Dax. "How did you snag him?"

"Actually, I have you to thank for that, in part."

Dax came to her, pausing just long enough to kiss her and smack her ass before going into the bathroom to leave the women alone.

"I heard you were asking around about me last night," Trudi said, sliding one foot forward to bear her weight on the rear one, she exuded attitude. "What do you want?"

"I want to know if it was worth it. How much did you get for setting me up?"

"You still pissed about that? Look, it wasn't my idea. Carlos told me to give you that address. I didn't know what was going to happen."

"You knew it wasn't going to be anything good," Ivy said.

Going to the bedroom door, she locked it and kept her hand on the cool metal when she turned to press her spine against it.

"What are you doing?" Trudi asked, glancing at the bathroom door. "You better not think about hurting me, I have a guy downstairs who—"

Ivy laughed. "You got a good look at Dax, didn't you? Do you think I'm afraid of whatever pussy bodyguard you have sitting in the hotel bar? I don't think so, honey. Besides, we have you for a full hour. Think about all the damage we could do to that pretty face in an hour."

Trudi prickled; Ivy gave her some credit for not wilting. Her former roommate would resort to feminine pleading before she'd think to stand up for herself.

"You're not going to hurt me," Trudi said as Ivy came closer. "I know you, there's no way that you—"

Backhanding Trudi, she didn't care about the woman's squeal of pain. Trudi cradled her cheek; an expression of shock swathed her face. Her pouting lips, still glistening with gloss, parted to take in another breath.

Behind Trudi, Dax materialized in the bathroom doorway. He didn't make a sound, just folded his arms and leaned on the doorframe to keep an eye on proceedings.

"You fucking bitch!" Trudi exclaimed and lunged forward to grab a handful of her hair.

The bite of Trudi's nails cut into the side of her neck, but Ivy wasn't the bitch fight type. She bypassed the hair-pulling and scratching to slap Trudi again. Trudi screamed and tried to kick, but was pulled back by Dax, who'd come out of nowhere.

Ivy wrenched her hair out of her ex-friend's grasp, and while shaking it back from her face, she braced for another hit. But Dax was still there, holding Trudi back with little effort. He kept Trudi's arms locked behind her back.

When Trudi tried to kick again, Dax's powerful leg swept around, taking the hooker's feet from under her, sending her to her knees. Dax went down to maintain his grip on Trudi's arms; one of his shins clamped Trudi's calves to the floor. There was nowhere for Trudi to go, no way for her to fight for herself.

Even without his intervention, Ivy was confident she would've come out on top. Either her husband hadn't wanted to see his wife get hurt or watching such a pathetic excuse for a fight irritated him.

While still holding Trudi, he looked at her, wearing a cool, aloof expression. One of the underground fighting rules was not to hit a man while he was down. It was not sportsman-like. So as much as she'd like to knock a few more lumps out of Trudi for betraying her, she got down to business.

"Do you know Darryl?" she asked Trudi.

"What? Darryl?" Trudi asked, giving up her squirming. "No, who is he?"

"You only dealt with Carlos?" Ivy asked. "Did Carlos ever mention anyone else?"

"No, I didn't ask questions. You don't question Carlos, you follow his orders, and that's it. Girls who question him don't last very long."

"So how did you get away?" Ivy asked. "You're not working for him anymore."

"He sold me off to his cousin when they started this new deal. Carlos still gets a cut because he ponied up a heap of cash to get it moving."

"Yeah," Ivy said, bending to get into Trudi's face. "Money he got for setting me up."

"Seemed to work out pretty well for you from where I'm standing."

Except it could have so easily gone the other way. Making eye contact with Dax reminded her how lucky she was to have him. If it hadn't been for his love, she would be living in the Stark mansion right now, married to Trystan and living her version of hell.

"You're useless to me," Ivy said, backing off. "This is quite the life you have for yourself, Trud. Did you ever think about having a bit of self-respect?"

"Oh, yeah, 'cause it's just so easy," Trudi said. "You always thought you were better than the other girls on our block. Always saying you wouldn't make a living on your back."

"Like you said, it worked out for me, didn't it?"

Trudi's eyes slid in their sockets in Dax's direction. "Looks to me like that's exactly what you're doing. How many times did you open your legs for him before he gave you access to his bank accounts?"

Dax's grip shifted. One of his arms came around Trudi's throat, yanking her head back to growl in her ear. "Ivy's my jackpot, a cheap 'ho like you doesn't measure up."

Funny that Ivy had once thought about Dax being her jackpot, and now he was making the same comparison about her. She went to the door and unlocked it to open it an inch.

"Get out of here. If your little buddy downstairs wants to discuss any issues, Dax will be happy to talk to him in private."

She threw open the door and Dax stood up to lug Trudi across the room to throw her into the hall. Trudi rubbed her throat and hurried down the corridor without looking back. She didn't run, but her quickstep wasn't far from a jog.

Slamming the door, she exhaled, Trudi didn't have the information she wanted. That meant approaching Carlos. A nightmare come to life.

"I make ten grand in the ring on a poor night," Dax said. "You've got me beating on women in hotel rooms."

"I'm sorry," she said, going to sit on the bed. Doubling over, she retrieved her purse from the bedside unit. "You could've stayed in the bathroom. You didn't have to come out and—"

"The couple who threatens together, stays together, I guess," he said.

Pulling a black diary from her purse, she began to flick through the pages. Her husband came over to grab the book and toss it aside.

He hauled her onto her feet. "What's going on?"

Planning her next step would have to wait. "I just… I was going to take care of this myself. I meant to take off for a couple of days and be back before you noticed I was gone."

"I noticed," he said. "And I came here to take you back."

"Not yet," she said, shaking her head. "Please, we still have time before Mauri's party. If you want to go back and work with Serg, I understand, but… I have to do this. I don't know if I'll get the time to do it again."

"Like fuck I'll leave you here alone, you've got exes sniffing around and gangsters waiting in the lobby."

"I don't think Trudi really had a minder here. She just said that to scare us."

"You think?" he said. "You were planning to face that girl alone, she could have come armed."

Storming across the room, he pulled her luggage from the closet and opened drawers to stuff her clothes into it.

"What are you doing?" Ivy beseeched, running over to try wrenching the bag from him.

"You're not staying here alone," Dax said.

Unmoved by her actions, he carried on around the room throwing in the rest of her things before he went into the bathroom.

"You can't just issue a command and expect me to follow it! I am not going back to California, not yet." Being with a man whose boiling point was as low as Dax's led to dynamite sex and regular outbursts. "This is not about us! I am not leaving you. You can go back to LA, and I'll follow when I'm done in Vegas. I will always come to you!"

"What did I say about division?" Dax asked. Coming out of the bathroom, he zipped up the bag and tossed it onto the bed. "We should not be divided, not now, with everything that's going on."

Traversing the room, he hovered in front of her. His superior bulk blocked out the light from the window. Somehow, he'd managed to maneuver her so her back was to the bed.

"I have something I need to take care of," she said, fingering the hem of his tee-shirt. "It should only take two days, three tops."

"You think I'm going to leave you alone here for three days? I don't think so, Minx. What do you need to take care of?"

The trouble with asking for complete honesty was you had to give it back.

With a deep breath, she prepared to tell the truth. "It's something I can only do here."

"Tell me what you need so badly. What's here?"

"My life before Dax Harrow," she said. "I left everything here and I have some… ends I need to tie up."

"I'd wager it's nothing too important because you didn't come back here after you left my apartment and went on your seven-week adventure without me."

"Because I knew Vegas would be the first place that the Starks would look for me. It's no big deal, I… we have time, don't we? Mauri doesn't need us at the mansion until the party. I'll be back in time for that."

"Yeah," he said, pulling her hand away from his abs. "You will be."

He went to the bed and snatched up her black diary, but instead of reading it, he stuffed it into her purse. Gathering up both her purse and the sports bag he'd filled with her possessions, he came back to her.

"What are you doing?" she asked.

"Come on," he said, seizing her wrist he pulled her toward the door, but she dropped her weight down, trying to wrench herself free of his grip.

"Please, Dax, no, I don't want to leave. We can't leave Nevada until—"

He stopped yanking and turned without releasing her. "I have a suite upstairs, a better one," he said, glancing around at her budget room. "Trudi and your buddy Saul know where we are now. I'm not getting naked with you until we're sure no one is going to show up and start causing shit."

"Are you worried about fighting?" He raised an eyebrow, so she smiled. "I can do this alone, tough guy. You can go back to the Starks. I didn't want you involved in any of this. It's not your mess."

"If there's a mess, I'm going to fix it," he said. "You can fill me in upstairs."

Letting him take her up to the room he'd reserved would give her time to think about how to approach telling her story. He loved her and would accept any skeletons in her closet. She hadn't done any terrible thing that could shock him. Showing him weakness was what she feared.

Having him think she was weak or sentimental embarrassed her. She could stand up to any bully and had enough integrity to fill a football stadium. But showing her husband a softer, some would say weaker, side of herself had the potential to bring her out in hives.

TWELVE

WHEN THEY WERE SETTLED in Dax's suite, she washed her face and changed her clothes, then he took her hand and led her to the sumptuous couch in the living room.

"You're gonna give me the scoop, after that we'll eat, then we'll fuck."

She had once accused Dax of not being much of a planner. Tonight, he proved otherwise, knowing just what he wanted and when.

"We didn't have a room this big for our wedding night," she said, in an effort to delay her confession.

"We took what they had available," he said. "All we needed was a bed, and I provided that, didn't I?"

"You always provide," she said, linking her fingers on her lap. "You've got money and influence enough to look after yourself and me too. I don't have that. I'm not… I mean, I don't have a skill that I can use to support myself like you do."

"You've got mad skills, babygirl," he said with enough teasing in his tone to make her smile since she'd said something similar to him once. He took her hand out of her lap and into his. "If you don't start talking, I'm gonna assume the worst, and you know that doesn't end well for the next scumbag schmuck I see."

"My job at the GoldSpring is about as good as my life got," she said. "And the live-in job at that Vegas house that I was setup for, so the Starks could lure me…"

"Yeah?"

"Trudi, my ex-roommate, the hooker downstairs, she recommended the job. Her pimp took a payoff to get the information to me and I walked right into it."

"Carlos?"

"Yeah," she said, sagging back into the couch.

"You were supposed to believe it," Dax said. "It has to look good, believable, so that the victim will walk in and accept the setup without suspecting anything's off."

"How many people did you set up?"

"Whoever Mauri told me to," he said. "Yeah, I've taken part in gigs like that before. I won't lie to you about my past."

"I had to come back to Vegas," she said. "Everything I own is here. I need to… it's time to consolidate my old life with my new one."

"No better way to do that than to keep the new life at your side." He took her hand to his mouth and kissed it, but when he tried to let her go, she captured his forearm.

"You can stay with me, here, in this room," she said. "But I need time alone to take care of… some things."

"Why? What are you so desperate to keep me away from?"

With half a shrug, she admitted the truth. "My ex-boyfriend."

Dax tensed and twisted their joined hands to bring her body flush to his. "That loser I met downstairs? You'll stay at my side. Why the fuck would you need to go near some loser that you used to bang? I'm here. I'll take care of—"

"I'm not going there for sex. Saul and I didn't have that kind of relationship anyway."

"You didn't fuck him?"

"I did. I meant it wasn't just sex. He did care about me," she said, avoiding eye contact.

Saul had seemed like a good guy when they started going out. For a time, he was besotted with her. But he always wanted to share in the next big thing and Ivy wasn't interested in being a part of any scene. Their relationship was doomed to never work out; they wanted different things.

"Is that meant to make me feel good? You were in love with the guy?"

"Not like I'm in love with you," she said. "If you want to meet him again, you can. What you can't do is invite him into the ring with you. You have to be nice to him, no threatening and intimidating him, he did me a favor when he didn't have to."

"What favor?"

"Nothing naked," she said, stroking the hairs on his arm. "I needed someone who could mobilize and disarm people. There's no one better at that than Saul. He knows tons of people, and he's so friendly, he can… he just knows how to work people I guess."

"So? Why did you need him to do that?"

"The night I left here, our wedding night—"

"You went to your ex-boyfriend on our fucking wedding night?" he shouted and shot to his feet.

"No! No, I called him. I went to my old place, Trudi was working, I knew she would be, I packed up the rest of my stuff there and then went… to the house where I had the live-in job. But there were new owners, the previous tenant was gone, and they didn't know where he was.

"So I was stuck there without cab money and no phone. I walked to a friend's place and used her phone to call Saul, and we made an arrangement."

"An arrangement?"

"He agreed to store my things for me, the stuff I'd picked up from Trudi's. I hadn't taken all my shit to the live-in job yet; I only took one bag. I didn't know if it would work out, and I'd paid rent to Trudi for the month. I wanted to make sure that she was looked after. Funny, isn't it? I was worried about her because I thought I'd landed on my feet with my new job. I was going to pick up the rest of my stuff from Trudi's later, then you know, everything happened.

When we were back in Vegas to get married, I took the chance and went over to Trudi's to pack everything up."

"Why did you go to the other house?"

"I left something there," she said. "I wanted to get it back."

"Something, what?"

"You won't understand."

"Try me."

"You're angry," she said. "I can tell when you bark at me like that."

"You went to an ex when we were together."

"I didn't see Saul on our wedding night. I left my bags from Trudi's at my friend's place, and he picked them up the next day. I came back here to you."

"But you didn't get that one bag? The things you took to your live-in job?"

"No, I didn't," she said, picking at her cuticle. "I was an idiot for going over there. I thought that… that Darryl Kay was a real person. He was probably made up. But I… I'm not ready to give up yet. If Trudi doesn't know him, then there's a chance that Carlos will. He'll be able to tell me who his contact was."

"No, he won't," Dax said, dashing her hopes. "We don't leave contact details and transactions like that happen in the shadows; chances are Carlos never saw a face."

"How can you—"

"Because I've been that guy, the guy offering a payoff to someone for carrying out a simple task. You said Trudi gave you the info?"

"Yeah."

"Someone went to Carlos with an envelope full of money and the details. He was told to give the information to Trudi and to make her pass it on to you. Carlos got his money and a piece of paper, that's it. He probably never saw the person before or since."

"Probably," she said, bouncing to her feet. "I have to take the chance. He might know. Trudi said she got the job details from a client. Maybe the person offering Carlos the payoff was a client, maybe he knew—"

"No," Dax said. "Being discreet is part of the job. Even if they were our guys, they wouldn't have approached a hooker they used or her pimp. They might make a recommendation on how to get to you, but someone else would make the drop."

"Great, way to break the news gently, Dax."

Seating herself on the couch again, she tried to think of other ways to get to Darryl Kay. But Trudi had been her ace, Ivy didn't have any other link to that job.

"Did you think about coming to me?" Dax asked.

"You?" she asked. "You weren't there. I would have remembered it if you were."

"Mauri kept me out of it because you and I interacted. But I have contacts of my own, I can find out how it went down."

"You can?"

"Maybe," he shrugged. "Pinning down the exact guy who made contact with Carlos will be tough, we're trained not to talk. But if he wasn't a top guy, he might be sloppy. If he's mouthed off to someone about working for Mauri, then I can find that out... though the chances are if Mauri's heard that the guy has opened his mouth, then the guy won't be around anymore, if you get me."

"I don't need to speak to that guy," she said, springing to her feet and rushing over to her husband. "I need to find out what happened to my things."

"The bag you never retrieved?"

She nodded. "Everything that's important to me is in it."

"Would Mauri have gotten rid of it?"

"Probably, if you were any other mark," he said. "But your role was supposed to be at Trystan's side, they might have sent your things to the California mansion."

"Damn."

"Damn? I thought that would make you happy, why does that disappoint you?"

"Because if Trystan has my possessions, then I'll have to ask him for access to them. He's never going to be nice and just hand them over. You know how he likes to play with people. He'll want to question me or make me beg."

"You don't have to do anything," Dax said, taking her hands to bring them to his shoulders. "If there's anything that belongs to you in Trystan's suite, I can get it."

"How?" She wouldn't ask Dax to beg for her, and she didn't want either of them owing Trystan any favors; he was a sick, twisted man, who could not be trusted.

"Don't worry about that," Dax said. "You should have come to me with this before coming here by yourself. What was the next part of your plan? Were you going to speak to Carlos alone?"

"If I had to, yes."

"Men like that don't talk to women; he wouldn't have answered your questions."

"Do you know Carlos?"

"No. I don't have to know the specific guy to know what they're like. Pimps like to exert power over women and are caught up in their own importance. Even if you did beg he still wouldn't give you the information. Who is Darryl?"

"Darryl Kay is the guy who owned the house that I worked in, at least I thought he was, he's the one that I worked for."

"That's a good start. I can call Mauri and—"

"I don't want us to owe them anything," she said, stepping back and dropping her hands. "If we ask for help, they'll expect us to fall in line. I don't want them to know this is important to me either, it's personal, and if they ask me to … I can't give them ammunition to use against me."

"I'll deal with it," he said, reaching for her hand. "Your name doesn't have to come up in conversation."

"So how will you get Mauri to—"

"To give up the man who tricked my future wife? Mauri teaches his kin young that disrespect is the greatest enemy. If I tell him that I want a face to face with the guy, Mauri will set it up. If he wants me to take over then he's going to have to give me everything I ask for."

"Are you still considering taking over?" she asked, hooking his belt loop to pull him back to the couch. "How did things go with Serg?"

"It was… like old times."

"Is that a good thing or a bad thing?"

"It felt good being out there again, I guess, you know, doing something. But once I knew you were here in Vegas, my mind wasn't on the job."

"I told Bri I would call and let her know we arrived safely," she said. Though they had arrived in California days ago, Ivy's newest friend had plenty going on in her own life so shouldn't have spent too much time worrying. But Ivy did feel bad that she hadn't phoned sooner.

"Okay, you phone her. I'll order room service then call Mauri."

"Can that wait?" Ivy asked, climbing over him to straddle his lap. "I want you to myself for a night. Since Brad showed up, we've either been fighting or avoiding each other, least that's how it feels."

Her husband made no secret about the fact that he was on guard and distracted tonight. He hadn't been in Vegas for long, and there had been plenty of drama already. She had to find a way to take his mind off the turmoil going on around them. Focusing entirely on each other might lead to a sleepless night, but it would be worth it.

BREAKFAST AT THE HOTEL was exquisite and far more extravagant than anything she'd had before. Waking Dax up had taken quite a while, but she was determined that they would share this meal together and then get to work. The food was delicious and the service impeccable, Ivy was disappointed to leave the table when they'd finished.

"Can we afford this?" she asked when Dax handed her a takeout cup of juice, brought by the staff before they left the restaurant.

"Sure we can," he said, raising the cup she held to his lips to drink while it remained in her grasp.

"It seems so unnecessary, to waste this kind of money, we might need it someday."

"You're the one who called this trip our honeymoon," he said.

Throwing an arm around her, he dragged her body to his and slid his shades over his eyes when they walked out into the desert heat.

"Is that why you bought the suite? Or are you overcompensating?"

He stopped, still under the hotel awning, and faced her. "You got a problem with the equipment you've been playing with?"

"No," she said with a flash of a smile.

"I'll drop my pants and fuck you right here if you need the reminder."

"No, tough guy," she said, tucking herself under his arm, against his solid form. "I'm not talking about your dick. I'm talking about us going to visit my ex."

"I've got nothing to prove," Dax said, swaggering onto The Strip. "I know this loser doesn't compare to me. He's shit scared of me anyway, just like he should be."

"He used to give me foot massages after I'd spent a long day on my feet on a shift."

"Hmm," he sort of grunted. "And since we've been married, have you been on your feet for a whole day?"

"No, but—"

"Fuck foot massages, I massage the more interesting parts of your body."

His hand opened over her breast.

She nudged her hip into him. "I'll take you over a foot massage any day," she said, kissing his arm. "Orgasms were hit and miss with Saul."

Giving him that boost made her feel better. As soon as the men came face to face with each other again, the testosterone would fly. Grateful as she was to Saul, her husband was the better man. There was no better man as far as she was concerned. Though she wouldn't tell him that, his ego was already healthy enough.

"I hit your mark every time, babygirl."

Often more than once, it helped that their lives together served as constant foreplay. "Yes, you're better in bed, does that make you feel like a stud?"

"I fuck better than him and I fight better than him," Dax said. "Fuck yeah, I am the man."

His arm came up around her neck when she laughed, and she turned her mouth down to it. "Yes, you are."

"Now where is this lesser guy?"

"We need to get a cab," she said. "And when we get there, I need you to say nothing, not a word."

"I do strong and silent better than other dudes as well."

"Yes. You're quite the catch. I'd suggest that we run off together and get married, but…"

"You're too late," he said, wiggling his occupied ring finger in her face. He moved them off the sidewalk and hailed a cab. "Let's get this over with then I'll call Mauri."

Dax was so eager to say goodbye to her past but at the same time he clung fiercely to his own. Letting go wasn't so difficult for her, perhaps because she'd done it so many times before.

THIRTEEN

THIS SAUL GUY had a nice bungalow with a huge yard fit for entertaining. Dax had propped himself on a railing by the pool with a view into the concrete shed Saul opened to reveal Ivy's stuff. She went inside to pick out her bags, so Saul had handed over an ice-cold beer and joined him in his wait.

"You're a lucky guy," Saul said to him.

Fixated on his wife's ass as she bent over to look in a bag, he took a mouthful of beer.

"Yeah," he said.

Ivy had told him not to say much, which suited him. He had no intention of getting buddy-buddy with the prick who used to fuck his wife.

"Ivy's great," Saul said.

"Yeah."

They kept drinking their beer. Despite projecting patience, he was eager to get Ivy's shit and get the hell away from there.

"So… any fights planned while you're in town?"

"Nope," Dax said.

"I could… you know, I could hook you up if you wanted…"

Lowering his chin, Dax peered over the top of his shades at the eager puppy. "You think I need help from a guy like you?"

"No! No, I... I was just saying... I know people and I could... I could get you a good deal."

"Shit," Dax exhaled and didn't hide his smile as he pushed away from the railing to cross to Ivy's ass, which was still in the air. That skirt of hers licked the top of her thighs inviting him to whip it out of the way and slide into her real deep.

After all this time together, his dick shouldn't react to her so impulsively. When he got there, he smacked her ass, and she immediately righted herself to peek over her shoulder.

"Don't do that in front of Saul."

"Why?" Dax asked, happy her body came to rest against him. "The guy's a loser, what did you see in him? Forget it, I don't want to know."

The last thing that he wanted to hear was his wife talking about the positive attributes of her ex.

"Don't be stupid," she said, bending again, this time deliberately pushing her ass into him.

"If you'd told me this needed done, I'd have sent guys over here. I don't want you here."

"You don't want to be here," she said.

Slipping a hand under her skirt, he pressed the length of his cold bottle against her panties, and she gasped in a breath that reminded him of how she breathed in in his bed.

"You're not going fast enough," he said.

His body blocked hers from the view of the yard, she was still half-in, half-out the shed. He fingered aside her panties and touched her core with the condensation covered bottle.

"Don't do that," she said, but when she tried to stand up, he splayed his other hand on the small of her back and held her down.

"Take a couple of steps forward. I'll close this door and fuck you right here."

"We are not having sex at my ex-boyfriend's place," she hissed.

"Why not? Worried about upsetting him?"

"No, but I am not a trophy," she said, groping around she found his wrist and pulled his hand off her back.

When she stood, he took the opportunity to seek her breast, fondling through her dress. Kissing the scratch Trudi left on her neck, he flicked her earlobe with his tongue.

"This fucking heat, doesn't it turn you on?"

"No," she said, using her body to move his around, remaining flush with him while bringing the pool into their view. "But I do think that we should get a pool."

"At the apartment?"

As it stood, they didn't have a fixed abode. They had been living in North Carolina, then flew to his apartment in California. Mauri wanted them to live at the mansion. Right then, they lived in a hotel in Vegas. Putting in a pool wasn't an option anywhere.

"Wherever we end up," she said.

He didn't like the way she sighed as she spoke. She had to be fed up with his ties to the Starks after everything they put her through. Turning down Mauri should have been his first instinct, but he couldn't be stupid enough to ignore the chance Mauri was presenting. If they took over the Stark empire, he'd be able to give Ivy everything she wanted.

He had money from the many fights he'd taken part in over the years but wasn't dumb enough to think he could fight for the rest of his life. Eventually, he'd have to retire, probably sometime soon. His bank account was healthy and would support them if they chose to live a modest life. He didn't want modest for her and wanted to take care of his wife in the best possible way. Living in the opulence of the Stark mansion would give her the luxury she deserved.

"Why don't you go inside and call Mauri," Ivy said. "I'll finish up out here."

All she was doing was transferring her things from several smaller bags into a larger one and a suitcase that Saul had given her. It shouldn't take her too long, and she didn't want to be party to his conversation with Mauri anyway.

Leaving her alone, he went inside, passing Saul without speaking to him, and picked up the phone to dial

Mauri's direct number. Few people had direct access to Mauri, Dax was one of the lucky ones.

"Hello?" Mauri answered the phone and wouldn't have recognized the number, so his audible suspicion was understandable.

"It's me," Dax said. "I need something."

"Anything."

"The guy Ivy worked for in Vegas, who was he?"

"Darryl Kay," Mauri said. "He's on his yacht, sailing in the Pacific now."

Men like that didn't own sailboats, they owned ships that were filled with luxuries. Staying in Vegas had no doubt been a step down for the man.

"He owed you something?"

"Several somethings," Mauri said. His connections were global, and he kept a running tally of who he'd done favors for over the years. Maurice Stark had no shame in calling in a favor when it suited him. "What do you want with him? Did he touch Ivy? Hurt her?"

The concern in Mauri's voice was no doubt meant to curry favor. Why hadn't it occurred to him to question what Ivy had gone through in the three days she worked for Darryl Kay?

"He just did you a favor?" Dax asked.

"Yes."

"When did he leave Vegas?"

"Not long after we took Ivy," Mauri said. "The man had a weak stomach."

"If Ivy left something in Kay's place, where would it be now?" Dax asked.

"Is there something in particular—"

"Do you know the answer to my question?"

"I can look into it," Mauri said.

Standing in Saul's kitchen, Dax dropped his fist to the countertop. There was no way that he had to "look into" anything, he already had the answer. At that time, Mauri expected Ivy to be his daughter-in-law, that kind of op wasn't left to chance.

"You're forgetting who you're talking to, Mauri," Dax said, lowering the bass of his voice. "If you want me to trust you, show me some respect. I can walk any time I want."

Mauri exhaled. "Yes, I know. I'll have her things ready when you come to the party. I'll find out where they are and have them brought to your suite."

Their suite? So Mauri was expecting them to move into the mansion after the party. Growing up there, he'd lived with staff, not in the main body of the house like Brad and Trystan. Mauri was going to great lengths to make him feel special. Why was this so important to the old man?

"Good," Dax said. "You do that."

After hanging up the phone, Dax remained in the kitchen. Keeping watch out of the back window, he made sure that Saul didn't go anywhere near Ivy while she sorted through her possessions.

Slugging more beer from his bottle, he fixated on her ass again. Knowing that Saul was also enjoying the view irritated him. After this day, his wife wouldn't go near any man who had touched her in the past, he would make sure of it.

FOURTEEN

IVY HAD HER DOUBTS Maurice Stark would deliver, but Dax was confident. Her husband had been conditioned from a young age to have utter faith in his mentor; that kind of unshakable trust confounded her.

After witnessing Dax's turmoil when Mauri failed to accept their relationship, she worried that Dax would crash if he was disappointed again. During their early days, Dax had been convinced that Mauri would embrace their marriage once he knew how much they cared for, and loved, each other. It hadn't worked out that way at all.

When she requested that they stay in Vegas for the week instead of rushing back to LA, Dax yielded. It gave them time to relax and enjoy themselves without the watchful eye of the Stark network.

But on the Saturday of Maurice Stark's party, they flew back to California with Ivy's possessions in tow. Having her clothes and knick-knacks back was great, but what she really wanted was the bag Mauri had promised would be at the party.

They hadn't been back at the apartment for very long. Dax had gone straight into the shower, leaving her to deal with the unpacking and laundry. Now in the bedroom closet sorting through their apparel, she heard him come out of their bathroom and move into the bedroom.

"Are you ever going to tell me what happened?" she shouted just loud enough for her voice to carry through the open closet door.

When he came into the doorway, he was already clothed though his hair was still damp. "Tell you about what?" he asked, clipping the metal strap of his watch closed.

"What happened between you and Mauri at that midnight meeting?"

"That was months ago," Dax said. "The meeting when I told them to go to hell then spent seven weeks trying to find you?"

"Yes," she said. Folding a clean tee-shirt into a drawer, she closed it then set her sights on him. "You saw Mauri alone then you came back here to tell me he had commanded us to go to a meeting at his mansion. I told you Mauri would want you to hand me over to Trystan, so you let me leave here, to escape from them. But you went to the meeting by yourself. Something happened at that meeting. Something which made you walk away from them. You followed me across the country after that. Why did you come after me?"

"I figured out I loved you."

"You already knew you loved me," she said, hooking her hands onto a shelf behind her. "You had already married me."

"Yeah, but I hadn't lost you yet. I only married you so he couldn't."

At least at the time, he'd told himself that, Ivy would never have married him if she hadn't been sure he reciprocated her feelings.

Dax turned to leave, but she sprang forward to hold him back. "You went to that midnight meeting; you told me that you did."

"Yeah," he said.

"What happened?"

"I told them to go to hell, told them I wanted to be with you, and I didn't care about them anymore."

"What did they say to you?" she asked. His countenance betrayed there was something he didn't want to share, he got irritated, and his attention went everywhere except to her. "Please, tell me, it will sound better coming from you, whatever it is, I'd rather know. Was it about me? Were they disrespectful? Do you think you're protecting me?"

"I am protecting you," he said. "You know everything you need to know."

Removing her hand from his arm, Dax continued out into the bedroom.

She trailed after him. "Just like that," she said. "You expect me to just accept that?"

"I expect you to keep your mouth shut. I don't answer to you."

"Oh, so you're going to get defensive and start snapping at me? Yeah, that really tells me nothing happened. Dax, we're going over there tonight, and I don't know what's going to happen when we get there."

"It's a party," Dax said, taking his phone and his wallet from the nightstand to stuff them into his jean's pockets. "There will be music and dancing and food, it's a fucking party."

"This might be easy for you, but I am going back to a place… the last time I was there they were fitting me for a wedding dress, remember? I was locked in a room and told I was expected to be part of the family, to be Trystan's wife. Has all that slipped your mind?"

"You're not in danger when I'm around," he said.

"Really? Because I seem to remember you telling me you'd take care of everything and we ended up hightailing it out of there on your motorcycle, hoping no one would catch us. You took me to Vegas and married me because you were too scared to stand up to Mauri."

"Except I've done it now," he said, heading for the door. "I'm going out."

"What about the party?"

"It's not for a few hours. I'm going to the bar to talk to Serg. I'll pick you up at nine."

"Nine," she muttered because he was already storming out, slamming the front door behind him in the process.

Going back to the Stark mansion set her on edge. This wasn't easy for either of them. Being married to a man as masculine as Dax, he wasn't the type to sit and talk about his feelings. She didn't need his reassurances, what Ivy needed were the facts. Something had happened at that midnight meeting. Something he felt the need to hide from her.

Dax was a straightforward guy under normal circumstances. When he wanted something, he took it or found a way to get it. Ivy had been living the easy life with him back east, they went to work, came home, enjoyed each other, and then did it all over again the next day.

When it came to his upbringing, or their day-to-day lives, Dax had no trouble sharing with her. What had happened at the midnight meeting was the only thing he refused to talk to her about.

The meeting must have been difficult for him, Dax went into the mansion to explain her conspicuous absence and he must have assumed Mauri would accept his explanations. Except Mauri was a master manipulator, he'd managed once to convince Dax the relationship was a sham and that Ivy had used Dax to ensure her own safety.

Regardless of that, Dax had let her walk away alone, so he hadn't gone to the midnight meeting expecting to cut ties with the Starks. If he had, then they could have arranged to meet up somewhere safe after it instead of going their separate ways.

Something went on that night, and she was completely in the dark as to what it was.

FIFTEEN

RIGHT ON TIME, Dax came back to the apartment at nine o'clock, and although she smelled liquor on him, Ivy didn't begrudge him needing the courage. He took a shower, and she was ready by the time he emerged, dressed, from the bathroom.

Seeing him in a suit made her smile. "What are you smiling at?" he asked as she put in his cufflinks for him.

"You're not usually so put together," she said. "Seeing you like this reminds me of Vegas."

"When we got married, I was wearing jeans."

"Not then; the night we met," she said, finding his eyes. "You were dressed up that night, sitting in the corner of that couch, you kept looking at me."

"You were the one who couldn't take your eyes off me, babygirl," he said, resting his fingers around her hips.

"You weren't like any of them," she murmured, stroking his arms. "They were all drunk idiots, but you… I could tell you didn't want to be there. That your purpose wasn't to get drunk and laid like Trystan's."

"I used to babysit him all the time, parties like that were normal."

"And how many other hotel employees did he violate?"

His intense gaze exuded pain. "I was in deep. You were right when you said I was desensitized to what was going on. Trystan's a jerk, and I promise you that you'll never be in that position again. I won't let any man harm you; I promise you, babygirl."

"I know," she said, levering up to kiss him then wiping the gloss residue from his lips.

At nine fifteen, a limo, sent by Mauri, pulled up outside their apartment. It remained parked outside until they went down about twenty minutes later. Neither said much in the back of the car, Dax poured her a flute of champagne, but he didn't have anything to drink himself. He probably assumed she'd need some courage too, but she didn't really want any alcohol, still, she sipped it throughout the trip.

By the time they drove through the open Stark gates, Ivy had finished about half of her drink, but she didn't mind putting it aside when Dax took her hand and helped her out of the limo.

The mansion was as imposing as it had been the last time she was there. But with the glittering white lights around the driveway and entrance, it did seem warmer than it had when she was imprisoned there.

Once they were inside, she was given another glass of champagne. Dax refused a drink. There were plenty of people milling around; her husband didn't wait to speak to anyone. Instead of being forced up the stairs, as she had been the last time she was there, Dax took her down a corridor into a grand double-story space filled with people.

Women wore beautiful gowns and glittering jewels that drew her eye. These people wanted to be admired, they wanted to be respected and revered, but Ivy felt no sense of wonder.

Ensconcing themselves in a far corner, they separated themselves from everyone else. Ivy tightened her grip on Dax's hand to get his attention.

"What's wrong?" he asked.

"I want to go home."

She wasn't even sure where home was, she had started to think of her home as the man as opposed to any specific location. Dax had told her they belonged next to each other, and that was right, but this was the enemy lair, so relaxing here was nigh on impossible.

"We just have to stay long enough to be seen," Dax said.

Turning to observe the room behind them, his frown remained static. He kept her back to the wall to shelter her from the false smiles and handshakes which accompanied the string quartet in the opposite corner.

This was a crazy scenario, the Starks were crime bosses, meaning everyone else in the room was either a criminal or turned a blind eye to the glaring fact that everything there was bought with dirty money. Did these people know how Maurice Stark made his fortune? Or did they believe the companies built in the Stark name to launder drug money were legitimate?

Dax certainly didn't seem interested in talking to anyone. His permanent scowl didn't speak of a comfortable man, happy to be there. When his expression got even harder, she peeked around him to see Trystan striding over.

"Shit," she said and gulped the champagne.

Her husband's hand slid low on her back. "You don't have to say a word," Dax muttered into her hair and kissed her temple as he turned to face Trystan.

"Hello!" Trystan declared loud enough to draw attention to them. "It's the happy couple, check you out!"

"What do you want?" Dax hissed.

"I came to offer my congratulations," Trystan said, snatching Dax's hand from his side to shake it.

After dropping the handshake, Trystan leaned in as if to kiss her cheek. Threatened by his proximity, Ivy recoiled on a gasp. Her reaction prompted Dax to grab Trystan's lapels and pin him to the perpendicular wall.

Pressing his forearm across the width of Trystan's chest, Dax got in his face. "You stay the fuck away from her."

"Oh, the jealous type," Trystan said. "I thought it worked out that we shared everything. Isn't that how you ended up stealing her from me?"

Ivy didn't budge from the wall, but murmurs from around them caused her to peek beyond her husband. The mumbling party guests were catching glimpses of the unfolding drama.

"Dax," she whispered, stroking his upper arm.

"Yeah," Trystan said. "Listen to your little woman, you're causing a scene, you know how my father feels about that."

Attention was what Trystan craved, so ignoring the others in the room, she gripped Dax's elbow. "Why don't you knock him out, maybe crack a few of those veneers, then we can go home?"

"With pleasure," Dax said.

Her husband's fist didn't rise more than a couple of inches before Maurice materialized with a beautiful woman on his arm.

"You boys will need to learn to get along," Mauri said. "Trystan go away from here; I have business with Dax and his wife."

Dax twisted to shove Trystan back toward the party guests, but once he'd recovered from his stumble, Trystan walked backwards smoothing out his suit.

"Guess you can't teach class," Trystan said then widened his grin again to disappear into the throng.

"I'm sorry about him," Mauri said to her.

Being addressed directly caught her off-guard and she wasn't sure where to look. The only time they had spoken in the past, she'd lied to him and pretended to be something she wasn't.

Dax returned to her side and flopped an arm around her to haul her body to his. No, he wasn't particularly refined, but he did know how to put his mark on her. She loved that about him.

"You should've kept him locked up," Dax said to Mauri. "We won't be staying long if that's the way your guests behave."

"I will have another word with him," Mauri said, then he whispered something to the woman on his arm and she melted away, leaving the three of them alone. "I told you I had a gift for you."

"A gift?" Dax said.

"My plan to persuade you," Mauri said, he kept smiling at her, and Ivy wasn't sure she understood or appreciated the attention. "I have a gift for both of you. You can consider it a belated wedding gift."

"Okay," Dax said. "Show me."

"It's next door, in the social drawing room, will you join me?"

Mauri started to walk out, and Dax followed, keeping her pinned to his side. Departing the ballroom, they moved down the corridor and stopped upon reaching the next door. Mauri paused to look at Dax but neither man spoke, then Maurice opened the door to enter with them in tow.

A large window took up one wall of this new room, and bookcases lined the two side walls. Two women, standing in the center of a large square rug, surrounded by four couches, were the focal point. Maurice crossed to stand between the women, leaving Ivy and Dax at the door. Neither of the women said anything, but Ivy recognized the one to Maurice's left.

"Rosie?" Ivy asked. Dax's arm had loosened enough to let her take a step forward, but when his arm left her shoulders, she grabbed for his hand. "That's my sister."

Her sister grinned, but she didn't move. "Ivy! Oh, wow, look at all this you have now!" Rosie exclaimed.

Maurice lifted the hand of the second woman. "This is your mother, Dax," Mauri said. "She can verify everything we told you. It's true, son."

Ivy hadn't seen her sister for a long time, but that was nothing to Dax, who hadn't seen his mother since he was in diapers. It was unmistakable though. Ivy recognized those piercing blue eyes because they matched her husband's. Ignoring her sibling, Ivy turned around to see how Dax was reacting to this bombshell.

His frown was more of a glare, his nostrils flared

when he inhaled, then without a word, he turned around and walked out of the room alone.

SIXTEEN

MAURI HAD JUST PRESENTED Dax with a threat he couldn't beat out of his way. Given Mauri's penchant for reuniting family members, it shouldn't be a surprise he'd pulled this stunt, but his mother was the last thing he'd ever think of as a gift.

Storming out of the family filled room, Dax began to head for the exit but stopped mid-stride in the entrance foyer to spin around. Ivy. She was still in that damn room, and he couldn't walk out of here and abandon her in this place. She hadn't even wanted to come to this party, but he had insisted nothing untoward would happen, how wrong he had been.

"Hey," Brad said, rushing over to Dax, who was staring at the end of the corridor he'd just come from, hoping Ivy would emerge. "What's going on?"

"Fuck off," Dax said.

If Ivy wasn't following him, he had no choice except to go back for her.

"Not in the party mood?"

In need of an outlet for his anger, Dax hauled Brad up, off his feet. Rushing his adopted brother backwards until he hit the nearest wall, a crystal statue beside them wobbled and fell to the floor. The smash of crystal was accompanied by the squeals and gasps of party guests, but Dax didn't give a fuck about their audience or the decor.

"You knew about this?" Dax asked. "You fucking cock-sucking bastard. You didn't give me this piece of info before asking us to jet back over here?"

"Excuse me, sir."

Someone touched his shoulder and Dax whipped around, landing a punch on the security guard, knocking him out flat. That one move alerted half a dozen other security men, and they all began to rush through the guests toward him. Great, Dax actually smiled and widened his stance as he pulled off his tux jacket and ripped the cuffs of his shirt open. Ivy could take as much time as she wanted in that room with her sister. He had enough to keep him occupied out there.

The men running at him were nearly on his position, he was braced and ready to take them on.

"No!" Brad said, skirting around to block the men from reaching him.

"Get the fuck out of the way," Dax growled. "I'll take them all at once, I need the workout."

Brad's head twisted, but he kept his body as a barrier. "You'll murder them, you asshole. You think that's smart with this many witnesses?"

"I don't give a fuck."

"You want Ivy to come out here and find this?" Brad asked.

The party guests were forming a wide arc around him, Brad, and the poised security guards. Still, Dax couldn't bring himself to care about the shock on their faces. "Ivy won't give a fuck."

His wife knew who he was, knew his skills, and loved him despite the harm he'd caused others in the past.

"I think she will in front of your mom and her sister." So Brad did know what Mauri had set up. "Go back to your posts," Brad said to the security guards. "Apologies everyone, my brother is just a little riled. He'll calm down now."

The chatter returned, and the security guards did as they were told. Brad turned around and put a hand on his arm.

Dax through it off. "Don't fucking touch me!"

"Okay," Brad said, lowering to pick his jacket up off the floor. "Do you want to go back to your wife now?"

"I want to go downstairs."

The gym down there was state of the art, but the only thing he needed access to was the punching bag.

"Okay," Brad nodded. Dax hadn't expected him to agree. "Let's go."

Brad again tried to touch him in order to guide him, but he lifted his arm away and didn't move in the direction Brad wanted him to go. "What's going on? What is Mauri playing at?"

"You'd have to ask him that," Brad said. "All I know is bringing these people together was important to him. He doesn't have much time, Dax, and tracing those women sapped a lot of his energy. He was very hands on with making this happen, he had to be. Your mother was reluctant to come here."

"Good," he said. "She can fuck off then. Go in there and get Ivy for me."

"My," Brad said, wearing a smile Dax wanted to rearrange. "Dax Harrow isn't afraid, is he?"

"Afraid? No, but I'm done with the games. Mauri couldn't have done a worse thing, Ivy was already against coming back here, and you've just given me the excuse I need to walk away."

"Walk if you want to," Brad said. "But Ivy doesn't appear to be as eager to get out of here, does she?"

That could have been Mauri's goal, he wanted to tempt Ivy by bringing these women back into their lives. Ivy might change her mind now her family could be a part of their supposed new life. Coming to Mauri's call had been a mistake, his wife had been right all along.

"Get out of my way," Dax said, sweeping Brad aside to march back to the room he'd left Ivy in.

Going back down the corridor, he tossed open the door but didn't venture much more than a foot into the room. "Move," he said to Ivy.

All of the women were seated in the wood framed couches arranged in a square formation. Mauri was alone on the head one in front of the window. Their relatives were seated together on the couch to Mauri's right. Opposite, Ivy sat on a third couch with a man who hadn't been present before, a man he didn't recognize.

"Dax," Mauri said. "Come in and join us."

"No, thanks," he sniped, keeping his focus on Ivy, who hadn't said a single word though her attention was trained on him. "What's the matter with you, Minx? Move."

"I think Ivy wants to stay," Mauri said. "You should join her."

"You want to stay?" Dax asked her.

"Yes, she does," Mauri said.

Releasing the door handle, he came another couple of feet into the room while remaining in the shadow of the door. "You keep your fucking mouth shut, old man. My wife has a tongue in her head, and she's very capable of using it."

"Your wife is very beautiful."

The unfamiliar female voice drew his eye for a second. The words had come from the woman Mauri claimed was his mother.

Dax wasn't going to entertain her, that was exactly what Mauri wanted. "Minx?"

Ivy's lips parted to speak, "I…" her body jolted an inch, and her feisty eyes snapped around to the man at her side.

Taking in the scene again, Dax kicked himself for not sensing the danger sooner. "Take your fucking hands off her," he said, striding toward the man beside his wife.

The drawing room door closed, but he didn't bother looking to see who had closed it. It should have been obvious his wife sitting on the couch without expressing a word or opinion was wrong. His mind was mangled by Mauri's revelations. At least he had some legitimate danger to vent his frustration on.

Before Dax got to their position, the man rose and hauled Ivy to her feet, keeping her body pulled into his side. The gleam of a gun barrel was pressed under her ribs.

"Now everyone calm down," Mauri said, rising from his seat.

The man holding Ivy inched back until they were aligned with the patriarch.

Dax paused next to the couch they'd been seated on and made eye contact with Ivy. "I should've fucking known."

"Not your fault," Ivy said and managed a smile. She wasn't saying much and was maybe a fraction paler than normal, but she didn't wear fear or have tears in her eyes. "They took exception to me wanting to come after you… apparently there's more they have to tell you."

"We didn't want to resort to this," Mauri said. "All we want you to do is hear us out."

Us. That was a joke. Mauri was a puppet-master who tugged on everyone's strings whenever he wanted, and Dax had just got his Ivy embroiled in the old man's sick theatre.

"Do you think threatening my wife is going to tempt me into agreeing with you?"

"Who would you rather we threaten?" Mauri asked. "She has you hypnotized."

"Pissed I stopped dancing to your tune?" Dax asked. "Ivy doesn't give me instructions and expect them to be followed blindly. She taught me respect, something you never showed anyone."

"You're lashing out, I understand that," Mauri said, glancing at whoever was behind Dax.

He didn't want to take his focus from Ivy and the weapon in the room. As it turned out, he didn't have to, his girl acted as his eyes.

"It's Brad," she said. "He doesn't have a weapon though. I trust you can take him."

"Like he just tried to take half a dozen security guards in the lobby," Brad said. "The guests know something is going on."

"We don't care about them," Mauri said. "Everyone we care about is right here."

"Trystan might take exception to that," Brad said.

"Oh, let him, the boy is nothing but trouble," Mauri said.

Dax had seen him annoyed before, but this was more than that.

"He's giving you a run for your money now," Dax said. "You thought Ivy could get him to shape up before you died, doesn't look likely now."

"No," Mauri said. "But he will be your problem when I am no longer here."

"He's his own problem," Dax said. "I don't give a fuck about your empire or your family. You let mine go, and we'll be out of the state by sunset." Turning to Ivy, he held out his hand. "Come here."

She tried to move forward, but the guy at her side wrenched her back, prodding the gun deep into her side until she winced. His upper lip twitched with the angry revulsion taking him over. He would remember every detail of that motherfucker's face. If he ever saw the guy again, he would make sure he never drew another breath.

"Is this what it's like to have two men fighting over you?" Ivy quipped.

"He's not going to hurt you," Dax said, taking a step closer. "You think Mauri would take the risk of hurting you, babygirl? It won't happen."

"I'm expendable," Ivy said.

"Not to me," he said. "That diamond cost a small fortune."

"Well, I want to be buried with it, so you're out of luck," she said, smiling again. "No refund or return for you."

"Damn. I knew I should've gone with the zirconia."

"Then I might have said no."

"You're not going to say no now, are you?" he asked, elevating his hand. "Come here."

The guy with a hold of her looked at Mauri when Ivy began to move away from him. The threatener didn't yank her back, but he kept his hand on her arm.

"You don't want Dax to get over there, dad," Brad said to Mauri, prompting the guy gripping Ivy to let her go.

She bounded forward and put her hand in his.

"I'm disappointed, Mauri," Dax said. "You should follow your own advice. Never bluff in life, someone's always bound to call you on it."

Rounding, he went for the door, ready to get out of the house and away from these people forever.

"Your possessions are upstairs, Ivy," Mauri's voice sounded solemn.

Dax kept walking but had to stop when Ivy did. "What?" he asked her.

"I told you not to let them know how important that was to me," she murmured then let go of his hand to turn back to Mauri. "Where?"

"There's a bedroom ready for you and your husband upstairs, next door to the one being used by your sister. After you hear our offer, we will take you there. You will be free to have your possessions back, and I suspect there's a particular object of importance to you up there."

"What is your offer?" she asked.

"We don't care," Dax said, taking her upper arm. "Come on, we're leaving. What's up there can be replaced, I'll buy you a new one."

"You can't buy me," she said, wrenching her arm back and landing him with her ire. "I didn't marry you for money."

"Why did you marry him?" Brad asked, lowering to sit beside his father.

The man who had threatened Ivy went out a side door, but it wasn't over, he would take care of that guy at the first opportunity.

"I married him because I love him," Ivy said, folding her arms. "Is there another reason a woman would marry a man?"

"Dozens of them," Brad said. "You were sure it was love?"

"We've made it this far," Ivy said.

Dax came up behind her and brought his lips to her ear. "Stop engaging him."

"What's the worst they can do?" Ivy asked. "They've proven they're not going to hurt us, even if they threaten it, we know it's not in their best interest to try scaring us."

"You didn't appear to be scared at all," Brad said. "Even with a gun aimed at you point blank, you didn't blink. Most women would be weeping and pleading."

"Ivy isn't the weeping type," Dax muttered.

If they were going to be stuck having this conversation until Mauri relinquished Ivy's possessions, then they had better be comfortable doing it. Dax led his wife to the couch she had occupied when he entered and seated them both. As long as he maintained his focus on Brad and Mauri, he could just pretend the other women weren't present.

"There was nothing for me to be afraid of," Ivy said. "That's the great thing about being married to a man like Dax. Few people take the risk of threatening my life because the consequences would be grave."

"As we've just highlighted," Mauri said. "I am sorry we had to take such measures. But if we had allowed you to run after Dax, you would not have heard us out."

"You mentioned an offer," Ivy said.

Dax rested back on the couch, lifting one ankle to the opposite knee. Ivy twisted her body toward him to address Mauri and Brad and pressed her hands into his thigh.

"You're not interested in their offer," Dax said to her.

"No, I'm not. But they said we had to hear it, then I could get my things and go. So, the sooner we hear it…"

"We want to offer you the chance of a vacation," Mauri said. "Two weeks in the California sun."

"Why would you want to—"

"We can afford our own vacation," Dax said.

"We want you to spend two weeks at the beach house, with your relatives," Mauri said, glancing over at the silent women.

"You want to facilitate some big reunion?" Dax asked. "Sorry, we're not interested."

"You have to be," Brad said.

"If you do this, you'll have the time to consider the offer I made to you before," Mauri said. "Then if at the end of it you choose not to agree, we'll provide you a million dollars, no strings attached."

He didn't like the way Ivy shifted. He wanted to throw the offer back at Mauri without any hesitation. But the offer of money did bring clarity about why their relatives had come.

"How much are you paying them?" he asked, bobbing his head in the direction of the other two women. "That how you got them here?"

"Financial incentive is effective," Maurice said.

"What's the point of this?" Ivy asked. "What do you expect to happen?"

"Family is important, I've always believed that, but it's become more relevant to me recently. When I'm gone, Dax won't have a parental figure in his life anymore. He and Brad have always tolerated each other, but we know what his relationship with Trystan is like. I don't want him to be alone in the world."

"And you thought bringing my relatives into it would tempt me to coerce him?" Ivy asked. "I don't have the influence over Dax you think I do."

"Yes, you do," Mauri smiled. "You're sitting here now negotiating with me while he remains silent because he will do what you tell him makes you happy. He doesn't want to lose you. He turned his back on his life for you."

"Not for me, because of you and your unreasonable demands," Ivy said. "If I had influence over Dax, we wouldn't be here now."

"I'm not expecting you to answer this minute," Mauri said. "We prepared your room and invite you to spend the night. We can complete our negotiations over breakfast. You're free to leave at any time, from here or from the beach house if you choose to. There is a lot at stake. It would be foolish of you both to turn your back on an offer of financial stability you won't receive again."

"Show us to our room, my husband and I have to talk."

Dax's eyes closed. This was an impossible decision. He didn't want to be Mauri's puppet anymore, but in a few months, Mauri would be out of the picture for good. Now they had the chance of a small fortune even if they didn't choose to take over the empire. He could use that money to take care of Ivy for the rest of their lives. She was right, they needed to talk.

SEVENTEEN

FOR THE FIRST TIME in a long time, it seemed like they didn't know what to say to each other. The party was still going on downstairs, but they had been shown upstairs to a beautiful room, which had a white carpet and blood red sheets on the four-poster bed. The grand space was at the front of the house, so it had a large window, currently covered by drapes matching the bedspread color.

Brad had given Dax his jacket back, but it was cast aside, as were his shoes and shirt. Now just wearing his pants, Dax strode the width of the room, checked out the bathroom, then came back and slid his hands into his pockets.

"Okay," he said. "You were right."

"You should get used to that," she said, pulling the pins out of her up-do and putting them on the dresser by the nightstand.

"What are we doing here, Minx? Why don't we just leave?"

"If you want to, we can," she said. "But a million dollars is nothing to ignore. And I don't want tonight to change how you feel about Mauri. I think… seeing my sister there was a shock, but he tracked down your mother. How does that feel?"

"When I came back here after Brad told me Mauri was sick, I was… I wanted to ask about my history, wanted to ask questions about where I came from."

"Now you can."

And now Ivy understood what that unknown other thing was that had been playing on his mind.

"Not sure I want to," Dax said. "She's a stranger."

"Your identity is tied into being an orphan. You've identified yourself that way for a long time, all your life. It's not easy to change your whole self-image in a single minute."

"Maybe I don't want to change how I look at myself," he said. "For all the shit I've been through, all the shit I've done, things worked out okay."

"Right now, you're my husband. You're a fighter, a friend, and you're an ex-enforcer, but… none of those have to change if you let yourself be a son too."

"You think this is a good idea?" he asked.

"I don't know what I think," she said, sitting on the bed, hooking her heels up on the frame beneath the mattress. "When I saw you storm out of that room… I wanted to follow you, then that guy came out of nowhere."

"I'll take care of that," Dax said, finding his scowl again. "Don't worry."

"That's not what I'm saying. I saw you were lost and hurt. I wanted to be there with you, to make you feel better."

Lifting her arms, she beckoned to him, so he came over to take her hands. "You know how to make me feel better."

Dipping down, he caught her lips with his and guided her hands to his hips. Sliding them around to his ass when he came lower, he hooked his hands under her ass and picked her up to move her further back on the bed. His solid form covered her, and he kept on kissing. His tongue slipped deeper into her mouth, and she kept on squeezing his ass enjoying the unyielding gluts she liked to grope at every opportunity.

His fist closed around the neckline of her dress, and she pushed on his chest to break their kiss. "Don't rip this dress, I have nothing else to wear."

"I don't give a fuck about that."

"In front of Mauri and his men, you will, especially when I'm standing in front of them wearing nothing but a thong."

Rolling off her, he dropped his hands onto his chest. "Take it off then."

Leaving the bed, she unzipped her silk sheath dress and let it drift onto the carpet. Some of his tension ebbed, but the intensity remained in his eyes, though that was nothing to do with what had gone on downstairs.

"Maybe we should talk," she said. Unhooking her bra, she discarded it, then bent to slide down her underwear. "There is a lot to talk about."

"Forget talking. Talking isn't what I need from you now," he said. Losing his pants took only a few seconds, he kicked them to the floor and curled his hand around his dick. "Have a seat."

"This is stupid." She smiled, climbing onto the bed. High on her knees, she hovered above the crown of the cock he was trying to direct into her. "We shouldn't be doing this here."

"I need this here," he said.

One arm swept around her, and he reversed their positions. Getting her onto her back, he was now the one high on his knees above her. She tried to sit up, but he took her move as an invitation. Cupping the back of her skull, he leaned back to guide his dick into her mouth.

Sucking on the bulb he'd pushed between her lips, Ivy held her mouth back, which was enough to make him mutter in his usual private fashion. Increasing his pressure, she was unable to restrain herself in the face of his strength, so she sucked, just like he wanted her to. But as soon as he relaxed his hand, she grabbed his shaft and took it from her mouth, working it with her hand instead.

"You think if you come, you'll be able to see things more clearly?"

"Your mouth has a way of reprioritizing my life," he said.

Snatching her arms, he pulled her out from under him and rested her on the pillows. "What are you—"

"Stay there," he said.

Lying above her, he kissed the side of her neck, and encompassed her in his arms. She sighed. When he kissed her like this, her whole body fizzed, her hormones took over, and she couldn't think straight let alone tease or argue with him.

Dax knew every part of her body, he massaged her breasts, using the tip of his thumb and the knuckle of his forefinger to work the nipple, pinching and pulling her into a peak he loved to suck into his mouth and catch in his teeth.

Running her hands through his hair and down his neck, she was pleased the endeavor gave him focus. Physical activity was what he needed and would keep his mind occupied for a while. Except her desire was thumping in her ears and the heat of fresh blood gushing through her veins opened every one of her nerves, each begging for his attention.

"Dax," she said, but he just grumbled around the breast he was sampling, which sent shivers of vibrations through her.

Locking her ankles at his back, Ivy regretted not taking her chance to ride him when he'd offered her the position. Lost in the deluge of pleasure she got writhing up against his solid member, she almost didn't notice when he stopped kissing her body and lifted his head.

"You really weren't scared down there?"

"While I was sucking your dick?" she teased, knowing exactly what he meant. He meant downstairs when the gun was digging into her. To that, there was only one response. "I trust you."

That answer wasn't a tease; he opened his mouth and kept on tasting her. His tongue glided down her abdomen. While he kissed and licked her navel, she squeezed her lips together, anticipating what it was a prelude to. When he was done tormenting her, he moved his attention further south.

Parting her legs wide, he pushed down on her inner thighs to give himself a panoramic view of her core.

Coiling her fingers around the pillows, Ivy watched him scrutinize her, and held her breath when he descended to taste her.

His skilled mouth licked and sucked on her until she was panting, then he came up over her to kiss her mouth, giving her the full flavor of herself while he sheathed himself in her. Whimpering against the scope of his reach, she relaxed when he moved out and then slammed back in, making no apology for stretching her passage for his own pleasure.

"I only need this," she breathed, taking handfuls of his hair. "I need… oh God, Dax, I only need you."

Opening her mouth wide, she screeched out his name and bucked up into his latest thrust. Orgasm clenched her abdominals, and as she rose from the bed, he took hold of the headboard, giving himself more leverage to pound in harder. One orgasm became two, and when his climax eventually conquered him, she was tossed over the cliff again.

"I don't want his money," Dax panted, resting his head on her shoulder while he regained himself. Then he flopped onto his back. She rolled onto her side toward him, keeping their bodies in contact. "I'm sorry, I put you through this again."

"No," she said. "We had to come and see this." He shoved an arm around her and tucked her head down under his chin. "If we don't want his money or the familial bribe, all that's left to consider is this: the mansion, the offer of taking over here."

"Brad must know something about it, but I can't see him happily signing over half the assets," Dax said. "Trystan too, he'll go crazy if he thinks I'm going to be in control of his budget, or any aspect of it."

"You think Mauri is setting you up or Brad will just pull the rug from under you when Mauri is gone?"

"Maybe, I don't know, the point is, I'm done. I told them when I walked out on that midnight meeting that I was through. I should've stuck to that. We should never have come back."

"I don't see my things here, do you?"

His head moved above hers. "No. What's so important to you in this bag?"

"My birth certificate, my pictures, my memory stick, my jewelry… things that can't be replaced."

Kissing her hair, he moved her body aside, away from his, and got off the bed.

"Where are you going?" she asked.

He was already getting dressed again. "Wait here, I'll get your things."

"How will you do that? Are you going to tell Mauri how we feel about his offer?"

"Not until after I've gotten your stuff back," he said, fastening his shirt and sticking his feet in his shoes. When he was dressed, he dropped a fist to the bed to balance his weight as he leaned down to kiss her. "Get dressed but stay here. I'll come back in a minute."

"I can come with you if—"

"No," Dax said. "I can be more persuasive if I'm alone."

Still naked on the bed, she watched him depart, then lay back to look up at the canopy over the bed. If they didn't want Mauri's money, family, or empire, they could leave there and close this chapter for good.

Recovering from the exertion of their lovemaking, she took an extra few seconds to herself before rolling off the bed to don her underwear. Being back there had been difficult for Dax. He'd had high hopes of what he would get from Mauri, like maybe some respect and a bit of reassurance. Instead, he had received none.

Ivy considered whether she should have been more forthright with her opinions of Mauri and what she expected, but it was difficult to dash Dax's hopes. The fact Mauri had trotted out Dax's mother was conniving. It was a whole new level of manipulation even she wouldn't have expected from Mauri, but as Dax had frequently reminded her, she didn't know Mauri well.

Picking up her dress from the floor, she was surprised to hear the door opening. Dax hadn't taken as long as she thought he would.

"That was quick," she said, unwinding the fabric.

"Thought the same thing myself."

The voice didn't belong to Dax. In an instant, she was off the bed and facing the door, with her dress held to her chest. Fear didn't invade her when rationale could be used to explain away the actions of men like Mauri. But the man who was in her room didn't work off any kind of sane rationale.

"Trystan," she said. "What do you want?"

"Don't worry," he said, grinning. "I'm not here for a replay of the night we met. You're safe."

"That's debatable," she said. "What are you doing here?"

"Came to say hello, to say sorry for the way things went down."

A grin like that didn't scream contrition.

"And you just walked into my bedroom to say that without thinking of knocking on the door?"

"Sorry," he said, swaggering to the foot post of the bed closest to her. "But it's not like I haven't seen those before."

Ogling her breasts, his grin morphed into something more salacious, and she stood tall, unwilling to shrink in the face of his intimidation. He'd seen her breasts before because he'd ripped open her shirt in Vegas, he'd violated her as that stare was intended to remind her.

"You've said you're sorry, you can leave now."

"Oh, I have more to say," he said.

Where he stood blocked her from the exit. She could make a dash for the door, but she'd have to pass him, and she didn't trust him not to intercept her. The last thing she wanted was his hands on her.

"Then say it."

"Dax was rough downstairs, don't you think?"

"He has reason to be."

"Sure he does, he's jealous. It's a shame things never worked out between you and me."

"A shame? I don't think so. You wanted a wife you could lock up at home to satisfy your father's urge to see you married. That's not the kind of life I could ever tolerate."

"We knew that. We figured it out," he said, nodding. "Dad came up with the ideal scenario, this could all have been settled if Dax had agreed to Dad's suggestion."

"What suggestion?"

"He didn't tell you?" Trystan asked. "You remember that meeting you were supposed to come to? That Dax was supposed to bring you to before he ran off?"

The midnight meeting. "Yes."

"Dad floated an idea I think Dax would have agreed to if it wasn't for the big bombshell he dropped at the same time."

She didn't like letting Trystan know he had power. That was what he was trying to exert by not just coming right out with what he had to say.

"Nothing you can say will interest me," she said.

"You sure?" Trystan pushed out his lower lip and took his eyes from her for a brief moment. "Seems you'd want to know when your husband agreed to share you."

"Excuse me?"

"Yeah," Trystan said. "I guess we could've worked out a timeshare or something. I mean you were mine first."

While he sauntered closer, she backed away until the dresser blocked her retreat. Though they were in shadow, she made out the unmistakable line of a scar on his cheek where she'd bitten him to escape in Vegas. She'd left a mark on him. Every time he looked in the mirror, he'd be reminded of her.

"I was never yours," she spat out. "And Dax would never share me."

"I guess not, I mean he'd probably worry that after you got a taste of me, you would never go back to him."

"Unlikely," she said, resisting the urge to laugh in his face.

Trystan was volatile, as displayed when his grin fell away and he laid his hands on top of the dresser either side of her.

He leaned down, getting in her face. "Dax would've given you to me. I'd have had you and everything would have stayed the same. You took him from dad, from me, from all of us, this is where he belongs."

"No, he's not your lackey anymore," she said. "Dax follows his own orders now, not yours."

"I've been locked up in this damned building for weeks. Weeks and weeks of nothing, all because of you and that damn betrayer."

"He's a better man than every one of you."

"Still think that, knowing that he would've handed you over to me? You'd have been in my bed, for me, for my pleasure and nothing else. He'd have given you up to keep me happy because he's a Stark under all the bullshit. He'd have done it if Dad hadn't revealed that Dax was the spawn of the guy he despised."

"I don't understand what—"

"Bruno," Trystan said. "Have you seen him around since you got here? No, you haven't. He took off a few days ago. Dad told Dax the truth, told him that Bruno was his father, and that the bastard never wanted a thing to do with the squirt. Imagine that? Your father turning his back on you."

The snarl in Trystan's voice made her go cold, but she wouldn't let tears form. She wouldn't let him see any weakness or let him know that her heart was pumping so fast she could feel it in her throat.

"You're lying."

"No, I'm not," Trystan said. "Dad signed Bruno's share of the will over to Dax, Bruno took off a few days ago after he and Dad had this huge blow out about it, we haven't seen Bruno since. You better watch your back, Lucky, Bruno holds a grudge."

"Like someone else I know," she said, trying to pass his arm, but he brought his hand to her hair and stroked down until his fingers reached her breast. Holding the dress against her, she couldn't use her hands to push him away. Her tone conveyed her disgust. "Get the hell off me."

"Dax isn't here to save you now, Lucky," he breathed, leaning in to whisper in her ear. "You're all alone, why don't you drop that dress? You give me what I want, and all the trouble goes away."

"You're the only trouble here," she said. As much as she wanted to push him away, Ivy didn't want to touch his body with her own for fear he would take it as an invitation.

"You give yourself to me once, and Dax can have everything he wants. He can have the family back, he can have the life he was supposed to have, the life that you stole from him."

The stifling weight of Trystan's body vanished. Bewildered by the sudden relief, her eyes opened just as Dax punched Trystan so hard he hit the floor, boom, unconscious. Another first-hand example of why living with a fighter could be advantageous.

"Did he touch you?" Dax had hold of her, but he couldn't capture her attention.

The prone man spread out on the floor transfixed her. "Dax," she whispered, he'd come in and taken care of business like it was nothing. Still caught in the adrenaline of having Trystan up close, it took her a few seconds to rest her hands on Dax's arms and be reassured she was back where she belonged.

"Tell me," he demanded, shaking her, forcing her attention onto him.

"Yes," she said, digging her nails into his arms to stop him going back to Trystan to finish the job. "His hands on me made me feel sick, but he didn't... he didn't assault me."

Pushing Dax aside, she dropped to her knees beside Trystan to check he had a pulse. Sorry that he did, she got back to her feet and stood over him, hands on her hips.

"What do we do with him now?" she asked.

"He'll wake up soon," Dax said. "Get dressed. We're getting out of here."

"You can't... I mean... are you just going to leave him like that?"

"Are you sorry I hit him?" Dax asked, snatching her dress from the floor to feed her feet into it.

He pulled it up and forced her arms into the straps.

"Dax," she said, grabbing his arm when he tried to pass her. "What did Mauri say?"

"That he'd have your things brought over to our apartment. I already told him we're not staying."

"You're sure?" she asked, touching his jaw. "You're sure that you're ready to walk away from this? From the Starks, and the fortune Mauri is offering?"

Linking his fingers with hers, he lowered her hand away from his face. "I've got my fortune right here." He kissed the back of her hand, waited while she slipped on her shoes, then they went back downstairs.

Dax knew his way around, and they exited the building through a side door, which prevented them from having to run the gauntlet of party guests. Mauri would figure out that they were gone eventually, probably sooner rather than later.

Ivy was proud of her husband for making such a bold decision, and he didn't seem uncertain of it at all. But something told her the Starks weren't about to give up on their prized asset quite as easily as Dax had given up on them.

EIGHTEEN

SPENDING THE REST of the night at Dax's apartment was stress-free for the first time. It had been a long night, so by the time they got back, there was nothing to do but go to bed and make love… slow. Much of the tension he'd carried over the last few days had waned, and he didn't mind taking his time to explore all of her.

It was reassuring when Dax slept in the following day. Just like at home, she got up to work out and shower then tidied up before making breakfast. It was almost noon by the time Dax fumbled his way out of bed and into the shower. She'd already eaten but brewed a fresh pot of coffee for him, which was ready by the time he joined her.

"Good morning," he grumbled and slugged great hulking mouthfuls of his coffee until the mug was empty, after which he held it out for a refill.

"Afternoon actually," she said. She couldn't even blame jetlag for his late hour because his shift at the club didn't usually start until late afternoon. If he was still on Eastern Time, he should've woken up earlier as opposed to later. "You missed your work out."

"Do we have plans today?" he asked, accepting the mug she handed over.

"No, but—"

"Then I'll do it this afternoon, I could use a run."

"I thought we might be leaving LA today."

He cleared his throat and yawned while placing himself on a stool at the other side of the breakfast bar. "I thought I'd call a realtor, get this place on the market."

"So we never have to come back. You're serious about this, aren't you?"

"And you're not?" he asked, taking another mouthful of coffee then setting the mug aside. "I know you want to get out of here. We can leave tomorrow; I'll tie up my loose ends and—"

"What loose ends?"

"You don't have your shit from Mauri yet, do you? I'll get it. I have to pack everything in the storage unit, we can have it shipped cross-country. And there's my bike… unless you want to ride bitch back east?"

"Uh, no," she said. Ivy loved his bike. After more than three thousand miles on the back of it, she might feel differently. "Do you want me to start packing the apartment?"

"Can if you want," he said. "But I figure we'll just sell it furnished, let the new owners figure out what they want to keep."

"There's nothing in here that you're attached to?"

"You," he said. Snagging her wrist, he pulled her into the space between his open thighs. "How do you feel about last night?"

She'd had some time to think about what happened at the Stark mansion. Time to think about what they were sacrificing by shunning the family. The Starks had saved Dax in childhood only to dragoon him into fulfilling their own nefarious needs later in his life. To say that she was angry at Mauri and the Starks for what they had put Dax through was an understatement.

Trotting out his mother and Ivy's sister had been a low blow meant to manipulate the couple. Maurice Stark didn't think about anyone other than himself. He would do whatever he had to in order to get what he wanted, which in this case was Dax.

"I don't like that my sister is staying in Mauri's house," Ivy said. "She has no idea what's going on or what the Starks are capable of."

She and her sister hadn't seen each other for years. Although they weren't close, Ivy would never wish her sister harm.

"We can get her out," Dax said.

Rosie did what Rosie wanted to, and no one would tell her different. "She won't do what we tell her to, she's headstrong."

"I never would've guessed," he said, brushing her hair aside to kiss her neck. "Must run in your family."

"I'm a delight compared to my sister," she teased.

"I love strong women, I'm sure she's a scream."

"Her chest is smaller than mine," Ivy said, arching her back to present her breasts with a smile.

He kissed the top of her cleavage, but his hands snaked around to cup her ass.

"You don't have to worry about me taking an interest in your sister. I found out recently that brunettes are my thing."

"Rosie is a brunette; the blonde came from a bottle."

"Oh, I should consider banging her then, huh," he said and stole her mouth when her jaw fell.

Dax wasn't an easy man to rile, but he sure knew how to press her buttons. There in his arms she licked the roof of his mouth and urged her body closer. Calling the realtor could wait until after she got her rocks off with her rock-hard man. Just to be sure that he was as willing as she was, she skimmed her palm down his torso to fondle him through his jeans.

"You should've joined me in the shower," he said, sliding down the straps of her dress.

She grabbed the bottom of his tee-shirt, but before she could raise it, his phone made a message noise. Resting an arm around her hips, he elevated his own to pull his phone from his back pocket. After he read the text, he slunk off the stool onto his feet.

"Who is that?" she asked, eyeing his cell.

"My mistress," he said, kissing her brow then easing her out of his embrace to put the device back into his rear jeans pocket.

"Your mistress is hanging from the reinforced beam in the spare bedroom," she said, drumming her fingers on the kitchen hutch.

His curious frown became amusement, and she rolled her eyes.

"You just exterminate any woman who looks at your man, do you? 'Cause I don't remember fucking any other women," he said. "You sure meant it when you said no second chances, didn't you?"

"I meant your punching bag. Fighting is the only thing you love as much as you love me. Though I guess it would be bad if I did mean another woman."

"You're all the woman I need, and now I've found out that there are two of you, I fear the apocalypse is coming."

She didn't laugh at his joke though he was pleased with himself. Dax left the room then came back a second later donning his leather jacket.

"Will you be long?" she asked.

"Maybe," he said. "I'll call the realtor while I'm out, you pack up whatever you want to keep or whatever you think we need."

"Okay," she said and went to him. Taking hold of the open edges of his jacket, she pouted up at him. "Will you call Mauri about my things?"

"Yes," he said, kissing her quickly. "I'll take care of everything. You just stay here." She nodded, but he took hold of her chin. "I mean it, Minx. Don't leave the state, don't get on any planes or buses. Stay. Here."

"As long as you do what you've promised, we have nothing to worry about."

"Good," he said and kissed her again, then he left the apartment.

That apartment wasn't her home. She'd never lived there but getting the chance to root around in Dax's possessions wasn't an opportunity she would flout. She'd call and request his gym equipment be shipped to the opposite coast. That would mean finding a storage unit; it wouldn't fit in their one-bedroom apartment back east.

Heading for the phone, she sought out a pen and paper then sat down to make her calls before she started packing. Keeping busy was a good distraction, she still wanted to quiz her husband on what Trystan had said the previous night. Yet once again her questions were left unanswered while Dax took care of his mysterious business. He had left without much of an explanation and in her past experience that never spelled anything positive.

NINETEEN

DAX HAD TAKEN A CAB to the storage unit to pull out his bike. Uncovering it to stand astride it again had been a buzz. After a few basic checks and a trip to the gas station, he was on his way to the bar where Serg had asked to meet him. The two of them couldn't be called close friends, but they had been through some trying times together. Serg was always available when needed, and he didn't ask questions, which was a major plus.

Being that might be the last time he was in California, possibly for the rest of his life, Dax didn't mind taking the time to talk to his old associate. He doubted that whatever Serg had to say would take long because the man was usually one of few words.

Parking in the alley next to the bar, Dax went through the chain link fence past a bunch of the guys who were barbequing beside the picnic bench. With a nod of acknowledgement, he strode past them and into the rear entrance of the hang out he and his men used between jobs. Pushing aside the metal link curtain, he strode onto the red tile of the private back room that was usually full of people, today Serg was the only one there.

"What's up?" Dax asked.

Serg hadn't even lifted his head from the books he was poring over when Dax came in, which was a stupid mistake. He should always be aware of his surroundings because in their line of work no one knew who was out looking for payback.

When Serg did raise his attention, it didn't stop on Dax, he stood up to get a better look behind him, which made Dax glance over his shoulder, but there was no one there.

"Where's Ivy?" Serg asked.

"Why would I bring Ivy here?"

"You brought her here before."

"Once and she's not with me this time," Dax asked. What was going on? Serg seemed agitated, which wasn't like him. "Why would you want to see Ivy?"

"You haven't heard?"

"Heard what?"

The conversation was frustrating. His colleague's sudden interest in Ivy, coupled with the odd conduct was giving him a bad feeling.

"Shit," Serg said, falling back in his seat. "Maybe it's just bullshit."

"What's just bullshit?" Dax asked, coming deeper into the room.

There were couches around the perimeter and the large metal table in the middle dominated the space. The walls were a kind of yellowing brown that had probably once been white. The gradient of the grimy color deepened the higher that it got, a slick layer of nicotine had built up over the years.

Serg nodded him over, and Dax went to sit perpendicular to the giant at the head of the table. Serg put a forearm down and leaned close, closer than the two men had ever been before. "I could get my ass handed to me for telling you this, maybe, I think… I don't know."

"Tell me already, I've got shit to do—"

"There's a bounty out."

"A bounty on what?" Dax asked.

They had never been the type to chase money, so he had no idea why the information would be relevant. Serg was paid well for what he did. As far as Dax knew, the guy had no expensive vices to eat up his income. Whatever the offer, he'd refuse, but he'd hear Serg out for old time's sake.

"Ivy."

Her name changed turned everything he was thinking on its head. Changed his whole demeanor and outlook. Sitting back, away from Serg, he absorbed. Who would want to harm his wife?

One thought spiked his fury.

"Is that why you were fucking asking about her?" Dax asked, standing up so fast, his chair clattered onto its back.

"No!" Serg said, leaping up ready to defend himself. "I was worried you left her somewhere she could be seen."

"What's the bounty?"

"Half a mill for her dead."

Dax could defend Ivy against anyone who came after her in person, but this was a different ballgame altogether. In a day or two, when word to spread throughout the community, every lowlife scumbag from far and wide would be on their tail. That kind of money was appealing to even the most loyal or cowardly of men. It would make anyone believe that going after the bounty was a risk worth taking.

"Who the fuck is on it?"

"I don't know," Serg said. "I got word this morning. I heard it, and I sent you that message to meet me. I thought you would want to know."

With eye contact and a nod, he gave his thanks. "Yeah," Dax said.

"Who would want this? Does she have enemies?"

Her only enemies were ones related to him. His thoughts briefly went to their time in Vegas. Trudi was pissed, probably Carlos too, if he'd heard his name was brought up in conversation. But they wouldn't flout five hundred grand on something like this; they just wouldn't have that kind of cash to burn.

Saul could have savings. Was he the vengeful type? According to Ivy, Saul had friends in every walk of life, so he would be able to set something like this up.

But pinning this on someone from Ivy's past was ignoring the obvious. Those angriest with her were his adopted family. Mauri might blame her for Dax's choices. Trystan was pissed that she'd rejected him. Again. Why would they go after Ivy and not after him?

"Is this Mauri?" Serg murmured. "Does he think you'll come back to the family with Ivy out of the picture?"

The man could be that deluded. Though it wasn't much of a delusion, Dax had set precedent. Mauri probably believed he could talk him into just about anything. Without Ivy there to keep him balanced, Dax might just be broken enough to let the old man win.

"I'm gonna find out," Dax said.

Spinning around, he set his destination as the Stark mansion determined to get answers. If this was Mauri's bidding, he'd find a way to have him call it off. Word was still spreading. It would take twice as long to call off the minions trying to chase Ivy down.

Before getting on his bike, he took his phone from his pocket. He couldn't tell Ivy what was going on, not over the phone, and not before he had all the information. But she was in danger and liked to defy his authority. She could be out on the streets that very minute, a walking target.

Dax called the apartment and was relieved to hear the line was busy. If she was home, she wasn't outside presenting an opportunity for every psycho with a gun. Opening his texts, he typed in his commands.

> *Stay home. No messing, Minx. Danger outside. Stay in the apartment.*

He expected her to call as soon as she read the message. Sure enough, before he started the bike his phone buzzed. For a few seconds, he debated with himself as to whether he should answer the phone. He wanted to get to Mauri and get some answers of his own. But if he ignored her, she was likely to ignore his message, so he picked up.

"What kind of message is that?" she asked before he had a chance to speak. "Are you being a dick?"

"I just got some information," Dax said. "There's trouble."

"What kind of trouble?"

"The kind that means you have to stay inside."

"Since you asked so nicely and all—"

"I mean it, Minx," he said, throwing a leg over his bike, he kicked away the stand. "Just stay inside."

"Tell me what happened," she said.

"I can't. I don't have all the facts yet. I'm going to find out what's going on, and then I'm coming home, hear me?"

"Dax," she exhaled.

In bed, she could say his name like she was worshiping an idol of pleasure. But that breathy whimper was absent now, this was a wife with a gripe she wanted to complain about.

"Yeah, I know you're pissed, babygirl. But I'm keeping you safe, I'll explain everything when I get home and then you can bitch at me all you want."

"We didn't talk about what happened last night, and now you're giving me more questions without any answers. We can't keep going like this, you have to trust me and hear me out. You can't just issue orders and expect me to follow them without any kind of explanation."

"Yeah, I can," he said. "Because I'm not gonna give you half a story, which might scare you, while I'm not there to reassure you. I don't care how pissed you are. I'm telling you to stay inside for your own good. I could've said nothing at all and just assumed that you'd stick to what you told me earlier, but I wanted to let you know that something serious was going down… I will explain, babygirl. Just trust me, stay in the apartment and don't let anyone in." When she didn't say anything, his concern grew. "Ivy?"

"Okay, I'll stay inside, but when you get back here, we are not doing anything else until you fill me in on everything, and I do mean everything, Dax Harrow."

"Okay. You got it."

She didn't hide her anger, but that was one of the things he loved about her. When Ivy was happy or aroused, she just glowed. But when she was pissed off, like right then, she made no secret of it.

She accepted who he was and had never tried to change him, although she had. The changes that he'd gone through had been those he chose for himself, and he preferred the man he was now to the one he'd been before. Except without Ivy, he wasn't sure there would be anything left of himself worth saving.

TWENTY

DAX DIDN'T WAIT TO BE ANNOUNCED. He went into the mansion and up the stairs to head for Maurice's private suite. The old man liked to be the wizard behind the curtain. Even if there was business to conduct, he would leave Brad to deal with it. Mauri only came out for the important matters, and it had been that way for a few years now. That didn't mean his influence was any less, he still pulled all the strings. But he didn't tire himself by dealing with those lower than him, which included pretty much everyone.

Security tailed him through the house. They were paid to take down any threat, but it had been so long since anyone had threatened the patriarch in his own home that security got complacent. As a result, Dax was able to enter the outer room of Mauri's suite, with its fireplace and red upholstered armchairs, while two security men were still running to catch up.

"Mauri!" Dax called out.

If he had to go into the bedroom, he would. But if he went in there, he was likely to end up murdering the man, and he couldn't do that, at least not until he'd called his dogs off Ivy. Security burst in at his back, and he spun around to defend himself. Taking one out with a punch, the other lunged at him. He got hold of the guy's arm, twisting it around and up his back, using it to toss him back out into the hall. The first security guard got up again, but Mauri's voice stalled the action.

"No more!" Mauri declared.

Despite a few growling glares, security left, closing the door to give them privacy.

"You—"

"I heard," Mauri said. "We found out about the bounty an hour ago, and we're doing our best to trace it."

Mauri was calm.

Dax couldn't hear himself think beyond the blood gushing at high speed through his body. "You expect me to believe you have nothing to do with this?"

"What would we gain? You lose your wife and blame me for the rest of your life? I want you with us and that means working together."

"Convenient."

"If this was my order, I wouldn't be making you the offer I'm about to," Mauri said, remaining in front of the bedroom door.

Dax was happy to keep his distance and maintain his position near the exit. "What offer?"

"Take Ivy to the beach house. She will be safe there. No one can approach without us knowing. I can post security outside; they will make sure she stays safe."

"And she's supposed to live the rest of her life there?"

"She can remain there until we uncover who is behind this. We neutralize the threat and then she can move freely again. You know yourself it will take a day or two to trace this to the source. Chances are he's using a middleman. We find that middleman and then we coax the information we want out of him." The coaxing part would be fun. "Once we know, we take him out."

"It will take time to spread the word that she's not to be harmed," Dax said.

Once the word of a bounty was out there, it spread. Putting the genie back in the bottle was no easy feat.

"She can stay in the beach house for as long as she needs to. You know that we can easily stock the place, and she can hole up there for months if necessary."

Ivy would despise the idea of being back there and of hiding out, but he couldn't come up with anything better. Moving her to Nevada or North Carolina wouldn't necessarily mean her safety, it would just mean the crooks would take longer to find her. Until they could stop the threat at the source, it would remain. They didn't know the threat's motive for wanting Ivy dead or if he could be reasoned with. It was just as possible that whoever had started this would rather die than retract the bounty.

"I can hide her," Dax said, trying to think of where he could take her and look after her alone while still trying to trace the threat.

"You can't do it alone," Mauri said. "You can't hide the girl and ensure her supplies remain fresh; you will lead the hunters directly to her. You're not naïve. You will be the first person others try to get to in order to find her. If she's at the beach house, then you can stay with her. It doesn't matter how many people follow you there, my security will keep them out."

Mauri had resources and manpower.

Two things he didn't have. "I have to find out who is doing this."

"And you can do that while my security team keep her safe. If you stick her in a cabin in the woods, you can't stand sentry twenty-four hours a day alone. You can't keep her in your sight and find out who has put up the bounty at the same time."

"No, I can't," Dax said, his rage cooling.

Every word Mauri said was right and ran in tandem with his thoughts.

"You will have all the men you need to look after her, and you could use my help uncovering the threat. Starks stick together. We'll find out who is doing this, and we will take them down, together."

"She won't want to go," Dax muttered.

Mauri came closer but posed no physical threat. "I appreciate the location may not hold happy memories for her. But you two found your love there, didn't you? She may appreciate a chance of a break and some peace; it is certainly preferable over the alternative of being on the run or hidden somewhere alone. This is just like the vacation I suggested to you last night, you can sell it to her that way."

His head came up. "The others, her sister and…"

"They are both there," Mauri said. "They travelled to the beach house this morning… Ivy would probably like to have some company while you are out hunting down the threat. She and her sister haven't seen each other for a long time."

Ivy had worried about Rosie being close to Mauri and staying in his house. If Ivy had time with her sister, she might be able to explain her concerns.

"Okay," Dax said. "We'll leave tonight, that should give me time to talk her round."

"Good, I will prepare everything and send a car for you. It will be safer that way. I'll make sure there is a full security team out there. We will keep her safe."

Safe from what? That morning they had been certain that they were leaving the Starks behind, and now they were about to walk straight back into Stark territory.

TWENTY-ONE

MURDER WAS NOTHING to trifle with. After the shock subsided, facing the truth was harsh. Someone wanted her dead; they were willing to pay big money to see her corpse. She didn't want to die and wasn't stupid enough to think she could defend herself against being hunted.

Freewill was a distant memory. One of Mauri's lackeys was outside the apartment, he'd arrived not long after Dax got home. By the time she learned the lackey was there, her husband had revealed what he knew. She was still languishing in the news.

Dax tried to question her, but she needed time to process. His questions had been about her enemies, about anyone who might wish her harm, anyone that she'd upset or angered recently. After some thought, she came up with a big fat zero. The only people she'd had run-ins with recently were the Starks, and they were apparently going to act as saviors.

She had made dinner, but they'd eaten in silence, and now she was packing up their things to go on this forced vacation.

"Are you pissed?" Dax asked, loitering in the bedroom doorway. "I can't get a read on what you're feeling."

She folded a sundress from the pile of clothes they'd dumped on the bed and placed it into the suitcase open beside the mound of clothes. "No," she said, carrying on with the folding to pack everything into the case.

"You're not saying much," he said, coming a few feet into the room. "If you want to get out of here… I mean if you want me to protect you alone—"

"You and Mauri figured it all out," she said. "I don't want anything happening to you either, so it makes sense to take advantage of Mauri's offer. I would prefer one of his thugs take the bullet than you."

"Not so long ago, I was one of his thugs," Dax said. "He's not doing this just out of the goodness of his heart. He wants something."

"He wants you."

"I don't think that's it."

"Are you willing to bet our future on that?" she asked, placing his shorts into their luggage. "We'll just go out there, play nice, and think of it as a vacation, just like Mauri said. We stay there for as long as we need to and then we get the hell out of there."

"Okay."

She carried on packing, and he sauntered toward the closet, he went in and came out, then retrieved some things from the bathroom before going back into the closet. Ivy kept turning over her questions in her mind, letting her thoughts grow until they reached critical mass.

She dumped an unfolded top down on the clothes. "You know what? I am pissed," she declared.

"There's a surprise," he said. "Doesn't it feel better just to say it?"

He left the closet and strolled out of the bedroom, leaving her to gape at his disappearing act. Not one to let him get away easily, she followed and found him in the kitchen retrieving a beer from the fridge.

"You can't ask me a question and then walk away when I answer."

Lowering the bottle from his lips, he took a breath. "I think I can. You want a beer?"

"No, I don't want a beer. Don't you want to ask why I'm pissed?"

"Isn't that obvious?" he asked. "But if you want to rant at me, I guess you're entitled."

"Rant at you?"

Leaving the kitchen, he went to the couch and picked up the TV remote. But before he could turn on the television, she rushed over and grabbed it from his hand. "I guess you want my attention while you rant," he said, flattening his hands on the couch at his sides. "Go for it then, babygirl."

"Why didn't you tell me Bruno's your father?"

With everything he'd revealed that day, she guessed that wasn't the question he expected. Getting his attention was her goal. He'd picked up the remote because he expected her to shout at him for getting her into this mess. But she didn't blame him for the actions of the crazy person. Anyone who wanted another person dead had to be crazy. She blamed her husband for concealing information. For lying to her by saying nothing happened at the midnight meeting all those weeks ago.

"That's why you're pissed?" he asked after he got over his surprise. "I come home and tell you someone is trying to get you killed, that we're going to a place where you were kept prisoner for months, and you're pissed that I didn't tell you something?"

"Trystan said—"

"And you believe what he says?"

"No," she said. "That's why I'm talking to you about it. I want you to know that I know. And I want to know why you didn't tell me."

"Because it's embarrassing," he said, leaning forward to rest his elbows on his knees so he didn't have to look her in the face. "It's disgusting. It's a fucking joke, that's why." Dax got up, looming close to her. "That sick motherfucker had his hands on you and if I think about—"

"Okay," she said. His fists clenched, she stroked his arms until they loosened. "I understand why you're upset. Are you sure it's true? How do you know Mauri wasn't trying to upset you? At the beach house, you'll have the chance to talk to your mother and—"

"Do you think she'll be honest?" he asked. "We don't know her. We can't be sure anything she says is the truth. I don't know anything about her."

"We can find out who she is. Trust takes time to build. I guess Mauri is giving us a chance to do that. I doubt you'll get to know her enough to trust her in the short time we're at the beach house." She hoped it was a short time. "But… it's a start."

"You're into this?" Dax asked. "You want me to let her into our lives?"

"I think it's worth taking advantage of this opportunity. Yeah, we were going to turn our backs on it, but things have changed. Now we're in it whether we like it or not. We might as well make the most of it."

"You don't have a great relationship with your mom, you haven't seen her since you were a teenager. Why do you think my mom will be different?"

"We're talking about two separate things," she said. "We don't know our mothers are the same. Besides, I'm not suggesting cozy Christmases together, all around the tree in jammies opening presents. I'm talking about having a conversation, finding out the truth about your past from the horse's mouth."

"Keeping you safe is number one, babygirl," he said, resting his hands on her waist. "How do you feel about going back to the beach house?"

"I think explaining the jail cell in the basement might take some dancing."

"Mauri knows we're going, he asked us to go there last night. He would have assumed he'd get his way so would've set the place up to receive guests. That cell wasn't always there. So don't be surprised if it's gone now."

"My sister probably wouldn't notice anyway, she's not had the best luck in life… kind of like me I suppose, until I met you."

"You said she used drugs."

"The last time I saw her, she was staying with my aunt again, and she was with a guy… Rosie is always with a guy, but, yeah, this guy was bad news, and he got her mixed up in all sorts."

"Do you think she's clean? She looked healthy last night."

"If she has, then being part of a family whose product is her vice might cause some problems. I can't see the Stark world being good for her."

"I'm not sure it's good for anyone," he said. His tune had changed so much in the time that they'd known each other, Ivy had to smile. "We'll keep an eye on her."

"What about Bruno?" she asked.

"What about him?" Dax asked.

"Trystan said that he and Mauri had a fight, then Bruno took off. Do you think that's true?"

"I don't give a fuck about him," Dax said, growing more rigid.

She wrapped her arms around him. "Use this time with your mom, tough guy, see if her story matches Mauri's. If we're going to be stuck there anyway, you might as well gain something."

"You see it as gaining something. I see it as nothing more than another hassle we have to deal with. My focus is on finding out who wants to hurt you, then I take the guy down, simple."

"You know… you can't discount that Mauri is behind this."

She didn't like to be pessimistic about Mauri. In their early days, Dax stressed his respect for him. Anytime she said anything less than glowing, there was always a chance of upsetting her husband.

"I haven't. I'll keep my eye on him. As long as you're safe at the beach house, I'll be investigating."

"He wanted us there, and now he's getting what he wanted."

"Yeah," Dax agreed. "But if he wanted you dead, he's had plenty of chances. He could have done it last night, at the party, or while we were alone in the drawing room. He told his man to threaten you but not to harm you."

"Which was before we left there in the middle of the night without a word."

"He knows where I live, and he knew that we'd be here," Dax said, she closed her hands together at his spine. "He could have sent someone here as soon as I left to meet Serg, before either of us knew there was a threat. Putting out a bounty isn't his style, there are plenty of guys on his payroll who would do that kind of work for him. He doesn't need to put the word out to the world, he'd keep it quiet and get it done… if that was what he wanted."

"I trust you, Dax," she said. "But you are the only one I trust. You've trusted Mauri before and look how that turned out. If he was as reasonable as you thought, if he had been as understanding, then he would never have asked you to share me with Trystan, would he?"

"What?"

"Trystan told me. Why didn't you tell me that piece of tantalizing information? You didn't trust me to handle it?"

No longer feeling like she wanted to be this close to a man she trusted with her life, she tried to walk away.

He caught her shoulder and brought her back. "Babygirl—"

"Don't," she said, trying to wriggle out of his grasp.

But her writhing prompted him to throw his arms around her and haul her body into his, giving her no choice but to accept his embrace. He was far stronger. Releasing her weight, she made no attempt to hold him as he held her, she just hung there in his arms letting him kiss her hair.

"I didn't tell you because I didn't want to upset you," he said. "What does it matter? I told them that was never going to happen. You're mine, you know that. I don't care what Trystan said, you know I would never share my female with another man."

"Do I get a say?"

Now his embrace did relax, he stopped trying to squeeze the life out of her. "You wanted to spend the night with him?"

"No, of course I didn't. But we're supposed to make decisions together, I… I don't know why you keep withholding information. What else aren't you telling me?"

"You know everything else," he said. "We don't have to deal with Bruno or Trystan anymore, and I guarantee you that after I've dealt with this mess, you will never have to deal with Maurice Stark or Brad ever again."

"You're so sure?" she asked, trying her best to lean back and look up at him. "That you don't want to take over Maurice's enterprises?"

"No," he said. "We're going back to our lives on the East Coast as soon as this is over."

She probably shouldn't be pleased to hear that, but she was. Dax had a chance to get to know his mother, to find out where he came from, but whether or not his mother would be a part of their lives after this mandated vacation remained to be seen.

Dax would dedicate his time to getting rid of the person using his wife as a pawn. It might be selfish of her, but she was looking forward to returning to the life they'd built together. Though at the moment, that life seemed incredibly far away and in more than just distance.

TWENTY-TWO

THE FIRST TIME Ivy arrived at the beach house, she'd been carted there in the trunk of Bruno and Dax's car. When she was hauled out bound and blindfolded, her surroundings were a mystery.

That was her first chance to get a good look at the place, except it was dark, and the internal lights blazed, obscuring the façade.

The waves crashed against the cliff far below, reminding her of their seclusion. Set out on a clifftop, surrounded by the ocean on three sides, they were so far from the road that it would be a trek just to get there. During her first stay, the isolation had terrorized her, it kept her prisoner, away from the world, against her will. Now it was a blessing. She needed the privacy to keep her safe against those who wished her harm.

They'd been chauffeur driven to the beach house. The motion of the car, coupled with the drama of the day, sent Ivy rocking to sleep in Dax's arms. When the car stopped, and she was jolted awake, the crashing reality made her extremities tingle.

They exited the vehicle, and she stood beside her husband on the driveway while the chauffeur gave him their suitcase.

They turned toward the house.

"You want me to knock this guy out and steal the car?" Dax mumbled into her hair as the driver went around to his side and got back into the vehicle.

"Why? So we can run off together and get married? We've already done that, remember?"

The lights that were on downstairs in the house displayed an empty room. The light upstairs came from behind a curtain. As yet, they didn't know who was there or where the occupants were located. Her sister and Dax's mother were brought there straight from the Stark mansion after the party.

"He shouldn't have picked this place," Dax said. "He has a place in Washington too."

"Are you kidding?" she said. The car that transported them there reversed and turned, leaving them alone in the moist sea air. "He picked this place on purpose."

"Yeah, does it bring back memories?"

Recalling her first arrival hadn't been a pleasant memory, but she didn't want to upset Dax by telling him that. "It makes sense for us to be here," she said. "It's close enough to LA for you to do your digging and still come home to me every night. I wouldn't want to be isolated from you, that wouldn't make me feel good… Do you think Rosie and your mom know what's going on?"

"Let's get inside and find out."

The nearer they got to the property, the tighter his arm around her shoulders became. Dax couldn't protect her from her own mind. His tight hold reminded her of what they were now in spite of what they were then.

"At least you don't have to give me instructions this time," she said, trying to help him relax.

Putting down the suitcase, he opened the front door. "I don't?"

"No," she said. "I'm used to being naked in bed with you now."

Dax lifted their luggage, then ushered them inside without responding to her quip. The abode looked the same, smelled the same, felt just the same. Her subconscious made her body tense. The sound of the door closing startled her. Spinning around, she opened it to reassure herself that it hadn't automatically locked.

"You're okay," Dax said, kissing her head and linking his fingers into hers while he closed the door.

Once that door was locked, there was no way out. She was all too aware of that and had tried to get out before without a key, and it had proved impossible. The positioning of the house on the cliff meant there was no way around from the back deck and pool. With the front door unlocked, she could get out; she wasn't a prisoner this time.

"Hi."

Whirling toward the voice, a slight woman stood just inside the living room, the kitchen threshold behind her. Dax's mom. According to Mauri. Her dyed blonde hair matched her complexion and wasn't garish like Rosie's hair.

She still had youth about her, though lines around her eyes and mouth betrayed her real age. Her fifties maybe? How old would she have been when she had Dax?

"I'm Carina," she said, examining the couple. "I don't know if either of you knew my name, we've never been introduced… Rosie and I are outside on the deck by the pool having a drink if you'd like to join us?"

"We're going to go upstairs first, get settled in, you know?" Ivy said, looping her arm around behind Dax, using their physical connection to reassure him. "We might join you later."

Dax didn't speak. He kept his arm around her and guided them both across the room and up the stairs into the bedroom they'd shared when they were last there. It stood to reason that Mauri would want them in that room, or maybe that was just the room Dax always chose when he stayed there.

He took her into the bedroom, and she closed the door while he disappeared into the closet to stow their suitcase.

"We have to talk about this," she said to Dax when he came back into the room.

"About what?"

"What do you want from her? If she wants to make the effort, you could get to know her."

"Mauri admitted he gave them a financial incentive. She is here to collect a check, then fuck off again and that's fine by me," Dax said. "We'll avoid each other. You and I managed to keep each other pretty occupied last time we were here." He stripped down to his jeans and crossed to sit on the side of the bed. "Come and stand here."

They needed to have a serious conversation, but the severe expression on his face loosened to a brief smile before he adopted it again. He had said that to her… sat in that place and said those exact words to her, all those months ago.

"What are you going to do?"

"Pick up right where we left off," he said. She sashayed toward him, slipping off her shoes and untying the halter of her dress on her journey. "Good."

The purr of arousal in his voice stalled her, and she held the ties of her dress straps over her shoulders so as not to reveal any of her flesh.

"What do you think is going to happen here?"

"Whatever the hell I want," he said. Leaning over to grab the fabric of her dress, he dragged her nearer to him.

Keeping her breasts concealed, she snatched the dress over her chest. "I'm not going to have sex with you," she said unable to keep the smile away from her face.

"Oh, I think you will."

"I will not," she said, curling her fingers around his shoulders, which gave him the opportunity to pull down her dress. She wasn't wearing a bra tonight, so when he pushed the fabric down over her hips, all that covered her was the pale silk of her panties.

Flattening his inverted hands on her waist, he drove his fingers south to scoop her thong down her thighs, leaving it around her ankles. He kissed one nipple, then still with a hold of her hips, he leaned back, forcing her to kneel on the bed astride him.

"Dax," she said while he enjoyed her breasts. "Is the ottoman still in the closet?"

"Yes, it is," he said, his mouth curled in a smile.

"Just in case, you know."

"I didn't forget."

That ottoman held the money he'd given her when they were there before. "You still haven't taken me to a fight."

"I think you've seen all the fighting you need to," he said.

The sound of his jeans being unbuckled carried to her ears. They wouldn't make it for drinks on the deck, Carina and Rosie would have to entertain themselves. After the day they'd had, it wasn't a night to play catch-up with long-lost relatives. It was a night for man and wife to enjoy each other, to reassure each other, tomorrow would be their chance to start over if that was what her husband wanted to do.

WHEN IVY WOKE UP, she was alone, just like the old days. She sat up in bed. The light streaming through the high windows to her right hurt her eyes. Dax liked to sleep in, usually she had to roll him out of bed in the morning with promises of giving him the world each day. The fact he was awake already meant either he hadn't slept at all, or he'd had a message that told him he was needed somewhere else for something else.

Crawling to his side of the bed, she reached for his phone and flopped back in the sheets to scroll through and see who had sent him a message.

Got a lead on Winlow. Pick you up at nine.

The message was from Serg and the time on his phone read eight forty-nine, so Serg would be there soon. Providing that Serg knew they were there, and he wasn't planning on picking Dax up at their apartment. In which case, he would be here a lot later than nine.

The bathroom door opened, and she tossed the phone onto the nightstand while rolling onto her side. "You're going to leave me here alone so soon?"

"Beats playing happy families, doesn't it?" he said, plucking the towel from his waist to rub his hair.

With a quick towel dry, he lobbed the damp towel across the room to land near her chest.

"Can I come with you?"

The answer was obvious. She was there to be safe from the threats that lurked everywhere. That didn't mean she liked surrendering or that she relished the idea of being there without him.

"Are you kidding?" he asked. "You're staying here until I'm sure it's safe for you out there."

"You can keep me safe," she said. "I'll just sit in the back of the car and not say a word."

"You don't know how to be silent," he said, sitting in a corner chair to lace his boots. "You wouldn't be able to help yourself."

"If it's the difference between being alone here and being out there, I think I could manage to be quiet. It's in my best interest, right? If I stay quiet, you'll have to take me with you tomorrow and so on."

"This is a safe place; Mauri has security on the property already."

"How do you know?"

"I called him when I got out of bed," Dax said, sitting back to examine her. "You're safe here."

"Maybe it's just being locked up again, it makes me uneasy."

"You're not locked in. I'll talk to security and make sure that the front door stays unlocked at all times. Will that make you feel better?"

"Maybe." She shrugged, dragging her gaze around the room. "Who thought we'd ever come back here by choice."

"Yeah," he muttered. "Wonders never cease. This is a temporary arrangement, don't get used to it."

"No chance of that. Who is Winlow?"

"Winlow is a sonofabitch who has a thing for knives. He also has ties to some of the LA gangs. I don't want to threaten anyone while you're around, I don't want them to know your face. I'm guessing you don't have much of a reputation around LA, you've never lived there. Tracking you will be hard if they don't know what you look like."

"But it's okay if they know your face?" she groaned. "What happens when these people who are out to get me find out that you're my husband? They'll use you to get to me."

"You think I'll let them hurt you to get myself out of a jam?"

"No," she said, lifting handfuls of the sheet then flopping her arms down. "They might hurt you. I don't want that to happen. I know you're too stubborn to tell anyone anything about me. But I'd rather you handed me over than you got yourself killed. Am I supposed to sit around here with my sister and your mother and sip tea while you get yourself into trouble?"

"Go for a swim, work out downstairs. Avoid them if you want to. I don't give a shit."

Dax went into the closet, and she lay on her back again, bringing his towel to her face, Ivy inhaled the scent of clean man and enjoyed how it blocked out the light.

"What's wrong with you?"

Dax's voice betrayed that he was back in the room with her, so she pulled the towel down. "Wrong with me?" she asked.

"Usually, you're up as soon as the sun hits the horizon."

That wasn't even close to being true. She could enjoy a nice lie in just like most of the population, but that was Dax's assessment because he was never awake himself to see how long she slept.

"I'd think my troubles were kind of obvious," she said.

"You never let the bastards get you down, never show fear or—"

"I'm not scared, I'm bored," she said. "I know I *will* be bored. There's no hurry to get out of bed. You're leaving.

I have no job to go to. I just have to stay here for maybe ever and do nothing. Maybe I should call Bri, find out if her and Blaser want to come for a vacation?"

"Are you going to explain how we got here? Why there's a bounty on your head? And who those women hanging around are?"

No, she didn't want to explain that. She wouldn't want to put her friends in danger either. If Mauri decided he didn't like uninvited guests, there could be trouble.

"Okay, well you go and beat on some people, maybe that will make you feel better. But you better be back here tonight. I don't want any crap that you went and got yourself into a fight or anything."

"I shouldn't need a fight," Dax said. "Not if we get our hands on Winlow."

A car horn blasted; Serg had arrived. Dax came over and leaned down to kiss her, but she covered her mouth with both hands, leaving him hanging there, his face a few inches from hers.

"What?" he asked. "You don't want to kiss me? Are you pissed?"

Elevating her hands just a little, she let herself talk but didn't remove the barrier. "I love you. But don't kill anyone today."

He scowled. "I'll try my damndest."

"They'll probably deserve it, but you know how important it is that I get mine."

Joking about sex was a potent reminder of how much she needed him by her side. The last place she wanted him to end up was in a jail cell.

Ready to leave and not put off by her hands, his fingers curled under her hip, and he flipped her onto her front before she realized his intention. He spanked her three times, then ducked down to dig his teeth into her flesh.

She laughed. "Dax!"

"Be good," he said, spanking her again then retreating from the bed to leave the room.

Ivy turned over to see his form disappear just before the door closed. Alone, she sighed and forced herself to get out of bed, now she had to go and make good with her mother-in-law.

TWENTY-THREE

THE KITCHEN WAS FILLED with fresh food and beverages and everything that they could need for a prolonged stay. Ivy picked some fruit from the bowl on the kitchen island then retrieved a bowl and a board to chop it on.

Casting her attention around, she focused on the drawer that had been locked during her last stay here. This time, it slid open without a hitch. Selecting a knife, Ivy went to work on peeling and chopping the fruit to put together a salad for breakfast.

While she was squeezing oranges, the kitchen door swung open, and Carina came in wearing an ankle length skirt and gauze shirt over a basic tank top.

"Good morning," Carina said.

"Morning," she reciprocated but kept on juicing.

"I'm sorry you and Dax didn't join us last night," Carina said, crossing to sit at the island.

"It was a long night. We just went to bed."

"I know this is difficult, for all of us."

"It is," Ivy said. "But there's no reason to make it more difficult than it has to be."

Pouring the last of the juice into the jug, she transferred it to the fridge. Scooping some of the fruit salad into an individual bowl, she covered the rest and put it into the fridge too.

"Is that for Dax?"

"The fruit salad?" Ivy smirked. "No, he likes his fruit whole, and the only breakfast he has is tar thick coffee and the occasional donut or three when they're around."

"He didn't look like the type to enjoy deep fried food."

"I don't think he's met a junk food he doesn't like," Ivy said, taking another mouthful of fruit. She chewed and sucked out the juice but eventually swallowed. "He runs and works out all the time, so he needs the energy. And he's a believer in everything in moderation."

As she said it, Ivy immediately thought of at least two things he didn't mind overindulging in, one of which was her.

"You must think this is odd," Carina said, smoothing a towel that lay folded on the counter. "I'm his mother, but I don't know a thing about him."

"Dax isn't an easy guy to get to know," Ivy said. "Why are you doing this? I mean, why are you here?"

"I haven't heard of him for so long and—"

"Look," Ivy said, shoving her bowl back to lean on the counter. "You won't win any points with me or Dax by bullshitting us, we have quite an accurate radar for that kind of shit."

"You're a tough woman."

To go with her tough guy, yeah, that made sense. But it wasn't her job to make friends with the mother of her husband, her job was to protect him, not to prioritize building bridges.

"You came here for money," Ivy said. "Mauri said it to us at the mansion. You'll get a lot further with both of us if you're honest."

"Mauri tracked me down," she said. "But that doesn't mean I don't want to get to know my son… and the woman he loves, of course."

The kitchen door swung open again and her sister, Rosie, swanned in with a grin on her face. "This place is immense! Your husband is related to zillionaires!"

The house only had three bedrooms, but the rooms were huge, and the furnishings screamed wealth. Rosie was older than her by two years. They were the same height, but Rosie's hair had been the same bleach blonde for as long as she could remember.

"Where did Mauri find you?" Ivy asked her sister who had already bounded over to snatch up the fruit salad.

"I was in Texas, singing in a club in Dallas," Rosie said, munching on an orange segment. "Where did you find that hunk of a husband? I didn't really believe the guy who picked me up in Dallas when he told me you'd got married. But, wow, Ive, you did good. He's a great guy."

Typical that Rosie would say such a thing having never exchanged a single word with Dax.

"You don't know anything about him," Ivy said.

"Where is he? Bring him in."

"He's not here," Ivy said. "He got called out to work." She wasn't going to be the one to tell Rosie and Carina about the gangs of people possibly looking to cause her harm. Mauri might have let them know. Until she talked to Dax about the merits of full disclosure, she was keeping her mouth shut.

"To work?" Carina said.

Something about the shift in her shoulders betrayed that she knew exactly what Dax did, or rather had done, for the Stark family.

"He'll be back tonight," Ivy said, tidying up the mess she'd made.

"Do you know that for sure?" Rosie asked, polishing off the last of Ivy's breakfast.

Yes, confident in Dax's return, he wouldn't want to leave her alone with all these variables floating around. He was also aware that he wouldn't get laid for a month if he abandoned her here.

"How do you know your way around this kitchen so well?" Carina asked.

"I've spent time here before, with Dax… and Bruno."

Ivy didn't have to wait long for Carina to react. The woman left her stool and took a hand to her chest. "Mauri said I wouldn't have to see him."

"You don't have to see him," Ivy said. "He's not been around; he wasn't in the mansion. Trystan said that he and Mauri had an argument."

"Trystan is cute," Rosie said, taking the empty bowl to the sink to dump it there.

"Don't even think about going there," Ivy said. Rosie went back to her stool. "You don't want to get mixed up with him."

"Could be fun," Rosie said. "He's a rich guy with class, I could do worse… hell, I have done worse!" Rosie laughed.

Carina was polite enough to smile, but the mention of Bruno's name had rattled her.

"How did you and Bruno meet?" Ivy asked, crossing to the sink to wash up the dishes.

"I don't… I'm not sure that I should talk about that… should I?" Carina asked.

"I met my last serious boyfriend in a public restroom," Rosie said, pulling the jug of freshly squeezed orange juice from the fridge. "And yes, that story is as distasteful as it sounds. Where did you meet Dax?"

"Vegas," Ivy answered honestly. "Why were you in Dallas? I thought you were staying with Auntie Jo?"

"I was until she got this letch of a boyfriend, yuck, he thought he owned the whole place, and Jo just let him take over. I was out of there as soon as he started laying down rules like I was some dumb kid."

Some dumb kid was exactly how Rosie came across. It was a bit rich of Rosie to pass judgement on how Jo was with her boyfriends because Rosie was exactly the same. She let her boyfriend's rule the roost and would let them get away with anything as long as they gave her attention. Rosie and Jo were just the same, their self-worth was directly tied to how much attention they got from the opposite sex.

Carina was tough to get a read on. She seemed kind of classy but was uneasy around others, and uncomfortable with direct questions, something Dax could be guilty of too.

"Have you heard from her recently?" Ivy asked. "Is she okay?"

"Last I heard, yeah," Rosie said, pouring out a full glass then putting the jug on the island while she sat on a stool and slurped from her glass. "I want to hear more about Dax."

"You'll hear about Dax from him," Ivy said.

It was unlikely that Dax would come back tonight and open up to a room full of women, but she wasn't going to give away information knowing how private he liked to be. They were married, and his secrets were her secrets, which was just the way she planned to keep them.

"What's downstairs?" Rosie asked.

Ivy's hands went limp in the dishwater. She drew in a breath at the reminder of what she'd endured in the space beneath their feet.

"Yes," Carina said. "Rosie and I had a look around last night, and we couldn't find the basement entrance."

"I think it's that door by the stairs," Rosie said. "It's the only one that wouldn't open."

"It is," Ivy said. "Dax will have a key." Though there was a chance that door was locked for a reason.

"It's weird they'd lock us out of just one place," Rosie said. "What do you think is down there?"

Possibly another woman inhabiting her cell, though she prayed that wasn't the case. "Last time I was here it was just a gym."

"A gym? That's disappointing. I was at least hoping for the family fortune, or maybe a private nightclub or something," Rosie sagged and dropped her head into her hands. "Can we even get down to the beach?"

"Not from here," Ivy said. "Speaking of the beach, I think I'll go for a swim in the pool, then I'll whip up something for lunch, does that suit everyone?"

She was draining the water from the sink and drying her hands but didn't wait for responses. She went back upstairs to her bedroom and flopped face first onto the bed.

The experience was draining her already, and Dax had only been gone for an hour.

TWENTY-FOUR

AS SOON AS DAX GOT INTO THE CAR, Serg updated him. Late last night, Mauri had called Serg to fill him in on their new arrangement. Having Serg on the case was reassuring, Mauri had chosen a point man Dax could trust. On the downside, Serg didn't excel at taking initiative, so Dax would have to drive this wagon.

That being said, when they pulled up outside an apartment block about an hour after leaving the beach house, Serg spoke with authority.

"Winlow's in there, top floor," Serg said, leaning forward to peer out of the top of the windshield. "Least that's what we've been told."

"Told?"

"He's wanted by the law," Serg said, sitting back. "No one's seen him in the flesh for a while. But you know Winlow, if there's a memo going around the ganglands, his name will be at the top."

"What do the cops want him for?"

"Knocked up some bitch then beat the kid out of her, that's what I've been told anyway. Her body was found in the park a few blocks down, she was fucked up."

So he'd killed his girlfriend and the baby she carried. Too many men in his acquaintance were pricks to the women in their lives. It made him sick. Then again, he could go and find himself a fight if Ivy was getting on his nerves, maybe that was an outlet he took for granted.

"Let's sit for a minute, see if anyone goes in or out," Dax said.

Winlow's associates were recognizable. If they were going in or out, he'd have confirmation Winlow was around. Taking his time, he wanted to be sure there weren't a dozen guys up there ready to ambush him. Although Serg carried a weapon and Dax was one, he didn't feel like working up a sweat on his first meeting of the day. He planned for this to be the first of many.

He'd talk to all the scumbags in the state to find out who had Ivy in their sights. The sooner they could eradicate the danger, the better.

"How is Ivy doing?" Serg asked. "Is she dealing or are you stuck on the couch?"

"The couch? My female doesn't pull that shit."

Ivy had never kicked him out of their bed. She would call him out on any issues before she would sulk and refuse to share her body or her bed with him.

"Lucky guy, I know a lot of women who would punish their guy for getting them into a mess like this."

Dax didn't need the reminder this was his fault. The more he thought about it, the more he was sure their relationship had put Ivy in someone's crosshairs. She had no associations of her own in that part of the country. If he didn't figure it out, he could lose her, and he'd have no one to blame but himself.

"Come on," Dax said, unclicking his seatbelt. "Let's just get this over with."

Dwelling on how they'd gotten there didn't solve anything, and he in the mood for a fight. Striding toward the apartment entrance, he walked inside and ran up the stairs, taking them two at a time. Usually, he saved that kind of zeal for when he was being paid. But the payment he wanted, his wife's safety, was far more valuable than any green.

Serg wasn't as quick up the stairs, so Dax had to wait because he didn't know which of the craphole apartments belonged to Winlow. Last he'd heard Winlow had made it big, he'd taken his poker addiction to professional levels. But the broken doors and graffiti covered internal walls didn't suggest he was languishing in the dough. Either the girlfriend spent it, or Winlow had developed another vice that sapped his winnings. At these kinds of extremes, Dax would guess drugs were that vice, which might explain why Winlow had wigged out and killed his girlfriend.

Serg pointed at a door. Dax didn't bother to knock and ask politely for Winlow. He marched forth and lifted a foot to kick the door in with one swift blow. Modern open-plan layouts made it easy to make an entrance. One window was boarded up, but the others were uncovered so there was plenty of light for Dax to pick out Winlow's stocky figure seated on the brown leather couch next to a skinny brunette who was wearing too much makeup for the time of day.

She squealed and leapt to her feet, but Dax held out a hand. "You just sit down, sweetheart, no one's gonna touch you." He managed enough of a smile to bend the brunette's knees and she fell back down to the couch. When she was resting easy, Dax switched on his glare and fixed it on Winlow. "You're the one who we want squealing."

With two paces, Dax grabbed a handful of Winlow's shirt, right under his throat. Twisting his wrist and flexing his bicep, he lifted Winlow out of the seat and turned to throw him against the wall behind a perpendicular armchair.

The brunette squeaked. In his periphery, Dax saw her rise from the couch. "Keep an eye on her," he said to Serg, not wanting some crazy woman beating on him while he was having a conversation.

"You got it," Serg said.

Winlow squawked when Dax bent down to lift him up off the floor with two hands. "I think you know why we're here," he said to Winlow.

"I… No… I…"

This kind of response was normal. It took people a minute or two to reorient themselves from calmly watching the television to having their head kicked in. If the bubbles of heat spinning and erupting beneath his skin were anything to go by, Dax needed a little action, so he would take his time.

"I've been told different," Dax said.

Winlow was in his thirties. His thinning hair and weathered face were a manifestation of the wrong choices he'd made and the struggles he'd had throughout his life. They weren't his concern. Things were going to get much worse for Winlow in a hurry if he thought about stonewalling.

Dax let go of his prey, which made him stagger. Balling his fist, he smacked the guy across the chops and sent him to the floor again. Winlow gagged and coughed, spraying blood over the back of his chair. But Dax crouched, propping his elbows on his knees, ignoring the crimson droplets.

"You got a thing for brunettes?" Dax asked.

"Don't fucking touch her!" Winlow exclaimed, spitting out more blood.

"Protective sonofabitch, are you? I can identify with that. See, I've got a pretty brunette of my own and word is she's not in a position of security. That concerns me… I'm sure that you can understand."

As Winlow flopped against the wall under the boarded-up window, he wiped the back of his hand over his chin to mop up the trail of blood that had slunk out of his lips. "I don't know what you're talking about."

"Oh, you don't, huh?" Dax asked, cracking his knuckles. "I heard you did. I heard you knew exactly who was trying to harm my girl… I'm an old-fashioned kind of guy, I think it's up to a man to protect his woman, but I guess that's a concept that's lost on you. I'm gonna be fair on you though, Winlow, and I'm gonna give you a choice, how does that sound?" Winlow nodded and clutched at his jaw. "Either I can believe you do know more than you're telling me now and keep beating you until you tell me what I want to know—"

"Don't hurt him!" the brunette wept.

Dax didn't bother to look her way, he just stayed right there, crouched by Winlow's sagging form. "Or I can believe that you're telling me the truth and that you don't know anything."

"I don't!" Winlow mumbled, the swelling in his mouth slurring his words.

"Okay." Dax nodded and rose to his feet, pulling the cellphone from his pocket. "What's the address here, Serg?"

"What are you doing?" Winlow asked.

"You're a wanted man, Winlow. What kind of citizen of this fair city would I be if I didn't let the law know I'd found a fugitive? You're FTA, aren't you? That's serious shit not to show up to court when you're wanted for murder."

"No," Winlow said. Using the chair and the wall to steady himself, he clambered up to his feet. "Don't call the police, I… I'll tell you, okay? I… I don't know much of anything."

"Why don't you start with what you want to tell me and then we'll move onto the details," Dax said, sticking his phone back into his pocket.

"Yeah, okay, I heard I… we had a card game, I was at a card game and… I heard it from a… I heard five hundred grand for her head, that's all I know."

"All you know?" Dax asked. Sweeping his forearm around, he thrust Winlow against the wall. "Who was at this card game?"

"Just three of us, me and Benny and… The Greyhound. No one else."

"That was it," Dax said, glancing back at Serg who was still in front of the brunette, his colleague shrugged, indicating he was happy enough with that information. Dax wasn't satisfied. "Who spoke? I want you to tell me exactly what was said."

Dax had to know how they'd identified Ivy to know what people were looking for.

"It was… it was The Greyhound, he was… he said he'd heard talk was all, he didn't say who told him."

"What did he say?" Dax demanded, pulling the guy forward to slam him to the wall.

"Just… just that there was a bounty out, told us how much, told us… he said, she… brunette, big tits, Ravager's wife, that was it."

"That was it?"

"Yeah… yeah, that was it. But come on man, I'm not gonna touch your girl, I'm holed up here. I can't go fucking anywhere, I'm stuck here. Your girl is safe—"

"From you maybe," Dax said, giving him another shove then letting him slither down the wall. "Piece of advice, if you're going to skip bail, haul ass out of the state, don't hang out in your buddy's old place and hope no one thinks to look…" Retreating, Dax nodded at Serg. "Let's go."

He and Serg left the apartment. Dax was preoccupied again, the Ravager. The Greyhound was a skinny guy known for his addiction to long distance running and chasing tail, hence how he got the moniker. Dax didn't have any beef with him, they didn't associate, but what was more interesting was the reference to his fighting name.

Benny frequented the circuit, so did Winlow when he was making money from his gambling. But as far as Dax knew The Greyhound had never been to a fight. He would know about Dax's ties to the Starks because he did some couriering for the family in his younger years. But if The Greyhound used his fighting name, whoever had told him about the contract had used it.

They might not know exactly who the source of this issue was, but they'd just narrowed it down. Whoever was doing this knew him from the fighting circuit. Ivy had never been to any of his fights, so he had his confirmation that the bounty was his fault.

"Where to now?" Serg asked when they got back to the car.

"We track down The Greyhound."

"We can go to Benny," Serg said.

Finding Benny was always easy. He didn't stay in one place for long, but he had never heard of discretion and practically announced himself in every room he walked into. Benny had various contacts but little respect, it was doubtful that he had been used as a middleman. The Greyhound, on the other hand, may be the guy Dax was looking for. Easily recognizable but discreet, yes, he would make a good go-to guy. At the very least Dax could squeeze him for information, if he had to trace this trail man-by-man, then he would.

But there was something else he could do. Something he'd told his wife he wouldn't. He could get himself a fight. If people were looking for the Ravager's girl, he had to get himself on a bill somewhere. Most guys would assume he would bring his brunette, which of course, he wouldn't. Tracking interested parties would be easier if he got them all together in one room. There was a chance one of them would slip up and say something to give himself away. If they did, he'd be ready.

Though if he were going to find himself a fight that night, he'd have to get back to Ivy that afternoon. His promise to return and not go looking for a fight was one he'd have to go back on, he'd have to soothe her snit. More than happy to do that, because it meant getting naked with her, the remaining buzz from upstairs fostered his need to seek out some private time with his wife after their next stop.

"Let's check out The Greyhound," Dax said. "You know where to find him?"

Serg nodded and turned the car at the next junction to take them toward The Greyhound's place, which it turned out was less than ten minutes' drive away.

As soon as they got to The Greyhound's apartment, it became obvious they were too late. Police tape was draped around the outer stairway of the building, and forensic analysts were crawling all over the scene. Dax waved two fingers at Serg indicating they should keep on driving.

"You think that's him?" Serg asked.

Examining the building, he noted the newly rendered facade and the freshly painted railings. A good block, unlikely there was too much crime around there.

"Whether it is or not, we're not getting in there without talking to a cop, you up for that?"

Serg didn't respond because he didn't need to. They were both of the same Stark school where if you saw a cop, you turned and walked the other way. Parking and trying to get in or ask questions would likely end up with one or both of their names in a notebook. That was the last thing that either of them wanted or needed.

"If The Greyhound was taken out because of this bounty then whoever is behind it is serious."

Yes, that was the proof this was no joke. "Take me to the mansion."

Going to Mauri was only a stop on his way back to Ivy. It was time to put his suspicions out there. If the old man didn't have any updates, anything tangible, it would be as good as signing a confession. When Mauri wanted information, he got it, unless whoever was behind this knew how to evade Mauri's grasp, but that was a rare thing for anyone outside the inner circle.

TWENTY-FIVE

MAURI TOOK LONGER than normal to come out of the bedroom. He looked frail like he'd had a rough night. It had been easy to forget how ill Mauri with so many other distractions around.

He'd paced Mauri's private drawing room for almost ten minutes, unable to sit down because of the unsated energy zipping through him. When Mauri did eventually come in, Dax stopped, and his tirade died on his lips.

Gaunt and tired, the lines on Mauri's face were etched deep. His usually proud stature was stooped. "I don't suppose this is a social visit," Mauri said, he coughed then brought a silk handkerchief to the corner of his mouth. "What did you find out?"

"I came here to find out what you know," Dax said, trying not to be affected by the sight of such a robust man wasting away.

"I told Serg what we discussed."

If Mauri didn't even know Serg had come to him, it was unlikely he'd done any digging of his own. "Yeah, we spoke to Winlow."

Mauri shuffled toward his armchair next to the fireplace. His steps weren't sure, they were unsteady, he fought the urge to go over there and support him.

"What did he say?"

"Tried to say he knew nothing."

"But you persuaded him to share?" Mauri asked.

Slumping into his seat, his relief became a smile, and he lifted his eyes.

Dax nodded.

His energy waned into the numb depths that sunk out of his guts. Mauri was going to die. Only now, looking at this shadow of his former mentor did he comprehend that in a few months there would be no more Maurice Stark. He wouldn't be around to offer advice and guidance; he would just be gone.

"He folded pretty quick," Dax said, glued to the floor.

"And what did he reveal?"

"He got the information at a card game, Benny and The Greyhound were there, it was The Greyhound who clued him in."

"Benny is a dead end. If he knew anything, he'd declare it in every bar he walked into, the man can't keep his mouth shut."

"Yeah."

"Did you follow up with The Greyhound?"

"His place is tied up. The cops are swarming; something went down there not too long ago."

"That's concerning," Mauri said, using the arm of the chair to support his weight.

"I thought the same thing," Dax said, forcing himself to leave his position by the door. He went to sit in the chair beside Mauri's. "But see what I can't figure out, is why you don't have a handle on what's going down. Nothing like this, nothing this big, goes down without you knowing someone who knows something."

Mauri exhaled what was probably supposed to be a laugh, but it became a wince. "As you might have noticed, I'm not quite at my full strength."

"No, but you've got Brad running the show. If he was to ask around—"

"I haven't given Brad all the information about this," Mauri said. "He's not happy about the offer I made to you. He would never contradict me in public, but behind closed doors… Ivy's war is not the only one being waged now, and I no longer have my favorite son to protect me."

"I wasn't your favorite," he said, shaking his head. "I was just the most pliable."

"Brad is proud and cannot be told, he thinks that he knows best and does not understand wisdom comes with experience."

"He doesn't listen to you," Dax said. "That's not new."

"And Trystan… well… you know what he's like."

"Yeah," Dax said. "You spoiled him, he thinks that he's invincible, which is why he thinks he can take whatever he wants."

"He was unhappy about you leaving the party," Mauri said. "I assumed from the bruising on his head that you and he had words."

"Not so many words, but action was taken. He puts his hands on my wife again and next time he won't bruise, he won't breathe either."

"I'll talk to him," Mauri said. "Do you believe he could be behind this bounty?"

"He has the means," Dax said. "I'm not taking anyone out of the running, including you."

"Me? I thought we'd discussed this," Mauri asked. "Why would I want to harm Ivy?"

"Could be that you think I'll take you up on your offer if she's not around. Maybe you just want to take someone with you when you go."

"Well…" Mauri said, examining the fireplace. If Dax didn't know any better, he would think the patriarch was hurt. "I'm sorry you believe I'm so callous. I wouldn't take your happiness from you. If I wanted to do that, I could have used the many other opportunities I've had with Ivy."

"You wanted us around, in the beach house, spending more time in California, and you've gotten your wish, that's a hard fact to ignore."

"Maybe," Mauri said. "But as you pointed out, I won't be around for long. If you don't have me, and you don't have Ivy, what would you do?"

Dax would tear apart every person who had harmed his wife and anyone that those people cared about. He'd dedicate his life to avenging her, because he would no longer care about his own life. There would be no future for him because Ivy was his future. Without her, nothing else would have value.

"Like I said," Dax said, brushing aside those thoughts of revenge. "It's hard to ignore that you got exactly what you wanted."

"What I wanted was for you to develop a relationship with your mother. If you're running around in the city trying to track down the threat to Ivy, you're not spending time with her, are you?"

"Why do you care about my relationship with my mother?"

"I realized after the meeting we had, before you left to retrieve Ivy… I realized telling you about Bruno, that he was your father, it must have raised questions for you. I can tell you everything I know, but that doesn't substitute what those in the relationship can tell you. Your mother is a valuable source of information."

"What does it matter where I came from?" Dax asked, propelling himself out of the armchair.

"It matters because you have a future with Ivy, and you can't embrace that until you understand the past. I worry… about you… I know how your temper can get you into trouble. The fighting, it seemed to give you a purpose and prevented you from getting into scrapes that could have landed you in jail."

Dax spun around. Mauri was brighter now that he was discussing the past.

"What are you talking about?" Dax asked.

"You used to fight, with the staff children here, then at school… it's why we started to school you from the mansion. You were always quick with your fists. Your father, the man you believed to be your father, had trained you to release that energy in the ring. As soon as we allowed you back into that ring, you began to excel at school again, you got along better with the other children."

Dax didn't remember a time that Mauri had tried to stop him fighting. The ring had always been a sanctuary for him. A way to get rid of the fury he often felt toward the world as a teenager.

"I don't remember that."

"It was only a few months," Mauri said. "But it escalated quickly, Brad and Trystan feared you. That was why it made sense for you to live with the staff children in the back of the house, we kept you apart for their safety."

The control he had over his urges to lash out was something he'd struggled with in his late teens and twenties, but he'd overcome that erratic side of his nature.

"I'm going to fight tonight," Dax said.

"I'm not surprised. You often need that vent when you feel overwhelmed."

"I am not overwhelmed," Dax snapped. "Winlow described Ivy as Ravager's girl. For someone to use my fighting name, in this city…"

"They must know you from those circles." Mauri nodded. "Tell me where it's taking place and I'll have men there to back you up, in case things get out of hand."

"I can handle myself," Dax said.

He'd called his scout on the way over so didn't know where the fight would be yet. But he would in a couple of hours.

"I understand," Mauri said. "You should take Serg at the very least. While you are in the ring others will be on the lookout for Ivy, someone should be watching for those people."

"I'll talk to him," Dax said. "He picked me up at the beach house, he'll need to give me a ride back over there."

"You can take any of the cars here. It might make sense for you to have your own mode of transportation, just in case any unforeseen circumstances arise."

"Security still at the beach house?" Dax asked. Mauri nodded. "Any incidents?"

"Not that I've heard about," Mauri said. "And I have had regular updates, last one was around an hour ago, and Ivy was in the pool."

It was reassuring to know Ivy was safe, but he wasn't sure how he felt about other men watching his wife, reporting on her movements.

"Good," Dax said, heading for the door.

"Where are you going now?" Mauri asked him. "Do you have more leads?"

"Right now, I'm going back to the beach house," he said. "I told Ivy I'd be back tonight, but if I'm fighting, I won't be."

Mauri smiled. "So you're going to break the news gently."

Dax reached the exit. "Gently and Ivy don't go together."

"You know," Mauri said, rising from the chair and moving around it to rest his hands on the back. "I didn't consider how you would change by finding the right woman. Brad has always been a serious person, and Trystan has always been wild. I hoped that he would settle down with the right woman at his side and some kids running around. But you... marriage and children weren't things I considered for your future."

"I was supposed to die young," Dax said causing Mauri to frown. "I remember you telling me when I was in my twenties that if I kept tearing around on the damn bike and walking into the ring night after night that I was inviting death. Back then I didn't care, I never considered my future."

"Until you met Ivy."

Shaking his head, he took his eyes to his hand on the door handle. "I married her to stop Trystan from getting his hands on her. I knew she was special... that I... that I felt something for her but... it wasn't about the future, it was a solution to my problem."

"And she knew this?"

"She knew more than I did," Dax said. "I think now that... the Trystan situation just gave me the excuse I needed to put my mark on her."

"So I did you a favor?"

"I wouldn't go that far," Dax said. "I'll be in touch if I hear anything tonight."

On leaving Mauri, his intended destination was the mansion garage. But as he descended the main stairs, he saw Brad enter with his entourage. As soon as Brad saw him, he stopped and said something to his colleagues, who glanced at Dax then all scurried away.

"What do you want?" Dax asked when he reached the bottom of the stairs.

It was obvious from the way he'd dismissed all witnesses that Brad had something to say.

"I heard about Ivy, about the bounty, I'm sorry."

"Are you?" Dax asked. He and Brad had a relationship of avoidance. They tried their best not to be around each other when either was in a sticky spot. Brad observed him with an interest that betrayed his true motive. "I'm not sticking around. You can keep your empire."

Brad relaxed enough to smile, though the gesture was false. "Mauri is known for always getting what he wants."

"You and I both know we're incapable of working together," Dax said. "We don't trust each other."

"No, we don't."

"So I'd hazard that's why you've kept your head down while Ivy and I have been around."

"I'm not going to encourage you to stay, although my father wants me to."

"You'd rather have needles stuck through your eyes," Dax said. "Don't worry, Brad. It's all yours."

Mauri did have a talent for encouraging everyone around him to defer to his wants. Brad didn't want Dax to stay, but he didn't want to go against his father's wishes by asking him to leave either.

"If you find out anything about Ivy's situation, I'd appreciate a heads up," Dax said.

Brad might be on the suspect list, if he could figure out his motivation. Brad wanted them gone, and he'd know Mauri would use this threat as a chance to keep the couple around. The possibility still existed that Mauri wanted Ivy gone, believing he'd fall into line without her. Another reason Brad had no motivation to get Ivy out of the picture.

Brad nodded and turned to depart the foyer in the direction of his staff. Dax continued his journey to the Stark mansion garage to get a car and drove off the property, heading for the beach house. It would take an hour or so to get there. Serg was still back at Mauri's, but there would be plenty for him to do. That night, they would need to be at their best to pick out the threat.

TWENTY-SIX

AFTER LUNCH Ivy had needed another distraction, so she went for a dip in the bathtub in the downstairs family bathroom, the only tub in the place. With waterfall taps and recessed lighting, the gleaming tile was dazzling, but the water felt good seeping into every crevice of her body. After an hour or so in there, she was beginning to prune, so she climbed out, drained the water, and wrapped a fluffy white towel around her body.

She ducked into the kitchen for a drink of rehydrating juice and washed her glass then went into the living room with ideas of going upstairs to the bedroom. When she was halfway across the room the front door opened, and she froze. Wearing nothing but a towel, she wasn't in the best position to defend herself against danger.

When Dax came in, her hackles fell, and her shoulders dropped as her smile rose.

With outstretched arms, she altered her path to aim for him. "You have never in the history of the world been early in coming back to me."

"You've been in the pool all this time?" he asked, scrutinizing her body.

"I was in the tub," she said, opening her towel to flash him. Tucking it back in, he blinked his eyes and smiled when she wrapped her hands around the back of his neck. "Does this mean that you've found what you were looking for?"

He kissed her and brushed some damp tendrils of hair from her forehead. "You naked is actually exactly what I'm looking for."

Tossing his keys into his opposite palm, Dax twined their fingers and led her up to the bedroom at such a pace she had to hold onto her towel to prevent losing it. He closed the bedroom door, dropped his keys then pulled her towel out of her grasp to whip it away across the room.

"Hey!" Ivy objected, but he was already taking her to the bed.

"Take that stuff out of your hair," he said, lifting one foot and then the other to pull off his boots.

She had her hair up so that it wouldn't get wet in the bath because she'd already washed it after being in the pool. Doing as he asked, Ivy flipped her head forward to shake her locks loose, and when she flipped back, he was shirking his jeans.

"I thought you had work to do today," she said.

Taking appearances as they were, he'd come home to have sex with her only a few hours after leaving her with promises he would return that night. Either he'd deciphered the threat already or something else was going on.

Dax enveloped her waist and walked her backward. Taking her weight off her feet, he laid her on the bed and lay on his side beside her. Scooping her hair up, away from her face, he began to kiss her neck. The attention of his hand went to her breast. Massaging her, he kept on kissing, and took his mouth over her jaw to hers, opening to tease her tongue, but her eyes hadn't closed yet.

"Dax," she said, turning her head to the side to break their kiss. That didn't put him off, he slipped one of his legs between hers and began to nudge her ankles apart then drove his thigh higher to press into her simmering center. "Dax, what's going on?"

"Hush," he said.

Removing his mouth from her breast, he forced a hand around the base of her skull, holding her in place to receive his kiss.

The press of his erection progressed inward from her outer thigh. Trailing its path with beads of his passion, he settled his pelvis between her thighs and kept on with the kissing. Sometimes Dax just needed to be active. If he was frustrated, action might help to bring him clarity.

Opening her arms and closing her eyes, she gave him his kiss back, surrendering to the want of her husband because explanations would come after. His hips rose then he was sliding into her, the occupying length of him took its time to reach its hilt. But he drew back and plunged in, the easy entry wasn't a prelude to soft love making, having softened her to his will, he found her wrists and took them in his hands.

Forcing them high above her head, he kept hold of her and elevated his torso. The fast pace of his hips matched the ferocity of fever in his focus drilling into her. Ivy might have touched his face or tried to soothe him if she had the use of her hands, but his fingers remained locked around her wrists. Exerting dominance over her body was something her husband did well. When he needed something from her, he took it, and that was what he was doing now.

He pushed in, bobbing back and forth. Keeping the oscillating movements short, he edged no more than in inch of himself in and out of her, remaining deep. The fountain within her gushed around him, easing his motion and aching for him to move with the same speed as he had before.

She was close to the climax he always delivered and didn't want to lose the brimming swell of pleasure aching to burst and send her surging into bliss.

"Get to it, big boy," she breathed, wheezing out the oxygen occupying her lungs. "Come on, give me what I want."

"What you want," he hummed and sucked in a breath before plastering his mouth over hers. His tongue drove into her mouth, the penetrating suction matched the mire of their joining and when he retracted his mouth, she gasped for breath. "You want cock, you just lay there and took it, no questions, no permission, you just want it."

Rocking his hips high, Dax shoved the head of his dick into her cervix, and she winced. "I've gotta let a guy like you get his rocks off," she murmured. "No lies here, the way you fuck me tells me everything about you."

"Yeah?" he snarled.

"Yeah."

"Or you're just a horny minx."

"Yeah, or that," she said, trying to wrench her hands free, but he didn't give her any wiggle room. "What do you want, stranger? Come on, give it to me!"

Her burst of volume made him grin, and she tried to free herself again. "Oh, she's getting testy, doesn't like it when she's not being satisfied."

"Don't bait me, you asshole, just fuck me!"

"Warm in here and tight, feels good, Minx. Squeeze me, go on," he said, grinding himself down into her, massaging her insides with his invader, increasing the need of her release.

Sucking her lips in around her teeth, Ivy closed her eyes and began to writhe up to match his provocative squirm. Giving him what he wanted, she clamped her pelvic muscles, and he groaned. Movement began again and the more she clenched the harder he tried to force his way into the passage she was closing around him.

Yeah, her orgasm was coming. It was coming again. Still with her eyes closed, she pushed out, trying to expel him only to have him slam in with such ferocity, she screamed. Her climax followed and wearing a satisfied grin, she opened her eyes to witness his reaction to the clamp that sucked his dick in so deep that he swore down at her.

Her release prompted his and from how he gnashed his teeth she knew his ejaculation was involuntary. He'd wanted to torment her some more, but her body had bled from his what it wanted.

While her cervix consumed his offering, she loosened to smile up at him. "That was unexpected," she said.

"I always come in you," he replied, letting her go and climbing off the bed.

"Not that, your arrival, the fact that you're here at all. I thought you were going to be gone all day."

"Change of plans," he said, taking his phone from his pocket to check it.

When he didn't see what he was looking for, he tossed the handset onto the nightstand.

"What's going on? You don't seem like a guy who located his man," she said, switching position to lie the correct way on the bed. "Did you find out who put the bounty out or why?"

"No," Dax said, sitting on the edge of the bed. "But I did find out that whoever is behind this knows me from the circuit."

"The fighting circuit?" Ivy scooted over in the bed to stroke his back. "What makes you think that?"

"It doesn't matter, it's a step closer to where we want to go."

"Progress isn't enough for you. You want results."

"Yeah," he said, tipping his head down to peer at her. "This is important, babygirl, probably the most important job I'll ever do. If I fail…"

"You won't fail," she said, sitting up to kiss his shoulders. "You don't know how to fail. You won't stop trying until you get what you want, and that's all you can do is try your best."

Dax exhaled a laugh and twisted to take a handful of her hair so he could join their mouths. "Thanks for the pep talk, mom."

Disregarding his mocking, Ivy referred to the real parental situation. "I asked your mother about Bruno this morning, but she clammed up. Whatever is going on, or whatever went on, it affected her deeply. Just the mention of his name was enough to make her blanch. I haven't seen a reaction that visceral since… well, for a long time."

"Don't get involved," he said. "Don't ask questions."

"I have to ask questions. I'm stuck here anyway; I might as well find out what happened. Did Mauri ever tell you why Bruno and your mom split?"

"No, but I never asked because I don't care."

"I care," she said. "What else am I supposed to do here all day?"

"Sleep, swim, work out, read, I don't care, just don't delve into my bullshit."

"Your bullshit is my bullshit now," she said, looping her arms around him when he tried to get up. "She's nice, you know, kind of classy, which surprises me."

He smiled. "That right?"

"Yeah, 'cause you're just a knucklehead. I guess you didn't inherit the refined gene."

"No, I guess not," he said, pinching her waist.

Ivy could keep on teasing him, but she didn't know how much time they had. "Are you here for the rest of the day or is this like a lunch break? Did you leave Serg in the car?"

"I got wheels from Mauri," Dax said, leaning over her to rest his fist on the bed on the other side of her hip. "I've got some time here, but I'm waiting for a call to tell me where to be tonight."

"Tonight?" Ivy collapsed back onto the bed. "That's why you're here? Because you've gotta go out tonight, where are you going?"

"Nowhere I haven't been before."

"Are you going to fight?"

It wasn't her keen detective skills that made her suspect he was going to the ring, it just made sense, and she didn't want to consider the alternative. At least a fight on the underground circuit was observed and had rules. If he went into some dark alley to beat up a lowlife for information, then there were no rules and no witnesses. Losing Dax was the worst thing she could imagine, and it made her take his knuckles from the bed and bring them to her lips. She kissed his wedding band.

"I'll stay at the apartment tonight. I don't know what time the fight will be over, and I might hang around to ask questions."

"Do you want me to come?" she asked. "We could draw this bastard out."

"No," Dax said, shoving her over on the bed so that he could lie down beside her. "The people who hurt you won't be the ones who have ponied up the cash, they're the ones looking to claim it. So getting you hurt, or using you as bait, is out. We want to go after the disease, not the symptom."

"It seems unfair that you have to get beat up just to keep me safe."

"Beat up? Nah, I'll keep it brief. Have you ever known me to lose in the ring?"

That was why he had the notoriety in the circles he did, he'd been doing it for most of his life. She'd seen him after fights and most of the time his injuries were minimal; he was quick and practiced. He could take his pick of opponents. If the fight was a means to an end, it stood to reason that he'd pick an easy opponent.

"I won't be there to nurse you back to health," she said, climbing up onto him. "Who'll take care of you when you get home?"

"I'll pick up a piece of ass while I'm there," he said. She dug her teeth into his nipple until he twisted her hair around his fist to pull her off. "Maybe we should send you into the ring."

"You think you could stand by and watch while I wrestled with a woman intent on killing me?"

"I think you held your own with Trudi in Vegas in that hotel room," he said. "Every guy's wet dream to be locked in a hotel with two scrapping hotties."

"A pillow fight maybe," she said. "But blood doesn't get every guy going, only you. It's a moot point anyway. If you won't let me watch you fight, I doubt you'll let me fight on my own."

"True," he said. "We don't need it anyway; I prefer you to take your frustrations out on me."

With her hands on his shoulders and her knees on his thighs, she rose onto all fours and growled down at him. "I've told you I can take you." His smile faded away to a more serious expression. "What?"

"The guy we went to see today, has a history of beating on women."

"That upset you?"

"Got me thinking about my… heritage. Bruno has a similar history. As far as I know he didn't have any women he didn't end up beating into submission."

"And you're worried he did the same to your mother?" Her knees slid off his legs and onto the bed on either side of him. "I suppose the fact that you've seen her, that she's a real person now, it would give you a different perspective."

"Her?" Dax said and quietened.

"What?" Ivy asked, nudging his shoulder to prompt him.

"I was thinking about you," he admitted.

The revelation subdued her want to talk.

"About me?"

"Yeah. In a couple of years, I'll have to retire for good. I don't fight half as much now as I used to… but when I stop… where will all that energy go?"

Pushing away, she crawled backwards until she was on her knees between his legs. "You think that… that you'll be like him? That because he's a bastard who beats women, you're going to be the same when you can't vent your emotions in the ring?"

Levering up, Dax crunched his abdominals. "I—" Ivy slapped her open palm across his cheek, and his words became silence. "What the fuck?"

He seized her wrist, but she wasn't going to hit him again.

"I'm more likely to be the one physically hurting you," she said. "Don't you dare compare yourself to him again, do you hear me? You are ten times the man that he is, and you would hurt yourself long before you would lift your hands to me in anger. You love me, and I wouldn't be here if I didn't believe my safety wasn't important to you."

"And you had to hit me to tell me that?"

"I had to hit you to remind you that I am capable of fighting for myself. I would fight back, and that would be one battle you'd be incapable of winning." Lurching forward, Ivy kissed the cheek she'd hit and nuzzled against it with her open lips. "You couldn't hurt me when it was Mauri's greatest wish for you to do it. I'm never safer than when I'm right here."

Bringing his arms around her, she rearranged their legs so that she was straddling his hips and rising up, Ivy sank down to bring him into her body again, their eyes locked as she rode him. Watching him doubt himself broke her heart, but she had conviction enough for both of them.

Their relationship was his priority. He'd proven that by walking away from his life for her. Being back brought back his hesitancy. He was reminded of what he was before, just one of Mauri's henchmen, doing what he was told, prioritizing Mauri's wishes above his own.

Bruno was a beast, selfish and callous, he acted in sadistic malice. She knew what it was to be beaten by him, she'd endured his cruelty. Dax was incapable of such hostility. Bruno's anger came from a place of blackness that existed in his every cell.

Dax had chosen her and been willing to protect her with his life. He wasn't evil, as Bruno was, she would never doubt him. Any time he needed reminding, she planned to be available to do just that.

TWENTY-SEVEN

DAX HAD STOPPED COUNTING the number of fights he took part in years ago. The buzz of the room was intoxicating. It was difficult to keep his mind focused. As soon as he walked in, it felt like everyone in the place was looking at him or wanted to talk to him. Nothing new. Except this time something was new. Instead of reveling in the atmosphere, he scanned the crowd trying to pick out anyone whose interest wasn't on him but on what he might have brought with him: his wife.

There was no danger to him there. Despite being a public arena, most of the faces were familiar. They were the same ones who'd come to these fights for years. More importantly, the spectators knew him. No one would dare touch him. He could take down anyone who wanted to fight, and his supporters would start a brawl with anyone who might try to tackle him. His wife's safety wasn't as assured.

He'd struck gold with Ivy. She wasn't happy he was leaving her alone in their sheets, again, but she didn't whine or give him shit. She accepted he was doing what he had to and let him go without giving him the guilt trip other women might have.

Thinking about their afternoon in bed wasn't productive. There in that crowded bar basement, Dax had to focus on finding the person threatening his peace. Too many faces blended together. Some men wanted to shake his hand while others wanted to talk about how he could make them some money. They tried to either tempt him into fighting on their premises or to throw a fight and make them a fortune.

Dax had fought in that bar before, so he knew where to go to get away from the clutching mass of people. Heading for the corner room, he went into the disused cloakroom and sat on the bench that ran along the back wall. Serg was going to meet him, he'd already texted his associate to let him know where to find him.

Unless someone approached him about Ivy, it would be on him to start a conversation without creating a fight outside the ring. Serg would have to keep an eye on things while he fought. In there, he had to concentrate. It wouldn't do anyone any good if he was handed his ass because he wasn't paying attention. As Ivy had said, she wouldn't be around to patch up any injuries he might sustain.

She always seemed kind of offended when he refused to bring her to a fight. This was exactly why he wouldn't, she was a distraction. Ivy wasn't even present, and she was all that filled his head. Before Ivy, he could come into a place like this and eat up every opponent thrown at him, and he could do it without breaking much of a sweat. All that mattered to him was the fight, taking down whoever stood opposite him, and collecting his money.

But it wasn't like that anymore. The money was unimportant. He didn't even care much about the win anymore; it didn't give him the same high. Now that high came from screwing his wife until she screamed like she had that afternoon. She stoked his kindling to a flame when she laughed or gave him that little half smile that told him she was thinking kinky.

Fighting was a thrill. It gave him a rush; he needed it to get rid of negativity he had always carried on his shoulders. Since surrendering to his feelings for Ivy that negativity wasn't as heavy as it used to be. Maybe it was the way she looked at him, but he didn't feel like the same lowlife he had been back then.

Putting her out of his mind, he thought about what lay ahead that evening. He got changed and went through his usual warm-up routine. When he was done with the fight, he would ask some leading questions and see what he could come up with. Ivy's wellbeing depended on him.

TWENTY-EIGHT

WINNING THE FIGHT was quicker and easier than he'd expected. Just what he needed. Serg had showed up just before he went in and had done his job. No one said anything about Ivy or the bounty though. Frustrating? Yes. Surprising? No.

"What now?" Serg asked.

Outside the bar, keeping to the shadows, they used the seclusion to pounce on anyone who came from underground. Being it was the end of the night, most people were gone now. The bookies were still down there settling up as security removed all traces that the fight had taken place.

"I want to talk to Robbo," Dax said, dropping his sports bag onto the asphalt between him and the building at his back.

Robbo was a bookie at the forefront of all the fights. There wasn't one taking place that Robbo wasn't a part of.

"Do you think he'll know something?"

"Maybe," Dax said. "He knew The Greyhound; they were tight for a while. If something went down at The Greyhound's apartment today, Robbo will know."

"Want me to go in there and pull him out?" Serg asked.

Patience wasn't his strong suit, but that came from his bulk and reputation. Few people would make a guy of Serg's size and build wait when he wanted something. At the very least people were eager to have him off their premises.

"We'll wait," Dax said. "If you want to head home, you can. I'll take the guy if I have to."

"Yeah, but who'll keep lookout while you dig the grave," Serg said. They shared the joke then Serg leaned back on the wall. "I thought Ivy might persuade you to stay home."

"She doesn't try," Dax said. "She knows this is part of who I am."

"A woman who doesn't try to change you? Where do I sign up?"

The back door of the bar was still closed, no one was coming out, so he turned to Serg. "That's the second time today you've asked me about her."

"So?"

"So why the interest?" Dax asked.

"You think I've got something to hide? If I wanted to off your wife, I would've done it this morning when I came to pick you up," Serg said. "The money might be nice, but I wouldn't get to enjoy it for long if I had you and Mauri on my ass, would I?"

"So why the interest?" Dax asked again. "You want to make friends with her?"

"Nah, I'm just… you never took much interest in women, no more than the rest of us. You fucked around. I don't remember you being tied to one bitch for more than a couple of weeks."

"Ivy's not like the chicks we screwed back in the day," Dax said, watching the bar door, waiting for it to open.

"I get that now," Serg said.

The door opened, and the tall, slender figure of Robbo came out with a couple of other guys. All members of the group were laughing as they came right their way. Dax slipped out of the shadows. The men stopped moving and laughing, none relaxed until Dax held up both hands.

"Got a minute, Rob?" Dax asked him.

That posse must be carrying some amount of cash between them. Someone lying in wait probably made them fear for their wad. But Dax didn't need their money. The men said their goodbyes, then Robbo came to him.

"I thought you left," Robbo said.

"You used to do a lot of work with The Greyhound, you heard from him today?"

"Not today," Robbo said, his eyes drifted to the street. "Cops found him this afternoon, run through, they say he died before he hit the deck."

"I'm sorry to hear that," Dax said.

Serg came out of the darkness to join them.

Robbo tensed. "What is it you want, Ravager?"

"You know who had business with him?" Dax asked.

"What's it to you? Did he owe Stark money?"

"No," Dax said, though he hadn't asked Mauri. "I didn't know he had a habit."

Robbo shook his head. "Poker was it."

"So who wanted him dead?"

"Other than his nutso ex-wife I don't know," Robbo said. "He lost big on poker."

"To Winlow?"

"No," Robbo said. "Winlow's shot, his nerves have gone to shit since he offed his old lady. What do you care?"

"He didn't lose to Benny," Dax said.

Benny had no poker face and only went to events like that if there was liquor involved, only increasing the likelihood he'd lose.

"Doubt it," Robbo said. "But they weren't the only two there."

Except Winlow had said they were. "Who else was—"

"I don't know," Robbo said, backing away a step. "Look, Ravager, I'm sorry I can't help you out. I would if I could, you know, but I wasn't fucking there. You want to know more go to Winlow or Benny, I've got to go."

Robbo retreated and turned to hasten down the sidewalk.

"Should I…?" Serg asked, moving forward.

Dax lifted a hand to halt him. "No, just leave him."

Winlow hadn't told the truth. He'd been dumb enough to believe the bastard and then tell him to split town. He just had to hope his advice hadn't been taken. Something told him that his luck was wearing thin.

THEY'D STOPPED AT Winlow's place, but it had been cleared out. No sign of him or the pretty brunette. It was too late in the night now to try hunting the bastard down, so Dax went back to the apartment and showered before he iced his hands.

It hadn't occurred to him to check his phone for a while. When he kicked his jeans aside to get into bed, his foot made contact with the device, so he leaned off the bed to pick it up. Ivy had sent him a text.

> *Win big for me, tough guy?*
> *Miss you.*

Dax had never bothered texting other women, but he liked that Ivy had thought of him, so he responded.

> *Always, babygirl. Send me a*
> *pic.*

Her message was timestamped more than two hours ago, so he doubted she would still be awake to respond. He pulled the sheet over himself and closed his eyes. Less than thirty seconds later, the phone rang.

Fumbling on the nightstand for the handset, he pressed receive and brought it to his ear. "Yeah?"

"I'm not sending you naked pictures," she said.

The smile in her voice made him smile. "I'll have to take some myself next time you're asleep beside me."

"Don't even think about it. If you want what I've got to offer, get your ass here and take it. Man up."

"Don't goad me tonight, Minx," he said, moving onto his back with a groan.

He might just drag himself out of there and take her up on that. Except he had to be up early in the morning to chase down Winlow. If that didn't work out, he'd go after Benny. The rats were scurrying for cover. Word was out he was hunting down the threat. His reputation meant no one wanted to face him when he was in any kind of rage.

"You sound tired," she said. "Tough fight?"

"No, it was over in a flash. But I found out that the guy I chased down today bullshitted me, and that pisses me off."

"How?"

"I believed him when he was lying."

"What did he lie about?" she asked.

"That there were only three of them at a poker game when there were more players."

"Oh," she said. "I would think that was good news."

His eyes opened though all he could see was darkness. "How could that be good news? He lied to me, and I bought it."

"Except he lied for a reason. So maybe the other person at the poker table is the one who put out the bounty. You're closer than you thought, tough guy. All you have to do is push that button one more time and you've got your answer."

She did have a way of looking at things that made him feel better. "But the guy has split. I don't know where he is."

"You'll find him, or one of the other guys from the game, I have faith. You win every fight because you don't give up. You're smart and play your opponents by staying several moves ahead. You can do this, Dax, don't feel sorry for yourself now. You're close to the prize."

"And what's the prize?" he asked.

"Me and my freedom, I'll be a very grateful woman if you can swing that."

"Naked picture grateful?"

"Maybe." She laughed. "Go to sleep. You need to rest. I'll talk to you tomorrow."

"Okay."

"Love you."

"I love you too, Minx. Be good."

Hanging up with her after such a short call, Dax rested the cellphone on his chest under his hands. Ivy had managed to turn around his thinking. Suddenly, he was optimistic about the day ahead. He would get this guy; he was closer than ever.

TWENTY-NINE

IVY HADN'T HEARD from Dax all day. Their middle of the night conversation sent her into a blissful sleep. she'd waited all day for word from him or for a visit. Neither had happened. Washing the last of the dinner dishes, she considered going for another swim until the sound of spike heels on tile drew her around.

Rosie was staggering around the kitchen isle with her hands held high above her head. She spun around, gesturing to her outfit. The short green dress was strapless and clung to Rosie's curves, leaving nothing to the imagination.

"What are you doing?" Ivy asked, drying her hands.

"I thought we could go out, you know, hit a few clubs."

"Why would we want to do that?"

"It's boring here. We've done everything that we can do and no offense, but I want the kind of fun that you and Carina just can't give me, you know?"

Carina had said she was going for a bath before Ivy started on the dishes. Rosie must have used that time to glam herself up, using every makeup brush in the pack from the looks of the layer of spackle on her face.

"You want to get laid." Ivy exhaled. "I suppose that means you don't have a fella?"

"I have a few." Rosie laughed. "But as it happens, I've got a guy in LA, and he wants to see me tonight. I can't pass that up, can I? Get changed and you can come out with us."

"I don't want to go out," Ivy said, having not told the other women about why she was there or what Dax was doing in the city that kept him from their supposed vacation. "I want to stay here."

"Is Dax coming back tonight?" Rosie asked, strutting over to the fridge.

She pulled out a bottle of wine and proceeded to pour herself a full tumbler of the liquid without even looking for the wine glasses that Ivy knew were there. When you came from a background of having nothing, you drank out whatever presented itself.

"I don't know, maybe."

"Call him, he can meet us at the club. I bet he's a guy who likes to have a good time."

Rosie gulped down the liquid then poured another glass, so Ivy went over to take the bottle away and put it back in the fridge. The only Dax she had seen in a club was one working security. He wasn't the type to dance surrounded by others, or the type to get drunk out of his wits. She imagined from his experiences with Trystan he was used to finding a suitable observation post and watching everyone else go wild rather than going wild himself.

"Don't get drunk," Ivy said.

They'd already had wine at dinner.

Rosie was on her way to tipsy. "Why not? Come on, it's cheaper to drink here than the fortune they charge you in the clubs."

Rosie tried to move her aside, but she kept herself in front of the refrigerator. "I thought you said you had a guy, he'll be paying for your drinks, won't he?"

"I guess." Rosie snorted. "He can afford it, he's stinking rich."

A guy with that amount of money would probably want his woman to conduct herself with some class. A woman he was serious about anyway. If he was just looking for a good time, Rosie was top of the bill. She could make a party come to life anywhere.

"I don't think it's a good idea to go into the city," she said, glancing at the clock. "It's already almost ten. If the guy has to come and pick you up and then drive back out there, it will be after midnight by the time you get there. How much fun can you have at that time?"

"Uh, loads!" Rosie declared. "Anyway, he's already on his way…"

"What?" she asked, snatching her sister's slender wrist. "You invited a random guy out here to the middle of nowhere in the middle of the night?"

She wasn't sure if she should be more concerned about how Dax would react to that news or about this random man's safety. If he drove up expecting to pick up a date and was descended upon by Stark security, he might not get out in one piece.

"You've gotta test how eager they are," Rosie grinned. "If he's willing to drive all the way out here to pick me up, he's definitely interested."

"You have to call him back and tell him not to come. No one is allowed out here. It's not our house, we can't invite other people to—"

"Dax won't mind, he's cool."

Rosie and Dax had yet to have a conversation. Once again Rosie was making up rules to suit her needs.

"I'm telling you that it's not cool. Phone him, Rosie, I mean it. Did you think about consulting me or Carina? We don't want a guy invading our space. Call him and tell him not to come or you'll be invited to leave too."

"Uh, fine." Rosie tsked, wandering away from her sister. "You're such a drag."

"I'm sorry, Rosie, but you can't just invite a party and expect the rest of us to deal."

"I'll call him, but you've got to promise we'll crank up the atmosphere here. Do you promise we'll have our own party?"

"I have to call Dax, but after that we can—"

Rosie whooped. "Let's have some fun! We'll have some wine and play some music, does this place have a sound system?"

There was a sound system in the living room with state-of-the-art speakers in every room, outside too, which could be individually controlled. But Ivy wasn't going to tell her sister that.

"I can't believe you've only been here a couple of days and you're bored already."

This was the recurring theme of her relationship with her sister who would much rather party than do most other things like have a civilized conversation or hold down a job. Though Ivy had lost her share of jobs too. Maybe it was more than just bad luck, and somehow it was engrained in their DNA that they would get themselves into frequent trouble.

"We're in California! LA is full of hot guys loaded with cash! We're wasting opportunities locking ourselves up out here. We could be in nightclubs, meeting people. Maybe we'd be discovered!" Rosie gasped and began to sashay around the room. "Who would turn down a chance to be rich and famous?"

Ivy didn't want to be the one to tell her sister that at the age of thirty-one she was a little too old to be discovered. Or more accurately that Rosie should be a little too old to fall for that line.

While Rosie amused herself by singing and dancing around the dining table, Ivy finished cleaning up the kitchen. "Go and phone him."

Rosie didn't miss a word of her song, she twirled her way out of the kitchen to the living room. Thank God for the peace, though she could still hear Rosie's singing from the other room.

She was about to go upstairs and phone Dax when Carina came into the kitchen, dressed but still flushed from the heat of the bathroom.

"She's in a good mood," Carina said, wearing a grin. "Is she always so happy?"

"Rosie is the queen of finding her happiness."

"I'm always impressed by people who manage to remain optimistic through their lives. We all have difficult times, but those don't seem to have affected Rosie."

It was an admirable quality. Rosie wouldn't let anyone else alter her mood. Carina retrieved the wine from the fridge and held it up in an offering.

Ivy shook her head. "Please carry on and enjoy it, I'm not much of a drinker."

"You're teetotal?" Carina asked, pouring wine into a wine glass she obtained from the top shelf. "Forgive me for asking, but did you have a problem?"

"With alcohol? No," Ivy said. Carina can't have noticed the glass of wine she'd had at dinner. "I just… I have to call Dax before I go to bed, and I'd rather be clearheaded to do it."

"He doesn't like you drinking. Does he direct a lot of your behavior?"

"You're asking if he's controlling?" she asked, pouring herself a tall glass of orange juice then going outside to sit on the deck with Carina following just behind her.

Ivy put her glass on the glass-top table between two wicker chairs and her feet up on the matching footstool. Carina seated herself in the other chair and held her glass close to her chest in both hands.

"I am curious about your relationship, you're very close and both very secretive."

"Dax is a straightforward guy. His barriers are just higher with you because… he doesn't want to get invested."

"Because I abandoned him once, he thinks I'll do it again. I can understand that. It's difficult to accept your son rejecting you. He holes up in your bedroom and avoids me."

Ivy wasn't sure what Carina wanted from her or from Dax. She complained about Dax's behavior but made no excuses for her own.

"You know, you haven't made your intentions clear. Until you are honest with us, you're unlikely to get any respect from us."

"Us? If I don't have your respect, I won't have Dax's?"

"I think I can be an ally, but I have to believe you'll be good for him. Soon, I'll be leaving, and I don't trust you, so I won't be arguing your case to Dax."

"You don't trust me?"

"When I've asked about your relationship with Bruno, you tell me you don't want to talk about it. So why should I tell you about my relationship with Dax?"

Carina finished her wine then took a deep breath. The sound of the ocean filled the echoing silence between the women.

"It's been a long time since I thought about him and longer since I spoke of him."

"Bruno?"

"Yes."

"Does that mean you haven't thought about Dax?" Ivy asked.

Dax could have used a mother when he was growing up. If he hadn't been abandoned by his parents so young, maybe he wouldn't have been such an easy target for Mauri Stark.

"I thought about him, but I thought he was with Ray." The man Dax thought was his father until Mauri revealed the truth of his parentage. "Bruno was... we were together for almost five years. For a long time, we were happy. He took care of me and made sacrifices for me."

"The dream guy," Ivy said, hoping her disdain wasn't too obvious.

"Oh no, he had his vices and after the bloom came off the rose... we fought a lot, and he didn't like it when I argued back... then the affairs started."

"He slept around?"

"Bruno did what he wanted when he wanted. At first, he made excuses but after a few months of enduring his flirtations he began to act like it was normal. He expected me to put up with his behavior without complaining. The sad part is that for a long time I did."

"Is that why you left him?"

"I found out I was pregnant. When I came home to tell him... I found him in bed with another woman."

Which sounded like it was normal behavior but from how Carina gazed out across the black ocean, lit by only the moon, something was different about that particular mistress.

"Who was it?" Ivy asked.

"Mauri's wife, Winnie," she said, forcing herself to smile and turn. The glaze in her eyes betrayed how real the pain was. Ivy's jaw fell. She wasn't quite sure how to respond to that revelation. Dax had never spoken about Mauri's wife, the mother of Brad and Trystan. By all accounts, the woman had been dead for a long time. "Mauri didn't know, and of course, I couldn't tell him."

"Why not?"

"Bruno warned me not to. He threatened me. I had to agree to keep the secret, Bruno was so angry at me for catching them like I did. The funny thing was, he fought more for her more than for me or anyone else. He didn't want his relationship with Mauri to change, but he also worried for Winnie's safety, for her wellbeing."

"Is that when you left?"

"I struggled because I thought the baby would change things. It didn't. I didn't tell him about it right away, but when I did... he told me to get rid of it, to get rid of Dax... I couldn't do that."

"Why did he want—"

"He wanted to keep seeing Mauri's wife. It would never have worked out between them, she would never have left Mauri, he could offer her a life Bruno couldn't. If Mauri had discovered them... he'd have cast them both out. Neither of them wanted that."

"How did Bruno react when you refused to have the abortion?"

"I didn't," Carina said, lifting her eyes to the moon. "I knew how he would react, and I knew he would force me to do it. I took everything I could, and I left, I never went back."

"That was... very brave of you," Ivy said. "You must have been scared."

"Before I was with Bruno I survived on my own for years. With a child it was... it was difficult and then I met Ray.

He was so good with Dax. They loved to spend time together. Dax was no more than a toddler when I met Ray, but they went everywhere together, like peas in a pod and… Ray made it look so easy."

"So you abandoned Dax? Why?"

Ivy's sympathy for Carina waned when she considered whether she could walk away from her child, the child she had sacrificed for before.

"I… I don't have an excuse. I was exhausted and… things weren't working out with Ray, he loved Dax more than he loved me. I thought it was important for a boy to have a father, that he have that male influence. I had struggled for so long, and was still terrified Bruno would find out I'd had the baby, if he found us… I didn't know what he would do. Ray and I were living in a trailer, struggling to make ends meet and… I got an offer from my cousin, she offered me a job in Boston… I couldn't have looked after a child and worked as well. So I just left…"

Rolls of moisture slid out of her eyes, and she made no attempt to brush them away.

"A child needs a mother too," Ivy said. "Ray sold him off to the fighting circuit when he was eight… I guess looking after a child that wasn't his took its toll on Ray too. Mauri didn't find him until he was thirteen."

"Mauri told me," Carina said, twisting in her seat to reach over and put a hand on the arm of Ivy's chair. "He told me everything he knew… Mauri found out that his wife was cheating, I don't think he ever knew who her lover was. If he did, I suspect he'd have turned his back on Bruno too. Trystan was only five or six when she died."

"How did she die?"

"Mauri didn't tell me," Carina said. "But it wasn't long after he discovered her affairs… read into that what you will."

"You think that Mauri…?"

"I know that he was a ruthless man in his hey-day. Even Bruno feared him, and he had a reprehensible reputation of his own."

Would Mauri have killed his wife for having an affair? Possibly. She'd have to ask Dax. With there being only a year between him and Trystan, he wouldn't have been in the Stark mansion when Mauri's wife died, so he might not know.

"Wait," Ivy said aloud. "There's only a year between Dax and Trystan…"

Carina said nothing to the unspoken question. It would be impossible to know if Bruno had knocked up two women a few months apart. Now she had a secret of her own. Ivy would have to tell Dax; she couldn't know and not tell him. If it turned out Trystan was his half-brother, Dax would go into self-destruct mode, he hated the guy.

In thinking about it, Trystan was nothing like Mauri and Brad, they were both dark haired and had a similar build and work ethic. Trystan was an anomaly. Maybe that came from being the youngest and spoiled. She had no idea what Mauri's wife looked like, what her coloring was, or her upbringing. Dax might.

"I have to call Dax," Ivy said.

Carina caught hold of her. "He's been through so much…"

"Yes, he has," Ivy said. "But he has to know the truth." Except with the bounty hanging over their heads, that maybe wasn't the time to split his focus.

"I'm glad he found you, that you two… that he has a woman in his life who loves him for who he is."

"I do," Ivy said. "None of this explains why you came back now."

"Dax was in his teens by the time I heard that he was staying with the Starks. I thought about approaching him, but I was too afraid of Bruno and what he would do if I tried to get into Dax's life. I didn't know what they told him about me… The Starks are a force to reckon with. If they decided I wasn't allowed to have contact with Dax, they had the means to keep us apart."

"You were worried for your safety but didn't consider Dax's?"

"Mauri has so much money and… he could give Dax a life I couldn't. I didn't know anything about how he was raised or where he was living. I knew the Stark mansion was impenetrable, what should I have done?"

"I don't know," Ivy said.

She didn't know what she would do in that scenario. Ivy had struggled to encourage Dax to stand up to Mauri when he was a fully grown man with nothing to fear. As a teenager, Dax would have been ensconced in the Stark ethos. If Mauri told him to cast out his mother, he probably would have… maybe in the most vicious of ways.

Despite that, Ivy tried to imagine what it would be to have a child in that place. If Mauri took her child from her and Dax, she wouldn't just walk away from him or her without a fight. But she also wasn't the type of woman to leave her son with a random boyfriend when she got bored of raising him.

"So you knew he was there, and you never tried to contact him?"

"I thought it was easier, that he had the life he wanted," Carina said, resting back in her seat and closing her eyes. "There are so many things I would have done differently, that I should've done differently. But Mauri made me think… he told me that now was my time to mend those mistakes."

"He got in touch with you?"

"I was surprised at first when I got the phone call. I was working in an accounting office, and Mauri just called me up and told me that he wanted me to visit. I shouldn't have been surprised. After a few more calls, I agreed. I just got into town this week. I had dinner with Mauri, he told me that he's been tracking me for a while."

Tracking her, made her sound like prey being hunted. Carina didn't seem to be offended or appalled.

"How long is a while?"

"I don't know. But he knew about my life, about things that have happened to me through the years. I don't know if he was watching me then, or if he somehow found out more recently. Mauri isn't the type of man to leave things to chance. He has full faith in what he does and likes to be prepared."

"Were you ever married?"

Carina nodded. "A couple of times."

"Did you have other children?"

Dax could have siblings out there that he might like to seek out.

"No other children," Carina said. "If I couldn't support my first child, it seemed wrong to… I couldn't bring myself to…"

Ivy supposed that was sensible. "I understand."

"You have to believe that it was never my intention to hurt anyone. And when I came back here, Mauri said Dax was married, he told me about his life and I… I was just desperate to meet him, to tell him how sorry I am. I do want to be a part of his life."

How would Dax feel about that? It took a lot out of him to admit his feelings, Ivy was blessed that he chose to be with her when it could easily have gone the other way. If it had, she would be married to Trystan by now. She'd be watching as Dax stood on the side-lines accepting Mauri's commands and carrying on with his life as though they hadn't fallen for each other.

"I don't know if that's possible," Ivy said. "I'll talk to him, but… when Dax makes up his mind…"

Carina's smile faded in again. "Just like Bruno and Mauri too… he's been surrounded by strong men who believe men shouldn't embrace their feelings or give in to any kind of weakness. Bruno used to say that caring made a man less formidable."

"One word of advice," Ivy smiled. "If you do talk to Dax or he does decide to let you be a part of his life…"

"Yes?"

"Don't compare him to Bruno, he won't take that as a compliment."

"No. Mauri told me Bruno was never on board with taking care of Dax. He wanted to leave him with the fighters."

"He was probably worried that having Dax back meant the possibility of you coming back into his life. If you held his secret about the affair…"

"Yes, maybe," Carina said.

The reverberation of a car engine broke the air, and Ivy sprang up. Though they were at the back of the house, the sound carried around to them from the driveway at the front.

"Is that Dax?" Carina asked.

God, she hoped so. If he knew he was going to be back, he wouldn't have bothered calling. Ivy would rather that Dax got his work done and came back to her than he interrupted what he was doing to call. That would cause him to take him longer in completing his task.

Dodging the table and Carina's legs, Ivy went back into the house and through the kitchen. When she got into the living room the front door was swinging shut, but there was no one in the room.

"Dax!" she called out in case he'd gone upstairs, but even he couldn't move that fast.

Shooting across the room, she opened the front door to witness a top-down convertible swinging a U-turn in the driveway. There was her sister in the passenger seat waving her hands in the air.

"Rosie!" Ivy called, rushing out onto the paving stones.

She stopped dead at the sight of the driver: Trystan Stark.

"Vegas here we come!" Rosie screamed and waved.

All she could do was watch the red of their taillights grow smaller as they disappeared down the driveway.

Trystan was the guy Rosie had met? He was coming to get her. He would have no trouble getting past Stark security. Trystan loved to mess with people. Going for Rosie was his way of attacking Ivy and Dax at the same time. Vegas would be a party for Rosie alright, but Ivy knew how Trystan Stark partied there.

THIRTY

"WHAT'S GOING ON?" Carina asked, coming into the living room from the kitchen as Ivy got back inside.

"Trystan fucking Stark is what's going on!" Ivy said, determined she wasn't going to take this lying down.

Going to Vegas with Trystan was the most stupid thing Rosie could possibly have done. What had Trystan promised Rosie to get her to take the trip? Whatever Trystan offered had to be better than the financial incentive Mauri had spoken about using to get Rosie there. By leaving the beach house, Rosie could be forfeiting.

"What has he done?"

"He's taking Rosie to Vegas," Ivy said.

Marching to the stairs, she went up into the bedroom and into the closet. Tossing her and Dax's things into their suitcase, she also retrieved the wad of money hidden under the ottoman during her first stay there. Brushing her hair, she pulled it back and then stuck her feet in her shoes.

Almost ready to leave, she returned to the bedroom to see Carina was in the room waiting for her.

"What are you doing?" Carina asked.

"I'm going to get my sister back before she does

something crazy… crazier than running off with a stranger anyway."

"They met at Mauri's party," Carina said. "They were dancing later in the evening. Maybe they're friends—"

"Trystan Stark doesn't have friends," Ivy said, checking her purse then throwing it over her shoulder. "He has worshippers and groupies. If Rosie tries to deny him—"

"Do you think that he would force her into…?"

"He will force her to do anything he thinks she should do. She hasn't used drugs while she's been here and going there with him… He'll get her hooked again and then, when he's bored, he'll abandon her."

"Maybe he cares about her," Carina said.

"Trystan cares about nothing except himself."

Carina exited the room. Ivy lifted the case onto the bed and unzipped it. She grabbed what she needed from the bathroom and brought it back to the case and pulled a few bills from the wad of cash to put them in her purse. If she needed money, she couldn't whip out a ten grand bundle and hope to be inconspicuous.

With her purse on her shoulder and the case on its wheels, Ivy headed for the exit. Should she leave Dax a note? She hesitated at the bedroom door. Without any idea of whether or not Dax would be back there, she chose not to leave evidence and instead decided to text him from the road. If she called or contacted him, he would tell her to stay put and that wasn't something she could do with her sister in possible peril.

Departing the bedroom, she got downstairs to find Carina waiting at the front door.

"We don't have a car," Carina said.

"We?" Ivy asked. "No. I'm going alone. If you want to leave, do it yourself, tomorrow, Mauri will send a car and—"

"I came here because I wanted to get to know Dax. You said it yourself that you can be an ally. I want to show you that I can be trusted. If you leave here now, you might not come back and… I'll lose Dax all over again."

"Okay." Ivy sighed, she didn't have the time to fight.

"Come if you want, but you have to do what I say."

"I will," Carina said, picking up her bag from the floor. "How do you plan to get there?"

Opening the front door, she noticed the single car in the driveway: the security guys' vehicle. Making a beeline for it, Ivy opened the door and climbed in, happy to find the keys in the ignition. Pulling her case over herself she got it into the back seat at the same time that Carina got into the passenger seat holding her luggage.

"This isn't your car," Carina said.

"Mauri's men won't call the cops," Ivy said, turning on the engine but keeping the lights off as she reversed and started to drive away from the house. "Keep your head down."

The security men wandered around on the property and only checked in at the house periodically. She hadn't seen anyone for a while. Trystan may have called them off so that he could stage his little escape with Rosie.

"How did you know the keys would be in the car?" Carina asked.

"If someone came onto the property, Mauri's men would want to be able to chase them away, and then chase them down. They'd want quick access," Ivy said. "They all arrived together, so this is a Stark company vehicle."

"I don't understand why Mauri sent security; do you think that crime is a problem out here?"

"Kidnap at least," Ivy said, switching on the lights when they got onto the road. But even if security saw them leave, they had no vehicle to follow. "Mauri isn't worried about crime."

"So why—"

"There's a bounty on my head," Ivy said, thinking maybe she should have told Carina that before the woman got into a car with her.

"A what?"

"It's why there's security at the house and why Dax has been gone all day, he's trying to find out who wants me dead."

"That's awful... But why...? Why would someone

want you to be killed?"

"That's sort of what we're trying to figure out," Ivy said.

"You have a full life," Carina said, hugging her bag closer to her chest. "You and Dax must have quite the adventures."

"Not really, it depends what coast we're on," Ivy said. "We prefer to keep to ourselves. But when we're out here, the trouble seems to seek us out."

"Are you afraid?"

"No." Ivy smiled. "No one will be looking for me in Vegas, and I have friends out there who can help us. Rosie doesn't have much of a head start, and Trystan Stark won't be hard to find in Vegas. He's a creature of habit and likes to make an impression. As I said, I have friends who should be able to help us locate him. I just hope we can before Rosie does something stupid."

"Like what? Marry him?"

"Oh, God." Ivy groaned. She hadn't thought about that. Mauri did want Trystan married and maybe if he got high enough, he would be up for it. Rosie would probably say yes because her sister believed any action taken in the name of a good time was justified. "Yes, like that."

"Weren't you supposed to call Dax? Will he worry when you don't phone him?"

"I'll phone him when we get there," Ivy said. "I'm more concerned about the welfare of the person who tells him we're not at the beach house anymore… I was supposed to be there laying low."

"So he'll worry for your safety," Carina said. "Maybe you should call him now."

"Wait until we've crossed state lines, that way we'll be too far away for him to drag me back by my hair." Carina said nothing, so Ivy glanced over at the woman's wide-eyed expression. "He's a worrier… when it comes to me."

Dax would be furious, but she hadn't been thinking about that when she packed to go after Rosie. No one would find her in Vegas, the friends she had would protect her. All she wanted to do was find Rosie. Once her sister was away from Trystan Stark, they would all return to the beach house. That was the plan, and she'd do everything in her power to make it happen as quickly as possible.

DAYLIGHT WAS BREAKING by the time they got to Vegas. Despite Ivy's attempts to call her sister, Rosie never picked up. After the tenth time, the phone started to go straight to voicemail without ringing first. Either Rosie had turned off her phone or the battery had died. There was still a chance Rosie had left her cell at the beach house meaning calling was pointless anyway.

Rosie and Trystan would be at the GoldSpring Hotel because that was where the Starks always stayed when they were in Vegas. Her instinct was to drive straight there and snatch her sister up. Except without a keycard or invitation, getting into the suite would be impossible. To get a keycard, they'd need a room, which would require a credit card. She couldn't risk using her credit card or being seen in the hotel. Anyone who might have tailed them from LA would find her in no time.

Trying to consider the bounty and be sensible about not walking into danger, the only safe place she could think of was Saul's house. Pulling into his driveway, she ran her fingers through her hair and used the rearview to check her eyes weren't too bloodshot. Scaring the guy wouldn't get them anywhere. Satisfied, she reached for the door release.

"Stay here," she said to Carina and got out of the car.

She had to knock on the door a dozen times before Saul answered. This was Vegas, the party had probably only ended a couple of hours ago. His hair was a mess, and he was wearing only boxer shorts.

Ivy grinned when he opened the door, trying to act as though it was just a normal, everyday visit. "Hey."

"Ivy…" he said and cleared his throat a few times. "I thought you were… I didn't know you were… didn't you leave?"

"I did," Ivy said, patting his chest and edging him aside. "I have a helluva story to tell you, can I come in?"

She was already inching around him, so he backed off while nodding. Getting him while he was still in a daze meant it took him longer to realize her inconvenient intrusion.

Working her way through the house to the kitchen at the back of the property, Ivy started making coffee to offer the pick-me-up as an olive branch. She was a good half-minute into the task before Saul came through to join her.

Seating himself at his breakfast bar, he finger-combed his hair and coughed. "What's going on? Why are you here so early?"

"I just got in," Ivy said, scooping more coffee than usual into the machine. "I just drove in from LA."

"Why? And where is Harrow?"

"Still in LA," she said, closing the coffee machine and spinning around to smile at him again. "I sort of need a place to stay, just for a day."

"A day?"

"Yeah," she said. "I was staying in LA with my sister, and she did something crazy... She took off with this guy, who is bad news, and came here to Vegas."

"Your sister?" he asked. "You never talked about her."

He kept blinking and yawning, following the conversation must be difficult when you were still half asleep.

"No," she said, "because I haven't seen her for a while."

"Then why do you care about what she does?"

"This particular guy could get her into a lot of trouble, and I just can't let that happen. So I had to come and stop it."

"Why didn't you go to a hotel? You did that last time you showed up."

"That's the thing," she said, creeping across the kitchen. "There's a bounty on my head."

His eyes landed on her, the yawning and blinking stopped. She smiled, hoping to encourage his understanding, but it still took a few seconds for him to react.

Licking his lips, Saul spoke in a dull tone. "Let me get this right," he said. "You were staying with your sister?"

"Yes."

"She took off with a creep, and you followed her here to Vegas?"

"Yes."

"But you can't go to a hotel because there's a bounty on your head?"

"That's right," Ivy said.

"Hmm," he said and pushed up to his feet. "I'm going back to bed."

"What? No!"

"This is obviously a dream, or I've slipped into a coma or something."

"No!" Ivy said. Leaping past the breakfast bar to grab his arm, she pulled him around to face her.

Just then a tiny brunette wearing a man's tee-shirt entered. "Oh," the brunette said. "Who's she?"

"This is Ivy," Saul said, pushing Ivy's hand away from his arm. Touching him didn't look good, so she let go and moved away. "Ivy, this is… uh…"

No need to worry about breaking up his deep and meaningful relationship if he couldn't even remember the girl's name.

"Brittany," the brunette said.

"Right," Saul said. "This is Brittany, Ivy, Brittany."

"Nice to meet you," Ivy said, reaching over to shake the girl's hand. "I'm sorry to interrupt your morning, but I… Saul and I are old friends."

"Whatever, I'm going to shower," the brunette said, scowling

She spun around and disappeared back the way she'd come.

"She's cute," Ivy said.

"I have great taste in women," Saul said.

Ivy laughed. "Yeah, I suppose that you do."

"Look, Ive, I'm sorry you're mixed up in some shit, but Harrow will kill me dead if he finds you here."

"I imagine he's already on his way," Ivy said.

She hadn't checked her messages but had read Dax's name twice on her phone screen. He'd certainly texted her. Ivy hadn't gone so far as to open the texts. They sure wouldn't be random, "*thinking of you*" messages.

"Exactly my point," Saul said and tried to walk away.

Ivy put herself in front of him. "He'll be grateful," she said to his glare. "No, really, Dax knows about the bounty, he's been trying to figure it out. I can't go to a hotel because it's not safe, but if you kick me out, that's where I'll have to go. If Dax finds out you've sent me into danger, how happy do you think he'll be?"

Saul thought about it for a second then lifted his hand and growled out loud. "Okay, fine, damn you. Stay if you want... Let me go and talk to Brittany."

"Okay. I'll get his mom."

She turned, but Saul snatched her shoulder to pull her back. "Whose mom?"

"Dax's," she said. "It's a long story and not important right now."

"You want to move in here with your mother-in-law?"

"I'm not moving in, don't be dramatic. We just need somewhere to freshen up and make phone calls. It would be great to sleep for a couple of hours too. The sooner I find out where Rosie is, the sooner we can get out of here."

"The sooner, the better," he said. "And don't accuse me of being dramatic, you're a fucking wanted woman, I'm one step away from harboring a fugitive."

"Don't be stupid, the cops aren't looking for me."

Saul folded his arms. "Yeah? So this bounty, someone wants you dead, right?"

"Yeah."

"Is it a big bounty?"

"Half a mill."

Saul whistled. "So every gangster and his bitch are going to be looking for you... I'd rather hide you from the cops."

"They won't look here. I'm wanted in LA."

"Yeah, 'cause that's a million miles away."

"Go and talk to your woman, then call the GoldSpring and find out if they have a reservation for Stark."

"I'm playing secretary again?" he asked.

"Not so much fun when someone else is calling the shots, is it?" she asked and spun around to get Carina from the car.

Saul was being nice, and he didn't have to be. He could've kicked them out, though what she had said about Dax was true. If she got hurt in an unsafe place because Saul hadn't offered a sanctuary, Dax would visit his wrath on the nearest person. Her husband was just looking for an excuse to beat on Saul anyway.

After retrieving Carina from the car, Ivy took her into the spare bedroom and set her up in the adjoining shower room. While Carina was busy freshening up, Ivy sat on the bed and opened the first message on her phone.

I'm thinking about collecting the bounty myself. Are you fucking insane? Where are you?

Someone had to have told Dax the cars left the beach house. Either he was told by phone while investigating in LA, or he showed up at the beach house and got the skinny on why the place was empty.

Much as Ivy knew he'd be mad no matter how he found out, she hoped he'd been called in LA. If he'd gotten all the way to the beach house before finding out, it would be worse for everyone involved. He would already be tired and hoping to slip into bed with his willing wife. Finding out that everyone had fled would have riled him.

She was holding her breath when she opened the second text.

Vegas. Again? On my way.

What she'd said to Saul had been right on the money: Dax was on his way, and he was pissed. She fired off a quick message to tell Dax where they were. Holding her phone, she waited for it to ring. Dax wouldn't be happy she was hanging out with an ex-boyfriend. Again.

The timestamp on Dax's second message was two hours ago, meaning he was probably still a couple of hours away if he was driving. Through the wall, the muffled voices of Saul and Brittany rose. If her cellphone didn't ring, she'd give the couple another two minutes then go through and apologize to Brittany. Hopefully distracting her for long enough to let Saul make the GoldSpring call.

If Saul confirmed Trystan and Rosie were at the GoldSpring, she could ride over there and persuade her sister to come back with her. Best case scenario, by the time Dax arrived, the problem would be resolved. Then they could all go back to LA as one happy family.

As predicted, her cellphone began to buzz in her hand, and she widened her smile before she picked up.

Squeezing her eyes shut, Ivy braced herself for his reaction. "Hey, sexy man, how are you?"

"You know I could do a lot with half a million dollars," Dax said. "Maybe I'll kill you myself and pick up the bounty. I could find myself a nice easy woman who'd be happy to stay chained to my radiator for the rest of her life."

"You're a true romantic at heart, Dax," she said.

"I can't fucking believe you did this. I said you wouldn't be safe in Vegas."

"We don't know that. I came to Saul's because no one will look for me here. We've figured out whoever put up the bounty knows me through you, through the fighting circuit, so there's no way that they'll know anything about Saul."

"He's an ex, all they have to do is ask a few questions and—"

"We had to come. I couldn't leave Rosie here with Trystan, you know what he's like…" She got up and wandered to the bedroom window to look out on Saul's pool and shed. "Who told you we'd left?"

"I was at Mauri's when he got a call security at the beach house had been left stranded. Someone had to go pick them up because someone else stole their car. That was when they said Trystan had come to the beach house and taken off with one of the women."

"You know what he's like, Rosie was already drunk,

and now he's brought her here to Vegas. If he asks her to take drugs… I don't want her to get mixed up in that again, he'll drop her as soon as he's bored." Ivy lowered her voice. "Rosie only came here, only met Trystan because of us. God only knows what he'll do to her, she'll have sex with him, Dax, and he's never struck me as the missionary position type."

"I get why you're worried," Dax said. "Why didn't you call me?"

"You're already dealing with one drama," she said. "I knew you would tell me not to follow her, but this is my sister, Dax. I can't leave her to a guy like Trystan, I had to act. You don't have to come out here to Vegas, I appreciate you're on your way, but I can handle this. You stay in LA and—"

"And what? Track down the person who wants to kill you?" Dax asked. "Keeping you safe is the priority, remember? I could only be sure you were safe at the beach house because security was there keeping an eye on you. But you ditched them and took off. Again! Not every mess can be fixed, and I'm sorry, but your sister getting fucked up because she screwed the wrong guy is not my problem, you are my problem."

She smiled and returned to the bed. "You've told me that before."

"And nothing has changed," he said. "I am coming there, to you, stay where you are, don't go outside—"

"But Trystan—"

"Is a problem I will take care of because you've forced my hand, understand? You can't go to The Strip. You can't hang out in bars and clubs looking for them. Someone will see you, and you're more recognizable there because you lived there, people in Vegas know you. All it takes is for one person to say your name and you'll have every criminal in the state parked in Saul's driveway, get me?"

"I know you're worried about me, but you're overreacting, I'll be safe here—"

"Okay. Fine. If you think you're safe at Saul's, then stay at Saul's until I get there. I'll come and check on you, get the story and then I'll go after Trystan. What are you planning to do with him anyway? Do you think he'll just hand over your sister and admit defeat?"

"What if she says no to him?"

"You just told me she wouldn't," Dax said. "She's a party girl, so she and Trystan are a perfect match. She'll be fine until I get there. I'll go to the GoldSpring and find her then I'll bring her back to you. After that, I'll be driving you back to the beach house. If I have to crack open the cell in the basement to keep you there, Minx, I will fucking do it."

His worry might be understandable, but that wasn't an appreciated threat. "Don't even joke about that, Dax. I'm sorry I upset you, but… that's not funny."

"I wasn't joking," he said. "I don't give a damn about your memories or about your fears. If I have to do it to keep you safe, to trust you to be safe, then I will do it. I don't care how loud you scream. You're my wife, and it's my responsibility to keep you safe. No matter what lengths I have to go to, I will keep you safe, Minx."

Pushing up from the bed, she rolled her lips and tried to calm her seething, but it was no use. "You fucking jerk, you would, wouldn't you? You would let me rot down there."

"No, I'll come back for you when I've taken care of the threat. But it's the only place I know where there are chains attached to the concrete foundations."

"I won't go, I won't go back there if—"

"If you go to Trystan now alone, he'll bait you. He'll ask you inside and rile you, he'll take pleasure in seeing you upset. He'll ask you to have a drink, you'll say no, but he'll make you a deal, you drink, and he'll send Rosie home with you."

"Fine, then I'll have a drink."

His laugh startled her. "That's what he wants, then it'll be 'have another drink, take a line of coke, take off your shirt, dance,' where do you stop? You gonna get naked for him? Kiss him? Suck him off?"

"Stop it," she hissed. "I won't do any of that. I can't stand the guy. I wouldn't be able to touch him or—"

"Then he'll force you, you've seen it before. You've fought him off once."

"And I'll do it again if I have to, Dax," she said.

Angry as she was, facing Trystan would be difficult. She wouldn't hold up well if he tried to ruffle her. Having Dax at her side was the only way to be sure she would come out of the scenario intact and unviolated.

"I don't know what drugs he has, he could have anything," Dax said. "If he injects you with something, spikes your drink, he could do whatever the fuck he wanted with you while you were unconscious. Do you want that?"

"No," she whispered.

"For all I know, he'll kill you and collect the bounty for kicks. You don't know him like I do, Minx. Please, just wait there, I will deal with Trystan."

"And if he hurts you?"

"I've been looking for an excuse to kill the guy for a long time, maybe today he'll give it to me."

"I don't want you to kill anyone," she said. "I'll wait here, and we'll go over there together."

"Wait there," he said. "That's what I want you to do."

Whether or not they went over there together was a fight they'd reserve for when he arrived. For now, Ivy had given him what he wanted. They would both have time to recharge their batteries and rethink their arguments before they were together again.

"Drive safe," she said, worrying that Dax on the road in a rage might not end well. "I'll be here, at Saul's. I won't go anywhere, I promise."

"Good," he said. "Try not to get into any more trouble."

"I'll try my best."

They hung up. She wouldn't go looking for trouble, but for some reason it always managed to find her.

THIRTY-ONE

ALTHOUGH SHE HADN'T intended to, Ivy had fallen asleep in the second bedroom after enjoying her shower. A hand pushed her bare shoulder, she moaned in protest, but it kept on shaking her.

"Dax," she said, throwing out an arm to toss aside the one prodding at her.

She blinked up at the person sitting on the edge of the bed to see that although she'd still been asleep her subconscious had guessed right.

"What the fuck do I do with you?" Dax asked but didn't expect an answer. Whipping her towel out from beneath her, he stood up to throw it aside, then pushed her onto her back. "I know you like to challenge me, but fucking hell, Minx."

"Can I have my towel back?" she asked, stretching. "Anyone could walk in here."

Digging a hand under her shoulder, he rolled her onto her front and smacked her ass. "Saul told me Carina went for a walk, and he's tied up with the piece of ass he picked up last night. Gives me some time to teach you a lesson."

"Come on, Dax we don't have time for this."

Much as she complained, it was nice to be together again. The sting of his hand on her ass warmed more than just the flesh he'd touched.

Climbing onto the bed, he knelt over her thighs and rested his weight on her. Despite her trying to hit him, he got hold of her wrists in one of his hands and held her imprisoned hands against the small of her back. Leaning down, he swept her hair away and licked the back of her neck, around to her ear.

"We have all the time I say we do, Minx. You ran away from me, again, came here to this place and put yourself in danger. You want to be hurt, you want to be punished, it's the only way I can figure it."

Sitting up on her thighs, he spanked her again, then rubbed his flat palm up and over the globes of her ass. Pushing her still locked wrists higher, he smacked the other cheek then leaned down again, urging the thick length of his denim-enclosed erection into the mounds he was punishing.

"I came to help my sister," she said, biting into the pillow, trying to stop herself from whimpering out the pleasure it gave her to be dominated by the man she loved. "You would've done the same thing."

"The only thing I care about is you," he snarled and smacked her one more time.

Rising on his knees, Dax released her wrists and flipped her over, keeping her inside the triangle formed by his thighs and the mattress. "I'm safe. You can see me, there's nothing wrong with me. Nothing happened to me."

"It's about to," he said, throwing off his tee-shirt, he unbuckled his jeans and took himself out of his underwear. "You think that you can lie around naked in other men's houses, and I'll just let it slide?"

"I fell asleep after my shower; it's been a long night."

"No more excuses," he said.

Still holding himself, he showed her two fingers then lowered them to her pussy. Massaging her clit as he passed it, Dax parted her lips and eased his fingers into her. There was no hiding her enjoyment, it was coating the digits he worked in and out of her.

"We don't…" she exhaled. "We don't have time for this."

Bowing down, he caught her lower lip between his teeth and licked her upper lip before he delved his tongue into her mouth. Their loud, desperate breathing was needed to fuel the fervor of their joining.

Her hands caressed his body, working their way around to his ass, still half in his jeans. He hadn't gotten naked, but already he was pressing the head of his dick into her. Widening her legs, she elevated her hips, begging him to move into her, to fill her now.

Just when she was about to give up hope, believing he wanted to tease her, he eased himself inside. She smiled, touching her fingertips to his lips. His lips parted, and he caught one of her fingers in his teeth. He bit her with just enough force to be uncomfortable, but he didn't break the skin, then he opened to free her fingers and concentrated on pumping his dick in and out of her pussy.

A quick fuck was all they had time for, and he was on his way to climax already, bringing her along with him.

"Yes, Dax," Ivy gasped out. "Oh, yeah."

That wasn't their house, and they weren't alone, but her husband wasn't asking her to be quiet, and she had no intention of subduing herself. With her eyes locked to his, she matched his thrusts, his depth massaged each secret crevice within her sending flames licking up through her womb, to her abdomen and into her heart.

A steady moan pulsed out of her as he took her closer, then just when she was on the edge of the precipice, he kissed her, swallowing the cries of orgasm she released into him. With a few more thrusts, he was right there with her, finishing himself and filling her with his precious nectar.

While she was still glowing and twitching through the aftershocks of orgasm, he rolled off her and flopped down onto his back beside her.

"They're at the GoldSpring," Dax panted. "I called before I got here. They're not in their suite now, so I'll have to keep trying. You're staying here until I've got Rosie, I'll take you both back."

"She won't go with you," Ivy said, rolling to her side and supporting her head with her hand. "She doesn't know you. Trystan won't let you take her either. He'll have plenty of snide jokes about you stealing another of his women."

"I don't care about his jokes and Rosie will come with me, if I have to pick her up and carry her, she'll fucking come with me."

"If you let me come with you, I can deal with Rosie while you keep Trystan at bay. We do make a good team, you know."

"You're forgetting about this stupid bounty. I don't want you out there because I don't want you to get hurt."

"Word won't be out here yet," she said, stroking her fingertips up and down his sternum. "It will be quicker if you let me come. You will draw attention to yourself if you take Rosie against her will. We can be in and out by tonight if we work together."

"You're so sure Rosie will come with you?" Dax asked.

"You can get us a room so we have a keycard. If we take a car and park in the hotel parking lot, we can take an elevator straight to their floor. Who will we come across in a hotel corridor? More than that, who would know to look for me there? No one in Vegas will have heard about the bounty yet. You said yourself word takes time to get around."

They were dealing with the drama caused by her sister and Trystan Stark, then they would have to go back to LA to deal with the bounty and with Maurice Stark. When would she have the time to talk to Dax about what Carina had told her? She would have to, but it didn't seem like the right time to bring up his mother and her history.

"Fine. I'll keep calling the hotel. As soon as we know they're there, I'll set up a meeting with Trystan."

"If they know we're coming, won't they run away?"

Dax exhaled and raised his arm to put it over her head and around her shoulders, bringing her body onto his. "You're missing the point. Trystan only went after Rosie because she was easy pickings and because he knew it would annoy us. He'll agree to a meeting. He'll want to see us running after him and begging for a favor. This is the kind of thing Trystan does to amuse himself.”

“He still hasn’t gotten over his grudge, has he?”

“Doesn’t look like it,” Dax said. “But don’t worry, we won’t have to deal with him ever again after this. I can talk to Mauri; he might send Trystan on a forced vacation of his own.”

Resting her head on his chest, she enjoyed her moment with him. They’d been few and far between recently. Mauri wouldn’t send Trystan anywhere, not while he was sick and could go at any time. But she had to admit that the idea of Trystan taking a long walk certainly sounded like a good idea to her.

THIRTY-TWO

IVY CAME OUT of the bedroom and closed the door. She had come to Saul's place and brought Carina too, yet she'd spent all afternoon in bed with her husband. That wasn't exactly polite. In an effort to be social, she entered the living room. Carina was reading while Saul was seated on a second couch watching sports on TV. When Ivy came in, both stopped to make her their focus.

"Where's Dax?" Carina asked, slipping a bookmark into her book.

"Asleep," Ivy said. "I'll wake him up soon."

"Glad everyone's so comfortable," Saul muttered and switched off the TV.

"Where's Brittany? Do you want me to explain that—"

"That what?" he asked. "That my ex-girlfriend showed up to track down her sister with her mother-in-law in tow? That my ex-girlfriend's husband came to protect her against the bounty hunters, but they ended up screwing in my second bedroom instead?"

Wincing against the obvious annoyance in Saul's voice, she crossed to sit on the couch with him. "In his defense, Dax was still protecting me while we were having sex."

"And I can't say a goddamn word that might upset you or scare you away 'cause there's a good chance your husband will kill me in my sleep if I do."

"Dax wouldn't kill you while you slept, that's like shooting a man in the back, it's not sportsmanlike."

"I'm reassured," he said.

"We appreciate this," Ivy said, reaching over to take one of his hands onto her knee. "And look on the bright side, you're making a new friend. Having a guy like the Ravager on your side could prove to be advantageous."

"The Ravager?" Carina asked, drawing their attention.

"It's the name Dax fights under," Ivy said.

"He's a pro on the underground fighting circuit. My ex-girlfriend married a man who knows a hundred ways to kill a man without making a sound."

Carina didn't exactly smile, but her eyes lit in amusement. Poor Saul was flabbergasted, but he could only accept his fate as it stood, because they needed him.

"We'll only be here a little while longer. Now Dax is here, he'll keep Trystan occupied while I talk to Rosie. I promise, we'll be gone by tonight. Brittany will appreciate a man who treats women right, she wouldn't like it much if you just tossed us out on the street."

"I think she'd have liked that just fine," Saul said.

"You didn't even know her name this morning, it's not as if I upset your great love."

"Maybe, we'll never know now, will we?" he asked then yawned, but it disappeared from his face when Dax walked in and made eye contact with her.

"Time to go," Dax said.

"Already?" Ivy asked, leaping up off the couch and throwing Saul's hand back to his lap. "How do you know that—"

"Trystan called; he wants to meet."

Ivy sighed. "You were right."

"Right about what?" Carina asked.

Dax didn't acknowledge her and wandered off in the direction of the kitchen.

Ivy answered. "Dax said Trystan would want to show off. That he would want to invite us to the suite just to annoy us."

"Brad is such a pleasant man," Carina said. "I can't understand how Trystan turned out to be so obnoxious."

"He's had a lot of practice," Ivy said.

Dax came back to the group. "Come on."

"What should we do with Carina?" Ivy asked, causing him to halt in the doorway.

"She can stay here," Dax said as though Carina wasn't in the room.

"But if we're taking Rosie home, we're not going to come back here, are we?"

"Maybe you should've thought about that before you brought her where she doesn't belong," Dax said.

"It wasn't like I had a lot of time to consider my options. I had to move fast."

"She's taken care of herself for years; she'll figure out how to get home."

He disappeared from the room and the front door closed, signaling he'd left the building.

"What a sweetheart, no wonder you fell in love with him," Saul said.

Ivy ignored him. "Carina, you stay here. I'll talk to Dax and—"

"He won't let me in, will he?" Carina asked.

"Now isn't the time to talk about this," Ivy said. "I need… time."

She didn't like to be rude to anyone, but it wasn't the right time to worry about Dax and Carina's relationship. If she was honest with herself, Ivy still hadn't figured out how she felt about Carina. She wasn't yet sure if using her influence over Dax to encourage him into a relationship he didn't want was a good idea. Carina might be bad news.

Sure, she came across as quite sweet and innocent, but the woman had walked away from her child when he was still an infant in need of a mother. Carina hadn't come back or followed up to see how Dax was. Anything could have happened to her son and what did happen to him wasn't at all pleasant.

Realizing she hadn't yet forgiven Carina for what she had done to Dax, Ivy left Saul's house alone. Going into the thick heat of the desert, she crossed the drive to reach the car she'd driven there.

Dax was in a different vehicle parked behind hers. Though he was wearing his sunglasses, he still managed to glower at her, and she glowered right back. Opening the trunk of her car, she unzipped the suitcase and pulled some bills from the wad of cash nestled in her clothes. Ivy was heading back into the house when she heard Dax exit his car.

"Give me the keys," he said.

She turned to toss him the car keys without knowing why he needed them.

Back in the living room, where she left Saul and Carina, she gave each of them a thousand dollars.

"You, for your trouble," Ivy said to Saul, then turned to Carina. "That should get you home, to wherever that is."

"It's over?" Carina asked. "But I didn't get a chance to—"

"The truth is there's too much going on for Dax to deal with this right now," Ivy said. "If you want to give me a phone number, I can talk to Dax. If he decides he wants to get in touch, I'll tell him to call you."

"A phone call," Carina said.

Ivy shrugged. "It's the best I can do right now."

With the bounty and Mauri's illness, it wasn't the time for an emotional reunion between mother and son. If Carina pushed Dax, there was no way she would get the response she hoped for. Dax would be abrupt, and he could be cold. His only reaction to Carina so far had been to ignore her, that didn't bode well.

Saul got them pen and paper so Carina could write down her phone number. Ivy said her goodbyes and went outside to see Dax enjoying the air conditioning in his car.

He buzzed the window down a couple of inches. "Get in."

Trusting that Dax had switched her things into his car, she did as asked and got in the passenger seat. "Is Trystan going to be a nightmare?"

"Yes," Dax answered. "Your sister knows how to pick 'em."

He backed out of the driveway and began to head toward The Strip. "Ironically," she said, fishing in the backseat for her purse, which Dax had flung in there. "She always went for the bad boys, and I always tried to avoid them."

"Why is that ironic?"

Peeking up from her purse, she smiled at his profile. "No reason, my baby-faced angel."

His scowl made her laugh, and she pulled her sunglasses from her purse. "Okay. So, I'm no innocent, but I'm better than Trystan."

"Hands down," she said. "Rosie just likes the attention. A guy like Trystan, with money, he could take care of her. If he was decent that is. I didn't know they were flirting until she vanished with him last night. Carina said that they met at Mauri's party."

"Why did you bring her? Why would you—"

"Carina came of her own accord. I packed up our things at the beach house and by the time I got downstairs, she was waiting for me. I didn't have the time to argue."

"I don't want you to make friends with her."

"I haven't. I spent most of the time avoiding her. But we did... we got the chance to talk before Rosie took off. I think you should listen to what she has to say."

"So now you know more about where I come from than I do?" Dax grumbled.

"If you'd taken the time to listen to her, you would know too," Ivy said. "Some of what she said was... I was shocked, but... it made sense too."

"I don't want to hear it."

Unsure if he was putting up the barriers just to be bull-headed, or because he was affected by his past, she started gently. "When she was pregnant, she left to protect you," she said, deliberately avoiding Bruno's name.

Though riling her husband then would mean his patience with Trystan would be non-existent. Fine by her. Great actually. Dax had shown Trystan plenty of patience over the years, too much in fact.

"Protect me from what? Getting involved in Mauri's world?" Dax asked. "That worked out, didn't it?"

"She didn't know Mauri had tracked you down and taken you in until years after the fact. She figured you wouldn't want to see her. Carina knows Mauri, knows the people in his world, and if they had closed ranks around you—"

"She didn't try, did she?" Dax asked.

"Did you want her to? Can you see yourself welcoming her? Look at how you're acting towards her now, if she had shown up when you were fifteen or sixteen, would you have fought against Mauri to keep her in your life? Be honest."

His jaw moved, peeved by the direction of the conversation. She returned her purse to the backseat and waited for him to respond.

"Mauri told me that… that he tried to stop me fighting."

"I didn't know that."

"Me neither. When he did, I got aggressive, and that's why he pulled me from school. He let me go back to fighting. That changed things, calmed me down, least that's what he said."

So Dax had been learning things about where he came from. Knowing that sort of made this whole journey worth it. They could have stayed away and refused to return with Brad despite Mauri's illness. But if they had done that, Dax would never have any answers to his questions.

Time had forced him to face up to where he had come from. Mauri had limited time left, and he was the greatest source of information. Bruno would never offer it, if anyone saw him again, and Carina had her own agenda. That being said, Mauri always had an agenda too. This time they knew exactly what it was, to have Dax take over the reins in line with Brad.

"I can imagine you as an angry teen," Ivy said. "All the more reason to doubt you'd let Carina in." Watching the road in front of them, an idea struck her. "Wait a minute, is that why…? You think that because when you lost the outlet for your anger back then that… that's why you thought you might hurt me when you retire from fighting now?"

"Makes sense," he mumbled.

"To who?" she sighed. "Dax. You're nothing like him, and you are nothing like the angry, hormonal teenager you were back then. You've grown and changed, even just in these months since we've been together, I've seen a change in you. You should be proud of what you've become, not fear it."

"I don't fear—"

"Yeah, yeah, you're a big brave man who fears nothing… I'm telling you that I'm proud of you, and I wouldn't have married you if I feared you. You can always beat the shit out of your bag and run as many miles as you want whenever I piss you off. When you give up fighting, we'll find something else to keep you occupied."

"Something else like what?"

"I don't know," she exhaled. "You can teach our boys how to defend themselves."

Taking his eyes from the road, he frowned at her. "Our what?"

"Sure. Now that I know you're not going to turn them into felons, there's no reason we shouldn't have kids." This time it was her stomach that was the focus of his scowl. "No, I am not pregnant… yet. But it's something to think about."

"If I can keep you alive long enough."

"Well, yeah, I guess there's that," she smiled. "I always worried that you brought more to this partnership than I did, you have skills that you get paid for and I just sort of tag along. But having babies… that's something we can do together."

"Okay, this conversation is too weird to have while we're on our way to do what we're going to do."

"Off to threaten together again," she said, sliding a hand onto his arm. "Don't worry, I'm sure Bri and Blaser will babysit if we have to do any threatening back home."

Bri and Blaser were their neighbors and employers in North Carolina. That was a friendship they could trust wouldn't turn into this kind of craziness. It was a friendship that Ivy wanted to get back to as soon as possible.

THIRTY-THREE

THE GOLDSPRING HADN'T CHANGED. Ivy worked there when she met Dax. Not all that long ago in real terms. They'd both changed and been through so much together that it seemed like a lifetime ago.

It was difficult to be there again because it was also the place Trystan had assaulted her. But that was part of the reason that Trystan was happy to keep coming there and spending his father's money. In that hotel, the staff would let him get away with anything as long as he kept coming back to splurge.

Dax parked in the private parking garage, took her out of the car and up in the elevator to the floor of Trystan's suite. With gold carpeting and gleaming white walls, the sweet smell of vanilla flowed down the hallway when the elevator doors opened. It was pumped in, the housekeeping staff had a specific, and large, budget just for the air fresheners alone.

"You stay quiet," Dax said, walking just ahead of her. "Stay behind me."

"I don't care what you do to Trystan," she whispered. "Just don't let him upset you."

"I know how to deal with Trystan."

The suite had double doors and was right at the end of the corridor. When they got there, Dax handed her the car key.

"Why are you giving me this?" she asked, tucking it into the pocket of her dress.

"Because I want you to get Rosie and get out. Don't wait for me. Just go."

"But how will you—?"

"I don't need you to look after me," Dax said.

"We can go back to Saul's and meet you there after—"

"No, go back to the beach house. You'll be safe there. Your things are in the car downstairs."

"I'm not leaving you here with him," Ivy said.

"I'll be right behind you," Dax said. "If it goes smoothly, we'll all be riding back together. But I'll give you cover if you need to—"

"You didn't bring this up until now, because…?

"Because now there's no time to argue about it," he said.

Turning to face the door, he knocked while pushing her behind his back again.

The GoldSpring-provided private attendant opened the door. She was blonde and in the same black and white uniform Ivy used to wear.

"Mr. Stark is expecting you," the blonde said.

Ivy was pleased the attendant didn't appear any worse for wear, but the night was young. The more Trystan indulged, the more unbearable he became. Her experience with Trystan Stark obviously hadn't prompted management to make any changes. Like to ensure that when Trystan was here only males were allowed to act as private attendant.

Though Trystan would probably request a female attendant. When a guest was willing to pay the kind of money that Trystan did, management would cater to their every whim. Trystan knew it too, which was how he got away with his abominable behavior so often.

The rounded window of this suite living room provided a location for couches, arranged to face each other.

The private attendant pointed to the furthest couch. "If you'd like to take a seat, I'll tell him you're here."

The attendant left by way of a side door, behind the bar area of the suite. That was a bedroom back there. Dax threw an arm around her and took her to the couch, seating himself in the corner and keeping her pressed to his side.

Scrutinizing every detail of the room, Ivy's attention eventually came to land back on him. "What?" he asked.

"You're sitting exactly where you were the night I first saw you."

"Don't think about that night," he said, yanking her closer to kiss her head.

"Trystan might have been a jerk that night, but I am sort of pleased things played out like they did. Being with you is the best thing that ever happened to me. I had to go through all the crap I did in life so that when I found you, I would appreciate you."

Bringing her hand to his face, Dax lowered his lips to hers. While that wasn't the time or place for getting it on, she wouldn't shy from loving her husband just because Trystan might comment on it.

It took a lot for Dax to be open with her. Ivy savored each time he trusted her and showed her affection. Spoiling her with gifts and soppy words wasn't where Dax excelled, he excelled in these moments. With the slightest touch, he conveyed how much he valued her.

A door opened, signaling someone had come in. The private attendant appeared first, she nodded and disappeared out of the suite giving Trystan the time to make his entrance. Trystan came in wearing a hotel-monogrammed bathrobe, strutting, and displaying a smile that conveyed his pride in his actions.

He was a handsome guy with sand colored hair and a square jaw. His cheekbones were sharp and still graced with the scar where she had taken a bite out of him to free herself from his assault. But that mark, and the bruise he'd received at Dax's hand, didn't dull his striking looks.

Trystan was taking his time to observe her and Dax, maybe he was trying to intimidate them into speaking first, but he'd never out intimidate Dax. Now she had the time, Ivy tried to pick out any of their host's features that might match Dax's. Carina's story had opened so many possibilities, but she didn't want to raise them with Dax until she could reach a decision on the veracity of Carina's claims herself.

Hearing he might be blood-related to Trystan would devastate Dax. He was still dealing with the idea Bruno was his father. Adding anything new to the mix would send him into a tailspin. There wasn't the time for him to fight his way out of that.

Finding out if the men were related was irrelevant. Dax would still despise Trystan just as much if it were a proven fact. But Ivy didn't like to withhold information from Dax so she would have to tell him that the possibility existed. She'd have to pick an appropriate moment to discuss it with him, and that sure wasn't the environment to be thinking about it.

"Mr. and Mrs. Harrow, what a surprise," Trystan said as he strolled the width of the room.

"You called us," Ivy said, not missing the chance to show him up.

"I heard you were in town, and we are all family, aren't we?"

Trystan settled his focus on Dax, Ivy glanced around to observe the frost Dax returned to his surrogate brother. They would try to stare each other to death all night if she let them. It was about as violent as Trystan would get with Dax; he wasn't quite crazy enough to believe that he could conquer her husband in a fight.

"Where's Rosie?" Ivy asked.

"Still asleep," Trystan said. "We had an eventful night."

When Trystan emerged from the bedroom in his robe, she'd feared what that meant. The glint in his eyes confirmed her suspicions.

"You had sex with her?" Ivy asked.

Dax's hand closed around hers, he must have sensed her desire to leap across the room and throttle the smug bastard.

"What can I say?" He grinned. "She wouldn't take no for an answer."

On coming there, she had worried Trystan would irritate Dax. She hadn't given full merit to how much he'd grate on her. Getting any kind of rise from another person as a result of his behavior was what thrilled Trystan and Ivy was his chosen target.

Dax body blocked her when they both rose at the same time. Breaking her view of Trystan was a relief but that didn't quench her need to see him exposed for the cruel coward that he was. She looked forward to the day that would happen, and she hoped to have a front row seat.

"Since we're all here," Trystan said. "What do you say to a swop? Hmm? Yours for mine, Dax?"

Grabbing Dax's waist, she took her turn to hold him in place, silently reminding him not to rise to Trystan's bait. "Not a chance," Dax said.

"You were happy to do it before when dad suggested it. You were happy to give up your wife to me then, just so you could stay in the family."

Dax started to move forward, but Ivy wrapped her arms around his torso and pressed her breasts into Dax's spine. "He wants to upset you," she murmured into him.

"You didn't tell her that?" Trystan asked. The smile in his voice was the sugar meant to make the poison slither down their gullets. "Yeah, Ivy, it's just one of those things, you know, Stark men share women all the time."

So she had recently heard. If Carina was right, Mauri shared his wife, though he might not have known it at the time.

"It's a good thing that Dax isn't a Stark then, isn't it?" she said, loosening her grip on her husband to slink around his body and into Trystan's view. "He's nothing like you. He's a better man than all of you."

"No way for you to know that unless you agree to the swop," Trystan said. "Rosie's in the bedroom, all warmed up for you, Dax. Don't you worry about the wife, I know just how to get her going."

"Going? Yeah, if you touch me, I am likely to leave you in my dust, just like I did the first time you tried to touch me, remember that? Does anyone ever ask you about your scar?" She pointed toward his face though he was still a good twenty feet away. "Do you tell them it's there because you tried to touch what wasn't yours?"

"I can have any fucking thing that I want," Trystan asserted.

His smile was long gone, he didn't appreciate it when the shoe was on the other foot, and he was the one in the irritating spotlight.

Leaning forward, her ass pressed into Dax, his hands slid onto her hips. "You can't have me," she murmured and widened her smile. "You are a sick fuck who seduced my sister because you thought it would be like having me, didn't you? But it's as close as you will get, Trystan. You will never have me. I will never want you. And you will live the rest of your life knowing you're far inferior to the street rat your daddy always preferred over you.

"Dax was Mauri's number one, and now he's mine too. No one wants you, and no one ever will, because you are a spoiled, pathetic mess still living off your daddy. Women want a real man. You are a joke; you can't provide for a family or protect them. Why would any woman choose you?"

"Your sister did," he snapped.

"While she was drunk and possibly high, we know what you're like. You love to drug your women and take advantage of them. You are a child stuck in a man's body. What are you going to do when Mauri isn't around anymore to protect you?"

"You're a fucking bitch," Trystan snarled.

When he stormed toward her, she didn't recoil, she didn't have to because Dax sidestepped and inserted his body in front of hers.

"You think about touching her and you'll regret it," Dax warned in a guttural tone. "I'll take you to pieces, I've been looking for an excuse to do it for years."

"And how will you explain that to Mauri?" Trystan barked. "You can't touch me."

"I'm not on Mauri's choke chain anymore, Tryst," Dax said. "For years I put up with your shit because I didn't think there was another way. Now I know there is."

The tone of his last sentence was a threat. Just like he'd done on the night they met, Dax had managed to make a threat without using a single negative word. Touching her lips to his arm, she grazed her fingertips down the back of his hand.

"Mauri would take you apart," Trystan said.

"You won't have him to hide behind forever," Dax replied. "You shouldn't be hiding behind him now. Ivy's right, you're spoiled and pathetic. Brad won't tolerate you risking his operation. He'll have way less patience for you than Mauri does. You're going to find yourself in the street without anyone to watch your back."

"I don't need anyone to—"

"Yeah, you do."

"Dad will look after me, when the will is read—"

"You're going to get a shock," Dax said. "He'll provide for you, but Brad will have the power and then what will you do?"

Trystan didn't have an answer. Dax was happy to remain silent and let the truth sink in. When Mauri passed away, he might leave money for Trystan, but Trystan would have no control of the business or the house and other assets. Mauri had offered Dax what he would never give to Trystan.

The youngest Stark was too irresponsible to be trusted with anything that mattered. Maintaining the business and reputation of the family was what mattered to Mauri. Trystan wasn't capable of that while his father was living and around to guide him, there would be no chance of it when the patriarch passed away.

For years, all of his adult life, Trystan had proved the only thing he cared about was himself. His antics had jeopardized the family more than any of their business dealings. Being spoiled and selfish, Trystan was happy to push boundaries and keep taking what he wanted without considering the consequences, or how it would affect the Stark name.

"I should go to Rosie," Ivy said. "I have to wake her so that we can get out of here."

"You're welcome to join mine and Rosie's party, I won't say no to sisters in my bed," Trystan said. "I can handle two of you at once, piece of cake."

"Dream on," Ivy said. "I'm going in there to get my sister back. I'll wake her up and get her dressed, then we're going to get the hell away from here, away from you."

"She won't want to leave," Trystan said. "She came here with me; she'll stay here until I'm finished with her."

"Until you're finished with her?" Ivy said, remaining behind Dax. "Do you think we'll just walk away and let you hurt her? You're forgetting who you're dealing with. We know what you're like. I won't let you pass her around to your friends after you get her high."

"You can't stop it," Trystan said, trying to regain the upper hand, but the arrogance he'd maintained when he came in was waning. "She'll want to stay right here. I can show her a good time."

"A good time? For as long as it suits you," Ivy said. "We came here to get her away from you, and that's what we're going to do."

Trystan wouldn't take on Dax, so Ivy left her shielded position to stand at Dax's side. The tension radiating between the men was so charged she told herself to hurry in retrieving Rosie. A brawl wouldn't end well for Trystan, and she didn't know how they'd clear up the mess if Dax started on Trystan.

Proving her previous point, she walked past Trystan, head held high, and he did nothing to stop her. She went to the bedroom but paused before entering to look back at the men. Dax and Trystan were frozen in their stare off again. If so much as a hair twitched, they'd snap and start working out some of their conflict in typical male fashion.

THIRTY-FOUR

PUSHING INTO THE BEDROOM, Ivy closed the door behind her to make sure that Trystan wouldn't be able to sneak up on her without at least some warning.

The huge room had a full wall of windows displaying the glitz of the artificial city in full widescreen. But it wasn't the vista that interested her, Ivy was focused on the centerpiece of the bedroom.

Crossing to the white and gold sheets, which gathered in waves on the bed, she began to pull them aside to uncover her sister's naked body.

Slumbering with her face pressed into a voluminous pillow, Rosie was out cold. Being in a slumber so deep suggested her sister must have been high the previous night.

"Damn it," Ivy said, giving Rosie a shake. "Come on, Rosie, wake up."

The room was a mess. She scanned around to see if any of the scattered items might belong to Rosie. Clothes were strewn across the floor, so she went to see what she could find. The mess wasn't hers to tidy, but it was a reminder of Trystan Stark's selfishness.

Empty champagne bottles clattered around, hitting each other every time Ivy lifted something to check for Rosie's clothes. She found her sister's underwear but couldn't find a dress or skirt to go over the top of it.

"Rosie!" Ivy called out, catching sight of the white powder scattered on the dresser nearest the bed.

So cocaine had been on the menu. As had lobster and something with a red sauce that was smeared into the carpet beside the fallen room service tray.

A flash of green near the bed drew her across the room. She fell to her knees to try pulling out the fabric, tangled in an electrical cable under the bed.

"God damn it, Rosie!" Ivy said, still fighting the cord for the dress. "Get up, get out of bed!"

A mumbling reply came from the bed, so she was reassured Rosie had heard her. But she had to wrestle with the dress for another minute before it came free. Exhaling, Ivy came out from under the bed and fell back to sit on her feet. Bra, panties, and the dress, it was a start. She would look for Rosie's shoes while Rosie was getting dressed.

For that, Ivy would need her sister to be fully awake, so that she could comprehend what was going on. Using the bed for support, Ivy climbed onto the mattress.

Shaking the slumbering form again, Ivy pulled Rosie onto her back. Her sister groped around for the sheet.

Ivy pulled it away from her reach. "No, Rosie, you are not going back to sleep. You have to wake up, we're leaving."

Rosie's eyes opened the smallest amount. "You're not Trystan."

"No, I'm not."

"Where is he?"

"In the other room with Dax," Ivy said. "You have to get dressed."

Putting Rosie's arms into her bra, Ivy slipped it up to her shoulders, but Rosie rolled onto her front again. "Go away, Ivy, we're having fun."

"Doesn't look like fun to me. You trashed this place. If Trystan ducks out and leaves you with the bill, how do you plan to pay for the room and all this mess?"

Ivy didn't think Trystan would do that, he had the funds to pay for whatever he wanted, and he liked to fritter that money away any chance he got. But making the accusation was enough to encourage Rosie onto her back.

"He wouldn't do that," she said.

Ivy smiled, pleased that Rosie's eyes were open, her face was smeared with makeup.

"Get your clothes on and then we can go out and check that the men are still here."

Rosie sat up, and Ivy handed over the clothes she'd gathered from around the room. Leaving the bed, she went to the bathroom and moistened the fluffy washcloth she picked up from the vanity.

"You should never have run off like that," Ivy called, wringing the water out of the washcloth.

"Don't start lecturing me," Rosie grumbled.

Returning to the bedroom, she found her sister wearing the bra and panties. The dress was proving to be more of an ordeal.

"I'm not lecturing you," Ivy said, sitting on the bed beside Rosie.

Using the washcloth, she rubbed away the traces of last night's makeup marring her skin.

Rosie put up no fight and flopped down to lie flat, closing her eyes to let her face be washed. Glad as she was Rosie was accepting her help, Ivy recognized her sister's exhaustion. All the indicators suggested a come down.

"You know, you should be careful," Ivy said, holding Rosie's face as she washed it.

"Trystan isn't as bad as you think," Rosie mumbled.

"He is," Ivy said. "But I'm talking about your recovery. You didn't use drugs at all when we were at the beach house. You shouldn't use them just because Trystan asks you to."

"He didn't ask me, he offered them and I'm sorry, Ivy, but I like to have a good time."

"This is more than that. You can have a good time without running away with random strangers and using drugs again."

"He's a good guy, and he's not a loser. He has money and—"

"Just because he has money doesn't mean he cares about you. He's using you."

"Using me?" Rosie said, opening her eyes. "Using me for what? Sex? I don't think so. We had sex at his father's big fancy house, and still called me the next day."

So after what had happened in the mansion bedroom, when Dax knocked Trystan out, Trystan had woken up and gone on a mission to seduce her sister. It shouldn't surprise her he would be so callous, but she didn't like to see her sister reduced to a piece on a game board.

"He wants to have sex with you because he knows it will hurt me. He's trying to lash out at me and Dax. We have history that—"

Rosie swiped Ivy's hand away and sat up. "You think a rich, sophisticated guy would only be interested in me because he wants you? Are you jealous?"

"No," Ivy said.

"Do you want Trystan for yourself?"

"Trystan attacked me," Ivy said. "The night he and I met, was right here, in this suite. He was drunk and high, having a party with a bunch of friends. I was working here; I was the private attendant."

"In this place?"

"Yes," Ivy said. "He tried to get me to drink and take drugs, I refused. Then he… he pinned me down and tried to force me."

"And Dax saved you?"

"Not even close." Ivy smiled. "I fought Trystan off and ran. I lost my job because Trystan told management to fire me. He holds a grudge, and he's a bad guy. I know you think you've struck gold, but he'll dump you as soon as he's finished with you. I don't want to see you hurt like that."

"It's not like I'm in love with the guy," Rosie mumbled and returned to fumbling with her dress.

Maybe they weren't in love, but Ivy could hear the hurt in her sister's voice. "He won't make you believe he's in love with you. Maybe he'll try making you feel special, I don't know what he does. What I do know is that if there comes a time when you want to say no to him, he won't hear it. If he wants you to take drugs, he'll make you take them. If he wants you drunk, he'll force you to drink. And if he wants to have sex with you… he won't hear no then either. He could hurt you, Rosie, and not just in your heart, but that beautiful face too… You see that?"

Ivy tipped her head back and angled it to point out the nick of a scar on the underside of her jaw.

Rosie touched the mark and lowered her hand. "He did that to you?"

"Yeah, he did," Ivy said, taking Rosie's dress and untwining the various straps that were meant to hang loose over the back. "And the mark on his face, that's how I got away."

"You left your mark on each other."

"Yeah," Ivy said, opening the dress with wide splayed fingers she guided Rosie's head and arms through the correct holes. "Every time I see his face I think about that night and how grateful I am I got away from him before he could violate me. I can't walk away from this room and leave you with a man I know to be dangerous. I just can't do it, Rosie. If he hurt you… I would never forgive myself."

Rosie wriggled the dress down and pulled her feet out from under the sheet to swivel around and sit on the side of the bed with her. "Why do you care so much?"

"Care so much?"

"Yeah, I mean, it's not like we're close or anything. We haven't seen each other for years."

"Yeah, but you're still my sister," Ivy said, putting an arm around her. "I want you to be happy."

Ivy wouldn't leave any woman in Trystan's clutches, much less her sister. She was too aware of his capabilities and how quickly he could turn on a person. Trystan didn't understand the word "no" and any woman he set his sights on would have a tough time getting away.

This situation was worse because Trystan could turn his hatred and frustration onto Rosie. It didn't matter that it was Dax and Ivy who riled him, Trystan would see Rosie as a way of venting those negative feelings.

"Dax, does he…?"

"Dax would never hurt me," Ivy said. "He and Trystan have history of their own, which is why I don't want to leave them out there on their own for too long. Are you ready to go?"

"Trystan might not let me just walk out of here," Rosie said.

In the sober light of day, Rosie was far more reasonable than when she was drunk. Until all this was over, Ivy would have to keep her sister away from the liquor cabinet in case she changed her mind and returned to Trystan.

She'd left the beach house to retrieve her sister, all she could think about was keeping Rosie safe and getting her away from harm. Ivy was grateful for Dax; grateful he had followed her to Vegas. It was only because of him that she could smile at her sister as they joined hands.

"Trystan can throw all the toddler tantrums that he likes," Ivy said. "Dax is here, and he will have no problem taking Trystan down if he has to. Do you have anything here that you need to take with you?"

Ivy stayed on the bed while Rosie darted around the room to collect her things, there were just a few makeup brushes and items of jewelry, no real luggage. Rosie found her purse in the bathroom and stuffed everything inside, then tucked it under her arm.

"Okay, I'm ready to go," Rosie said. "Wait, where are we going?"

"Back to the beach house," Ivy said, joining her sister near the door.

With Carina gone it would just be her and Rosie, they would have the chance to get to know each other again. They hadn't had a huge fight, they'd just drifted apart, each doing what they had to in order to get by.

A clatter from the next room startled the women. Damnit. Leaving Trystan and Dax out there alone for too long was guaranteed to lead to trouble. She wasn't concerned for Dax's ability to defend himself. But she didn't trust Trystan not to take a shot at getting Dax into trouble with the cops for doing it.

Grabbing Rosie, they dashed out of the bedroom and came up short in the living room. Dax and Trystan weren't the ones fighting. Three other men in the room were the culprits, two of whom were wrestling with a cursing Trystan on the floor. The other stood by Dax having a conversation as though the pandemonium on the floor at their feet was normal. That man, the one with Dax, was unmistakable, his height and stature gave away his identity: Serg.

"What's going on?" Ivy asked. Serg and Dax turned. "Why are you here?"

"Mauri sent us," Serg said. "We didn't know your man was here."

"You thought I'd come here alone?" Ivy asked.

"Is he a bad guy?" Rosie asked, pointing at Serg.

The note of awareness in her voice apparent.

"I don't know what he is," Ivy replied. "He's never hurt or attacked me like Trystan has, but I wouldn't say he's warm and cuddly either."

"Mauri heard about the beach house exodus," Dax said.

"He checked out Trystan's credit cards and traced him here," Serg said. "We were sent to bring him back. Mauri's not happy he stole your sister from the beach house and caused you to leave."

"Does he know I'm here?" Ivy asked.

Serg shrugged. "No idea. I just go where he points."

Making eye contact with Dax, she thought of when he had said something similar. "So if I hadn't been here, were you just going to leave my sister with the check?"

"It's been taken care of," Serg said. "We have to take Trystan to Mauri. Dax says that you'll take Rosie back. But we can—"

"No," Ivy said. "I'm not leaving my sister with you guys."

Serg, Trystan, and those two bulky guys lifting Trystan from the floor, might make for an interesting road trip, but it wasn't a guaranteed safe one. Mauri usually put up with Trystan's exploits and then chastised him for them afterwards.

"Dax probably figured that," Serg said.

His men had Trystan up on his feet.

Despite the split lip, Trystan was unharmed, except he wore an expression of thunder. "You set this up, didn't you, bitch?"

Ivy ignored him and kept Rosie's hand to lead her over to Dax and Serg.

"Is this normal?" Ivy asked. "For Mauri to intervene like this."

"No," Dax said. "Never heard of it."

"You've never heard of it because you were his check on the jerk," Serg said. "Mauri didn't have to police him when he had you doing it for him."

That made sense. Dax put an arm around her, holding her body to his. She felt like an anchor, though she wasn't sure what he was trying to hold onto, his anger or his restraint.

"Get him dressed," Serg said to his men who dragged Trystan into the bedroom.

Being told what to do was Trystan's worst nightmare. Although he swore out his objections to being manhandled, he did little to fight the men. That behavior exhibited his true colors, he'd get physical with a woman who he could overpower, but with men who were stronger and meaner, his true cowardice flourished.

Dax's phone rang. He let her go and walked to the window to speak to whoever was on the other end.

"I want to get going," Rosie said.

"We'll wait for Dax," Ivy said.

With Serg showing up to cart Trystan off, they didn't have to worry about travelling separately. Ivy had the car keys but wouldn't use them until she had her husband at her side.

"I'm going to check on Trystan," Serg said and left them to go into the bedroom.

"He's a giant," Rosie muttered, watching Serg go. "Do you think he's giant everywhere?"

Drawing her eyes to her curious sister, Ivy laughed. "Haven't you learned your lesson about strange men? They don't come much stranger than him."

Dax came back, putting his phone in his pocket. "Stranger than who?"

Ivy raised the keys and dropped them into his hand. "Who was on the phone?"

"Mauri," Dax said. "He wants us back at the mansion too."

"He snapped his fingers and thinks that we'll jump? What did you tell him?"

"That we were in Vegas and Serg had shown up to take Trystan home. We have to go back to California anyway, so I told him we'd stop at the mansion."

"We don't have to go back," Ivy said. "Why do we have to go back?"

"Because he says he has your things from Kay's place and until we find out who is behind the bounty and put a stop to it, you're in danger. I want this over before we go back home. Do you want to put our friends in danger?"

Appealing to her about their friends' safety was purely for her benefit. Dax would sacrifice anyone, all their friends and acquaintances, before he would let anyone harm a hair on her head.

"Okay," she said, taking his hand and turning to Rosie. "We'll give you some money, enough to get you wherever you want to go. I guess you're free now."

"No," Rosie said. "I want to come back with you."

"Why?"

"Because I want to know you'll be safe," Rosie said. "You came all the way out here to protect me when it could have cost you your life. Please, Ivy, let me see how this plays out."

"Okay." Ivy exhaled and glanced at Dax. "Let's go back to California."

Dax had responsibility for two women, but it didn't seem to annoy him. He'd rather have her and Rosie to worry about than deal with his mother again. So at Mauri's command, they headed out of the suite and down to the car in the GoldSpring parking garage.

It had been their intention to go back to the beach house anyway. It was impolite to use Mauri for his safe haven and then refuse to look him in the eye. Ivy tightened her grip on Dax's hand at the thought of going back there, not because she was fearful of her safety, but because she feared what Mauri would ask of him.

THIRTY-FIVE

"EVERY TIME WE DRIVE up to this place, I feel sick," Ivy admitted, watching the Stark mansion expand in her view as they drove closer.

Rosie leaned between the two front seats from her position in the back to see the house that Ivy was sneering at.

"I don't know why. You've never been harmed here, have you?" Dax asked.

"Never been harmed here?" Ivy said. Her head snapped to the side, taking the mansion out of her view, and bringing her husband front and center. "Are you crazy? The first time you brought me here, you spanked me in the driveway in full view of the house."

"You tried to run from me, and it worked, didn't it? You've never run away from me again."

"Except those seven weeks you spent chasing me across the country, are we forgetting about that?"

"Yeah," he said, bringing the car to a stop parallel to the front portico. "We are."

He turned off the engine and gave her the car keys again.

"Why do I need them this time?" she asked but put them into her purse.

"I don't know what Mauri wants, and you'll feel better if you have an escape route."

"I'll feel better, or you will?" Ivy asked him.

Twisting, he blocked Rosie out by resting his elbow on the shoulder of Ivy's chair, forcing Rosie to return to her slouched position in the backseat.

The back of his fingers met her temple, he stroked his thumb down her eye socket to her cheekbone. "You really don't want to go in there?"

"I hate what they do to you," Ivy said. "I don't want you going in there. I don't want either of us to be here. I would rather be at home, thousands of miles from here, with this in our past."

"We can't run now. If we do, the trouble will follow us."

"I know," she said. "But that doesn't make me any happier about this."

"We hear what Mauri has to say and then we split," Dax said.

"So we can keep the spankings private?"

"Yeah," he said, leaning over the center console to kiss her. "You ready?"

"To play the little woman again, yeah, ready as I'm ever going to be." He kissed her again, then exited the car. Ivy turned to address Rosie. "Keep your mouth shut in there. Mauri prefers to be the one doing the talking."

"I know it," Rosie said. "He gave Carina and me money just to keep quiet on the night of the party."

Bribery obviously worked, because the two women had been silent even as Ivy had been threatened. Her door opened, and she flipped around to see Dax waiting for her.

"Hurry up," Dax said. "Stop yapping."

"I am not yapping," she said, getting out of the car in time with Rosie.

Dax snatched Ivy's hand, so she snatched Rosie's, she wasn't going to leave her sister alone. Trystan would be home, and Ivy doubted he was pleased about what had gone down in Vegas.

Security didn't blink when Dax brought two women into the mansion, their arrival had to be anticipated. This was Mauri's home turf, and he'd had time to prepare for his guests. Despite the fact he'd never raised a hand to her himself, Ivy knew what Mauri was capable of. She didn't trust him and never would.

The route Dax took through the house wasn't one Ivy had used before. She had been downstairs at the party and in a couple of bedrooms, as well as in Mauri's office. This time they went up to the third floor and along a deep red carpet to a set of double doors with gold inlay and matching handles. Dax knocked and stepped away.

"Where are we?" Ivy asked.

"This is Mauri's private suite," Dax said. "Usually he doesn't see people up here. When I was growing up, this part of the house was off-limits unless you were personally escorted. Since we've been back in LA, Mauri has seen me in here."

"He's staying in his room," Ivy said.

It was so easy to forget that Mauri was dying and didn't have the strength that he'd wielded once upon a time. Regardless, Ivy didn't plan to underestimate him.

"I think he's getting weaker," Dax said. "He looked tired the last time I saw him here."

Her husband wasn't a guy who gave away a lot of insider information about his thoughts and feelings. But she could tell by his averted gaze that losing the man he'd considered a father for many years was taxing. Bringing her body into his side, she rested her head on his shoulder. Comfort wasn't an easy thing to give while they were in enemy territory, but she offered it nonetheless.

The door opened and Serg came into the hall. "Go on in."

"Tryst give you any trouble?" Dax asked him.

"Yeah, but it's what he's good at, right?" Serg said.

"Is he in there?" Ivy asked before Serg could leave.

"They're talking in the bedroom." The giant blocked out the females to get back to business with Dax. "I'll follow up on that thing we were investigating."

"Thanks," Dax said and then Serg walked off.

"What thing?" Ivy asked.

"Later."

Dax led her and Rosie into the empty drawing room. An unlit fireplace was the focus of the room and the large portrait above it appeared to be of Mauri, nothing like a narcissist to decorate a room. It seemed more likely that Mauri was Trystan's father as they both shared that trait.

Two armchairs to the left of the fireplace had a small table between them. There was a couch opposite the fireplace, and it was there Dax took her and sat her down.

"Stay here," Dax said and pushed Rosie's shoulders to sit her down as well.

"Where are you going?" Ivy asked, watching Dax cross past the two armchairs.

"To the bedroom, I'll be back."

He knocked again on a different door this time but didn't wait for a reply, he just went straight in and closed the door behind himself. Ivy and Rosie sat quietly until Rosie spoke.

"Do you think that Trystan will be pissed off?"

Ivy couldn't care less about Trystan's mood. "Why do you ask?"

"I don't want a guy like that annoyed at me, what if he comes after me?"

Ivy wanted to tell her sister she should've thought of that before running away with Trystan, but she'd given Rosie enough grief about that choice already, at least for today.

"Trystan isn't a fan of hard work," Ivy said. "Without Dax and other minions around to do his work for him, he shouldn't pose too much of a problem. Dax is on our side, we'll be fine."

Trystan could hold a grudge and when he did, the consequences could be grave. Scaring Rosie wouldn't get them anywhere, but she would be talking to her husband about Trystan's reaction to what happened in Vegas.

Rosie, Dax, and Ivy hadn't had time to disrespect Trystan in Vegas, Mauri had got there first by having his henchmen burst in to drag Trystan home. Trystan wouldn't go after his father. For one thing, Mauri would squish him like a bug if he tried. Father provided son with the money to go gallivanting around to suit himself and Trystan wouldn't risk losing that income.

"Dax is on your side," Rosie said. "I'm not going to be following you guys around forever."

"Don't worry," she said, taking her sister's hand. "We'll talk to Dax later and see what he says about it. He knows Trystan better than I do."

Dax had been the one to warn her about Trystan's tendency to hold a grudge. He'd been working for Mauri back then. At the time, his words were more of a threat than advice meant to protect.

The door Dax had exited by opened. Ivy sprang to her feet when Trystan came in with Mauri in his wake. Much to her relief, Dax wasn't too far behind, but he looked more pissed than ever.

"Hello, ladies," Mauri said, nudging Trystan along to stand in front of the fireplace. The two of them stood together, father smiled while son kept his head bowed. "I apologize for what has transpired over the last day or two. Trystan has something to say to you both."

It took him a minute and a grumble, but he raised his chin an inch to speak. "I apologize for my behavior."

"And to Rosie?" Mauri asked.

Throwing daggers through his eyes, Trystan glared at his father, but eventually exhaled to concede. "I shouldn't have taken you to Vegas."

"I went willingly," Rosie said. "I thought that we were… that there was something between us."

Trystan exhaled such a callous scoffing sound that Ivy glanced to Dax, ready to sic him on the disrespectful jerk. "You were easy, Rosie, that's all I wanted. I spouted off a few cheesy lines, and you fell for them. Talk about desperate. I don't know you, and I definitely don't care about a cheap piece of trash like you. You were a way to piss off your sister and that bastard over there. I used you, and you made it easy. The sex was just a bonus, though it was hardly worth the effort from what I can remember of it.

"They treated me like shit, so I gave it right back. Except even when I treated you like shit, you still lapped it up. I don't give a fuck about you, and I never did, never would. Why would a guy like me want anything to do with a tramp without class?"

"Trystan," Mauri warned. "That is an unacceptable way to talk to a lady."

"What? I'm just being honest. She's no lady. You wanted me to stand here and apologize, fine, I did it. But that doesn't change the fact that Dax and his bitch were the ones in the wrong."

"We were in the wrong?" Ivy said, her urge to lash out overpowered her. "You are a twisted bastard who tried to rape me. You attacked me, not the other way around. You're insensitive and unfeeling; a selfish prick who thinks of nothing but himself. All of you, you were wrong! Trystan, Mauri, Bruno, every single one of you! You hurt me, your friend, Bruno, beat me! You locked me up in that beach house for weeks like a zoo animal because I fought you! Because I said no, you thought that you could treat me like—"

Dax was at her side, pulling her away from the others. Ivy tried to twist her arm out of his grip, but he kept hold of her and dragged her to the far side of the room.

"Keep your mouth shut," he growled from the back of his throat. "This is not the time to—"

"It will never be the time," she hissed, jerking herself free of him.

But he snatched her waist and slammed her back against the wall. With an arm resting beside her face, he used the other to hold her in place, pressing it along her diaphragm.

"Listen to me, Minx. You won't get justice here. At the push of a button, Mauri can have a dozen guys in this room. You don't want me to be fighting my way through them while you and your sister are up here. There's no quick way out and while I'm occupied, you're exposed."

"Fine," she said, pushing his arm off her body. "I'll be quiet."

"Good," he said.

When he began to turn away, she grabbed his face and hauled him close to force his mouth down to hers. Sticking her tongue into his mouth, she used his return caress as a way to get out some of the anger she wanted to aim at Trystan and Mauri.

Arguing with the Starks might be crazy, Dax was right about that, and Ivy didn't want her husband to be hurt just because she had to state her case. But pushing more of herself into this kiss, she reminded him of their future. She didn't want his past to steal him back.

Pulling away, Ivy gasped in a breath and smiled at his confusion. "I told you that they couldn't have you. Don't forget who you belong to."

"Like I could," he murmured.

He tossed an arm around her shoulders and yanked her into his side, the more relaxed pose set her at ease. His frown was still there, but he was showing them he was proud to be owned by her and that lessened her need to rebel against the men standing on the hearth rug.

"Trystan apologizes for his behavior throughout this," Mauri said when she and Dax came to stand beside where Rosie sat. "There have been trials faced by all of us over the last year. Ivy, I am sorry many of the experiences you have had with the family have been negative. You are right. You were treated poorly."

That was an understatement, but Ivy had told Dax that she would be quiet.

"Why did you need us here now?" Dax asked Mauri.

"Trystan, leave us now," Mauri said.

THIRTY-SIX

THE STILL HUFFING TRYSTAN stormed out of the room, probably relieved he wouldn't have to uphold the contrite façade anymore. Trystan didn't know how to be apologetic. He felt no contrition because to do that he would have to first feel humility and compassion, neither of which were in his repertoire.

"Rosie, I apologize to you too, for my son's actions and for his disrespect," Mauri said.

Rosie had been very quiet since Trystan's outburst. "I'm going to get out of here," Rosie said, getting to her feet.

"Rosie," Ivy said, trying to console her sister by taking her arm. "I'm sorry you've been through this."

"No, it's my fault, Trystan was right, and you were too. I shouldn't… I should never have come here. These people have been horrible to you and it's not safe. I'm going to leave but call me and let me know that you're okay."

"I will," Ivy said, giving her sister a hug. "If you want to wait in the car, Dax and I will—"

"No," Rosie said, shaking her head and curling her fingers around her purse. "I can find my way home."

Rosie didn't have to be treated like a child, so Ivy let her go. For all the years they hadn't seen or heard from each other, Ivy assumed that her sister was savvy and could take care of herself. The sad thing she had learned today was that Rosie struggled with her self-respect.

Making herself into whatever her man of the moment wanted her to be took its toll on the once beautiful and vibrant woman. After this was over, Ivy would take the time to reconnect with her sister. Rosie needed to be reminded she was a worthwhile person with several wonderful qualities.

Now with Rosie and Trystan gone, Mauri went to the armchair closest to the fireplace and sat down. She had first met him just a few months ago, and while he didn't exactly look feeble, he did have a less imposing stature and that was as much to do with his attitude as his build.

"These events have upset everything," Mauri said. "I wanted you to come back to California to embrace your role in the family, Dax. Having you at the helm is the best way to ensure the family name remains respected. But it hasn't been smooth sailing reintegrating you into the family."

Dax still had his arm around her, and he guided her down to sit on the couch she had previously occupied with Rosie. "You said you had Ivy's things," Dax said.

She might have expected him to leap straight onto what Mauri had said and disclose what the marital couple had discussed about her husband not taking up a role in the Stark business. Instead, he asked about her things, telling her he wanted to be sure they had everything before he pissed off Mauri again.

"Yes," Mauri said and pressed a button on an electronic panel on the table.

Almost straight away, the bedroom door opened, and a steward came out carrying a blue backpack. Her blue backpack. Showing how eager she was to have it returned, she stood, her legs acting of their own volition. The steward paused beside Mauri, but he pointed to Ivy.

"Return it to Ivy," Mauri said.

The steward crossed to hand it over.

The relief at having it back, at seeing what she feared she never would again, was enough to relax her. She sat back down at Dax's side, tucking herself between her man and her bag, she rested a hand on each.

"Won't you open it and let us know what it contains that was so important to you?" Mauri asked.

At the party, he had implied he already knew which item she valued the most, she was not going to put on a show for him.

"No," she said, hoping her simple answer would be enough.

"She'll open it later," Dax said. "And if anything is missing—"

"Nothing is missing," Mauri said. "Now would you like me to arrange to have Ivy taken somewhere safe while we discuss business?"

"Somewhere safe is at my side," Dax said. "You're not taking her anywhere."

"You know we mean her no harm. I would think returning her possessions was enough to win your trust and show you we are serious about having her in the family as well. We will all have to learn to trust each other if we are to move forward and make progress—"

"We're not going to move forward," Dax said. "Ivy and I have already discussed everything."

"You discuss business with your wife?" Mauri asked.

"I discuss everything with my wife," Dax said. "Which is why I don't need you to usher her out of the room every time you want to say something to me you think she won't like."

"I have a feeling I am not going to like what you're going to say to me," Mauri said, pushing back in his chair.

"Probably not. I'm not coming back, Mauri. It's not going to happen."

"Simple as that?"

"Yeah," Dax said.

"We can't accept that; rejection is not an option. The Stark family needs you—"

"But I don't need them," Dax said. "It sounds like a great opportunity. This time last year, I'd have jumped on it. I'm sorry you're sick. But Brad will never accept my—"

"I can deal with Brad. I will talk to him—"

"And as soon as you're gone, we'll start butting heads," Dax said. "I won't take orders from him. I never respected him because he never respected me. I'm tired of Trystan, he'll cause more problems when you're not around. Brad can't control him, and I won't be his babysitter anymore. And Bruno—"

"Is no longer around."

"Because of me," Dax said, sitting forward. "He doesn't like me, doesn't respect me, and the feeling is mutual. He has the means to ruin the family, he might not do it when you're here because he still has respect for you. But I guarantee as soon as you're not here, we'd be dealing with blackmail and extortion. He knows all the family secrets and unless we give him a position of power or a load of money, he can blow the whistle to the cops or start in-fighting among the men."

"You've thought about this."

"I used to take orders, do what I was told because I respected you, and I wanted your approval. I don't need your approval anymore, and I don't need any part in what you do. Brad lives to run the business, and Bruno can be his problem. There's no incentive to come back."

"You will have financial security for life."

"I'm an easy fall guy, if that's not your intention now, it will be Brad's when he's tired of hearing my input. We don't need you, Mauri, any of you."

"You need us now. We can offer protection for Ivy against these bounty hunters. She is in serious danger. You have to keep her safe, it's your job as—"

"I know what my job is," Dax said. "I'm not going to stop looking for the person responsible for the bounty, and I know how to keep my wife safe."

"You don't have the resources we can offer you," Mauri said. "You can stay here at the house; Ivy will be unharmed. At the beach house, we proved that Ivy's wellbeing is important to the Starks, our security men—"

"Let Trystan come in and take her sister away," Dax said. "Your men are loyal, and they follow orders. But they don't know the history. You would never let anyone know what you did to Ivy, what Trystan and Bruno did, what I took part in. That would bring shame to you and the family and despite all he's done, you still defend Trystan."

Mauri's cool expression switched to her. "You have changed him."

"He did all the work himself," Ivy said. "And he's not changed, he's just a better version of himself."

Dax had learned not to follow orders without question, being with her had taught him he was more than what Mauri and the other Stark men saw him as. Dax knew he was valuable, just for being himself. He didn't have to work for her or run any operation well enough to make her proud.

"You are very lucky," Mauri said to Dax. "I'm surprised you found something real and sustainable in such oppressive circumstances."

"He didn't oppress me," Ivy said. "Dax embraced who I was just as I embraced him. You wanted him to change me, to make me a different person, to break me. But he didn't."

"I never even tried," Dax said, bringing his focus to hers. "No one changes you, Minx."

"Can't mess with perfection." She smiled and rested her mouth on his arm. "Dax has kindness and modesty under that hard-ass, arrogant-as-hell exterior, and those are qualities he didn't learn from you or what you do. We have a new life together, and it's one that won't involve any of this."

"I'm curious," Mauri said. "If he had wanted to return, would you have allowed it?"

"You're asking if she's the only obstacle to my agreement," Dax said. "She's not. I told you I wanted nothing more to do with you before you ever made this offer."

"So why come back?"

"Brad said you were sick, and it seemed like the right thing to do. I was curious too about... I always thought meeting you at that fight when I was thirteen, I thought that was an accident. To find out you were looking for me, that you meant it… You lied to me through my whole life."

"Bruno didn't want to accept you," Mauri said. "He saw you as a threat though I didn't know why. I wanted him to embrace fatherhood. I thought it would change him, make him realize there was a softer way to be. He's often too heavy handed and impulsive. Having a child makes a man reconsider his life, at least it did for me."

"Didn't work for Bruno," Dax said. "I'll never accept him as my father, but I would like to know how you found out about me."

"When Carina was pregnant, she kept it to herself at first. She told Bruno, and when he reacted in a negative way, she fled. At the time, I didn't know that she was pregnant, I found out later."

"How did your wife die?" Ivy asked.

The worst he could do was refuse to answer the question.

His answer was an evasion. "Trystan was only five," Mauri said. "It was a long time ago."

"You found out about her affair with Bruno," Ivy said.

Though she could feel Dax's stare, she kept her attention on Mauri.

"I see that locking you in a house with Carina was not a wise decision," Mauri said. "Why did she tell you?"

"I wanted answers to Dax's questions," Ivy said without admitting she and Dax hadn't discussed his questions. "Carina kept evading my questions. I put it to her that she couldn't expect trust if she didn't show honesty."

"She told you?"

"Yes," Ivy said. "She didn't know if you knew."

"I didn't at the time."

Locking her fingers between Dax's, she filled him in. "Carina caught Bruno sleeping with Mauri's wife at around the same time she found out she was pregnant. Bruno didn't want the truth to come out and by that time he was beating her regularly. He didn't want to have a baby with her, which is why Carina left, to protect you."

"How long did the affair last?" Dax asked.

"I don't know," Ivy said, shaking her head and turning to Mauri.

"I don't know when it started," Mauri said. "I wasn't aware they were together at first. I discovered them together not long before Winnie, my wife, died."

"Did you kill her?" Dax asked without any of the tact or hesitation. "Did you kill her for sleeping with your best friend?"

"No," Mauri said. "Bruno killed her."

That was unprecedented, if questionable, honesty.

"Why?" Ivy asked. "Why would he do that? Carina believed he was in love with her."

"Maybe he was. Winnie who confessed Carina's pregnancy to me. When Bruno found out she broke his confidence, he was angry. After that, when they were resolving their differences, I found them together. Winnie asked me to cast him out, he was violent and unpredictable. When Bruno heard she had turned on him, he turned on her. He was angry and holding a gun…"

"He shot her?" Ivy asked.

"Only one of them could have survived in my inner circle," Mauri said. "Bruno knew that."

To speak of the death of his wife without emotion was chilling.

Dax seemed to understand. "It was one or the other," he said. "You forgave him?"

"It was that or lose him too," Mauri said. "I told him we had to find his child, and we spent years tracing you. Bruno was never interested, but he listened to me. By the time we found you, most of our issues had been resolved."

Bruno might have loved Winnie, but it didn't seem Mauri loved her very much. Maybe he had in the early years, or maybe he stood by her because she was the mother of his children. But facing his mortality, he made no apology for covering up the murder of his wife. Men in his line of work had to be detached.

She was pleased Dax wasn't cut from the same cloth.

"This is why we should remain together as a family," Mauri said. "There is a rich history between us all. One Ivy will be a part of now too."

"Ivy and I want to build our own family, not be a part of anyone else's," Dax said, rising from the couch, taking her and her backpack with him.

Mauri sprang up portraying panic through his expression. "You cannot just leave."

"I can, Mauri," Dax said. "Thanks for… I have a lot of respect for you, and I'm sorry you are sick. This is a time when you need to embrace your family and I'm not a part of that anymore. Ivy is all the family I need."

"We can give you money and security and—"

Dax skirted the couch, taking her to the door, which he opened before he looked back at Mauri. "The Stark trade will carry on without you and without me. Fate will decide how it works out. Take care, Mauri."

Ivy stayed quiet when he led her out of the room and through the house to the exit. The Starks were no longer a part of their life, they would never have to be there again.

The car was still in the drive when they got outside, Dax took their things out of it and left the car keys on the front seat. Looping her purse up over her head and putting on her backpack, Ivy smiled when her husband put an arm around her.

"What are you grinning at?" he mumbled at her as they made their way down the drive towards the gate.

"I love you," she said. "And I'm so proud of you."

"Yeah? You just remember that while I'm trying to keep you alive."

"I will. I don't doubt you're capable of fixing this, not for a second. I have faith in you."

"I'm glad one of us does," he said.

Pulling her closer to kiss her head, Dax guided them out onto the street where they could call for a cab. They'd dispensed with one dilemma. One more remained: the bounty.

THIRTY-SEVEN

THE CAB TOOK THEM to Dax's storage unit to retrieve his bike. There was no point going to a car rental place or even buying a new vehicle, because she hoped that they wouldn't be in California for that long.

"We could just go back east," Ivy said as soon as they got back to Dax's apartment. "Or we could leave the country entirely and take up residence on a deserted island in the South Pacific."

"For half a mill, I know a couple of guys who would still manage to find you," he said as they made their way into the bedroom.

"Do you have a plan?" she asked, leaning on the inside of the bedroom door after it was shut.

"I've been thinking about that since we left Mauri's," Dax said, sitting on the end of the bed, with his feet far apart, he rested his hands on the bed behind him.

"And what have you come up with?"

"If you want me to go back there, to tell Mauri I'll stay and do what he wants—"

"No, why would I want you to do that?" she asked, crossing to kneel on the floor between his knees, resting her head against his leg. "I don't want you going back there, not for anything."

"What he said was right," Dax said. "Mauri can keep you safer than I can, he has the resources and manpower—"

"I only need one man and that's you. For all we know, Mauri wants us to go crawling back, if he's the one behind this—"

"I thought about that," he said, stroking her hair down her cheek. "If he had put up the bounty, he would've shown his hand in that last meeting. He'd have told us he knew something or someone that would make it go away."

"He would've blackmailed us?"

"Yeah. I doubt he'd have come out and confessed to being the one behind it, but we'd have figured it out—"

"When he was magically able to make it go away."

"Yeah," Dax said. "But he didn't, so I don't think he put the bounty up. For one thing, he could've gone higher, made the bounty a whole million or more if he was that desperate."

"So that leaves us with nothing."

"Not nothing. I'm still trying to track down Winlow. If I can find out who was at that poker game, I will have my guy, I know it."

"I can come with you. I can—"

"No, you're staying here, indoors. Outside, you're a walking target. If I'm going to be out there scaring my contacts, I need to know you're safe here. If I split my focus—"

"I'll stay here," she said. "If you promise not to go back to the mansion, not for anything, Dax. I mean it. Even if I drop down dead this minute, I don't want you to ever go back there."

"Why not?" he asked.

"Because they enjoy holding you for ransom. Trystan is beyond hope, and Brad cares only about his own interests. Mauri… I know you still respect him, but I don't trust him. He had that information about your mother and your upbringing, and he never told you any of it."

"He had his reasons."

"Yeah, because it kept you where he wanted you, right there, doing his dirty work. I love you, Dax. I know I encourage you to make your own choices, but please, tough guy, don't sink to their level again. You're better than that."

"I'd make a deal with the devil if it kept you safe."

"And I'm telling you not to."

"Telling me," he said, arching a brow. "You forget who owns you?"

"Not for a second," she said, rising up on her knees. "Did you forget who owns you? I told you they can't have you. Even if I'm dead, you still belong to me."

"Sure, until the first piece of ass comes my way."

Grinning at his attempted joke, she dug her nails into him through his jeans. "That should be your number one reason to keep me alive, 'cause if I'm not around, you're not getting laid."

Slipping both hands under her jaw, he angled up her head to bring their mouths close. "How you gonna stop me?" he asked.

"I'll haunt you and I'll haunt her. Do you think death would be enough to stop me from harassing and annoying you?"

"If I thought it was, I'd have offed you weeks ago."

"You are a clever boy," she whispered and leaned in to meet his kiss.

Ivy thought she gave her husband an anchor. He gave her one too. Making out with him never lost its magic. Using his grip on her jaw, he drew her up, onto the bed on top of him without breaking their kiss.

His mouth was never soft, it was his rough hunger that engorged her, whipped her into the depth of arousal that eliminated all fears and uncertainties about what they would face. Kneeling astride him, Ivy crossed her arms to whisk off her dress then helped him out of his tee-shirt. The jeans were next, and as soon as she had them both naked, she climbed back on to seat herself on his erection.

Time and peril dwindled away as she worked herself up and down on him.

"You see something you want, and you go get it," he said, skimming his hands up her thighs, her hips, over her waist to take hold of her breasts.

"You," she said, clutching his face and lowering herself to kiss him, he rose up to meet her halfway.

Their bodies came together and with his arms around her they switched positions. Dax took over the dominant role of the union to control the movement of their forms. By now they knew how to tilt, when to rise and when to fall. But no matter how many times they made love together, she never lost the addiction to the feeling of him gratifying her. The bulk of his arousal pushed into her without apology for its mass pervading her.

"Dax," she sighed.

His hand came over her mouth, and he locked his eyes onto her. "I'm going to protect you," he panted, still thrusting into her. "No one will take this away from me, and I'll kill any man who tries."

Digging her nails into his shoulders, her body seized around his, bucking up to keep a hold of his dick within her. He pumped on through her clamping muscles and gave her no space to vocalize her relief, but he growled out his own. Whipping his hand out of the way, he closed his mouth over hers, delving his tongue into her mouth, consuming every part of her.

When he was finished filling her with the liquid of his climax, Dax pulled away and pounced off the bed, giving himself no time to savor the moment, leaving her curious about why he wasn't lying with her to recover from his exertion. She was too busy breathing through the tingling aftereffects of her orgasm shimmering through her to move to question him.

As if Dax had somehow known it would, his cellphone started to ring. He crouched to swipe through their clothes until he came across the device.

"Yeah?" Dax asked the phone.

Opening her eyes, Ivy observed him standing above her at the foot of the bed. Because he was still close, she prodded his knee with her toe. Dax snatched the digit and pulled it high, forcing her legs further apart. During his phone conversation, his focus suggested he was watching the evidence of their previous union seeping out of her.

"I'm not on the job anymore, Serg," Dax said into the phone. "I told Mauri that I wasn't coming back… Okay… Great, I'll see you in five." He hung up and dropped her foot.

"What was that?" Ivy asked, gathering the sheet to wrap it around her body. "I can be ready in two minutes if we have to go out, but Serg… what did he say when you told him that you weren't going back to work with Mauri?"

"He said this was personal," Dax said, throwing the phone onto the end of the bed.

Leaving her, he went into the bathroom. Ivy was up and across the room in a flash, leaving the sheet in a discarded trail on the path she'd taken to get there. Dax switched on the shower then retreated from the stall to give the water time to heat.

"I'll grab a towel and—"

"You're not coming," Dax said. "I want you to stay here and stay away from the windows. I'll close all the blinds. If you keep the door shut, you should be safe."

"They could come here, anyone who knows where you live… Word will be out about the bounty now and—"

"Don't panic," he said, taking her shoulders to square their bodies. "I'm going to be as quick as I can. The only way someone will get through that door is to kick it in or blast their way through and in spite of the money at stake here, most criminals don't want to draw that kind of attention to themselves. This is a good block without many shootings. If anyone hears gunshots, they're going to call the cops."

"Great, except I'll be dead by then."

"Come here," Dax said.

With their fingers linked, he led her out of the bathroom, through the bedroom and into the closet. Reaching up to the top shelf, he pulled down a metal box, which he flicked open to show a nine-millimeter.

"Do you know how to use this?" he asked, checking the ammunition, and loading the chamber. "It's ready, loaded, and the safety is off. If you have to, aim and shoot, just squeeze the trigger."

"I've used a gun before," she said, taking the piece away from him.

"I'm not surprised."

"What does that mean?" she asked, the gun fell to her side when her arm loosened.

"I mean you have that kind of personality," Dax said. "I've thought about shooting you a few times myself."

"You don't use a gun; I've never seen you even touch one. Why would you use one on me?"

"I'm not going to hit you, am I? That wouldn't be right."

"But shooting me is okay?"

"I haven't done it yet, have I?" Dax asked.

"Yet?" she asked.

He didn't exactly smile, but his frown was far from sight. He squeezed past her, and she heard him move through into the bathroom to take his shower. She wasn't sure where he was going, but it was admirable of Serg to show such loyalty. That proved Dax's respect among Mauri's men outshone the loyalty they had to the Starks. She just hoped that was enough to help them get to the bottom of this.

THIRTY-EIGHT

IVY WAS GOING STIR CRAZY, it had been an hour since Dax closed the blinds and curtains then kissed her and left the apartment. There was plenty for her to do, she could watch TV and clear out the fridge, or finish packing Dax's belongings ready for them selling this apartment.

No matter what she did, she couldn't forget Dax was out there, in the streets, and a target himself. Anyone who wanted her knew her as Ravager's wife. So they might try to use him to get to her. Dax could take care of himself in a fight, but that didn't save him from bullets and knives.

Ivy was on the couch in the living room, tapping her cellphone on her knee when it rang. She jumped to her feet.

"Hello?" she answered, having not even checked the number.

"Ivy?"

The voice was female, definitely not Dax. The quiver of the tone made Ivy frown. "What is it? Who is this?"

"He… he's dead."

Her first thought was of Dax and the ice of the breath she drew in parched her lips. "Dead?"

"Yes, oh Ivy, I'm so sorry, I… I didn't know what to do. He said I could use the pool, and I came out and… I didn't hear a thing, but there he was on the carpet, in the living room, dead."

"Wait? Who is this? What are you talking about?"

"It's Carina," she sobbed. "I'm talking about Vegas. I'm talking about Saul."

"Saul?"

It disgusted her to feel relief. One wave crashed over her, and she immediately experienced revulsion. Hearing about the death of a man she once loved shouldn't please her, and it didn't, but she was pleased Dax was still alive.

"They must have come in while I was swimming, maybe they didn't see me, I don't know. But he's dead."

"Did you call the cops?"

"I… I called the cops then left, I hired a car and came back to California."

"You're back in California? Why?" Ivy asked, sitting on the couch again.

"Yes, I came back here to Mauri, I… I don't have experience with these things. I knew… I thought maybe bounty hunters were looking for you. I wouldn't have been able to answer the cops' questions, I… I didn't know what to do."

"You're at Mauri's? Now?"

"Yes!" Carina said. "He told me he would keep me safe. We're all in danger now, anyone who has been near you… Saul died because you went to him. That means Dax is in danger and me and Rosie and—"

"Rosie," she exhaled.

Her sister had left Mauri's without any form of protection. Anyone watching the house may have seen Rosie enter with her and Dax, that person could have taken her.

"It's okay. I'm sure she'll be okay."

"Rosie should be long gone by now," Ivy said.

"I hope so, Carina said. "Mauri said you should come here, you and Dax, it's just not safe on the streets."

She had no interest in going back to Mauri's, but if it was the only safe place, she Ivy would have to put her pride and personal prejudices aside. "Stay there, Carina, I'm going to call Dax."

"Call him? You mean you're not together?"

"Just stay there, Carina," Ivy snapped. "Worry about yourself."

Disconnecting the line, she immediately dialed Dax. He answered on the second ring like he too had been holding the phone waiting for it to ring.

"Dax?" she said the moment the line was active. "Carina called, she's back at the Stark mansion. Saul is dead, the bounty hunters got to him." She hated the panic in her voice, but guilt came with clarity. Saul was dead because of her, and the murderers could be right on their tail. "What do we do? Mauri said we should go over there, but—"

"Listen to me, babygirl, I need you to stay where you are. I need you to stay in the apartment."

"Are you coming here? Is everything okay? You sound like... Like you're on a mission."

"I am. It's a mission to keep you safe. We got him. We know who's behind this."

"You do? Who?"

"It's Bruno, babygirl. He's been hiding out at Benny's, worthless piece of shit. Bruno just left there, but we're on his tail. We've got him. This will be over soon. I need you to stay right there. Get naked and get into bed, 'cause when I get home, I'm gonna expect you to be very grateful to me for saving your life."

"Don't flirt with me when you're walking into danger, tough guy. I love you."

Gratitude didn't begin to cover the maelstrom of emotion warring in her now. Her love and guilt swirled together because the danger wasn't over yet. There was still a chance Dax wouldn't make it through this. If she lost him, it would be her fault.

"I can meet you, help you," Ivy said, trying to quell her desperation. "I don't want to lose you, Dax. I can't."

"You won't. Have faith and trust me. Of every time I've told you to stay put, this is the most important one. Please, babygirl, will you do as I say?"

She didn't know where he was or where he was going. But he was asking for her faith; she wouldn't give it to anyone else. Through her life, Ivy had believed she was the only one who would act in her best interest. Altering that mind set wasn't so hard when she heard the hope in his.

"I'll stay here. Just be safe. Come home to me."

"I will. I'm not giving you an escape route because I plan to be at your side again. Soon." The line went dead. She'd been dismissed. Now all she could do was wait.

THIRTY-NINE

BRUNO HAD BEEN ONE of his top candidates, but Dax hadn't wanted to spend the time chasing down the guy until he had a clear lead that indicated him. Bruno could've been sunning himself in Barbados this whole time. He would have loved for Dax to show up ready to take him down for something he had nothing to do with. Bruno would take great pleasure in hearing Ivy was in danger and that Dax had wasted his time chasing a red herring.

But now he knew it for sure. That piece of shit Benny had folded like origami the moment Dax and Serg closed in on him. Benny never had the stomach for keeping secrets, and he loved his face too much to risk having it rearranged.

Bruno put up the bounty after he and Mauri had their fight. According to what Benny said, Bruno got a call from Mauri less than an hour ago, and he was on his way to the mansion. Exactly where Dax was going right now.

He'd promised his wife he wouldn't go back to Mauri's mansion, but this was a one-off necessity. Damn, she better listen and stay at the apartment. Whatever went down next would be wet. He didn't want Ivy to have blood on her hands. It could get messy enough that he'd worry for his own safety; he didn't need to be worrying for Ivy's too.

"I've never seen you this pissed," Serg said from the driver's seat.

It was a good thing he wasn't driving; he didn't have the inclination to stick to any speed limits and if a cop thought about stopping him… He was too in the mood for a fight for that to go down well.

Serg had never seen him so angry because nothing had been personal in the past. When they went after guys who needed to be taught a lesson, it was all business. This situation involved his wife, the woman that he loved, and their future. Someone thought they had the right to take that future from them, and now that someone had a name.

"Just get there," Dax said, judging time and speed, they were less than a minute away.

It wasn't smart to go in ready to combust, but he couldn't calm himself enough to be reasonable. Ivy would tell him to have a plan, to be prepared for different contingencies. In the ring he spent time predicting his opponents' next move and it was never a bad idea to be adrenaline-pumped there.

Security let them through the gate.

Serg drove up the driveway so slow, Dax considered practicing his craft. "Think about what you're going to do before you get in there."

"Fuck that," Dax said. "Stay out of it."

The car stopped, and Dax jumped out. Going straight to the front door, he was happy to dispense with anyone in his way. But there were no guys on the door to obstruct him. Unusual.

He found out why security was absent from the rest of the house when he got up to Mauri's suite. There were ten security guys in there, forming a barrier around Mauri, pinning Bruno to the wall near the door. Carina was on the couch, wailing about something Dax blocked out. As far as he was concerned, Bruno was his prey and that took his complete focus.

Snatching a handful of the first security man's shirt, he hauled him back and decked him. While that guy was rolling on the floor, Dax pulled the other one off and landed a knockout punch on him. Bruno was freed, Dax could hear Mauri's protestations and the thunder of security men closing in on him.

Bruno's smug face deserved a punch of its own. Dax delivered, knocking the man back against the wall with a thud. He'd had to contain the power of his fist because he wanted answers before he ended the man.

"Why?" Dax asked, balling his fists in Bruno's jacket, and slamming him back against the wall. "You tell me, you fucking piece of shit, why my wife was the—"

"The slut's got you on a leash," Bruno said, showing his teeth in a grin. "Here pussy, pussy—"

"Jealous you motherfucker?" Dax asked.

Bringing one arm back, he clenched his fist and thought about how much he'd enjoy ending this bastard's life.

"Wait!" Mauri exclaimed. "Dax, don't!"

"Why the fuck shouldn't I?" Dax asked with his eyes pinned on the grinning Bruno.

"Daddy wants you taking over the organization," Bruno snarled. "That double-crossing bastard needs you squeaky clean."

"He is your father, Dax," Mauri said. "Family is—"

"Bullshit," Dax said, thrusting away from Bruno he turned to face Mauri. "You wanted me as long as I did what I was told. You don't want me now, you don't want me running the racket; you just want me to agree, so you know you still have me."

"You're here now," Mauri said. "This is where you're supposed to be."

"It was you he wanted all along," Bruno said, coming close enough to mutter in Dax's ear. The sound of a gun being cocked made Dax leap back a step, but when Bruno raised the gun, it was trained in Mauri's direction. "I gave you my life, and you favor this piece of shit!"

Dax was forgotten in Bruno's mist of psychosis. Bruno strode toward Mauri. Some of the security men backed off, while others closed in around Mauri. Carina bounced up to her feet, and Dax kept backing away, widening his field of vision so no one could take him by surprise. There wasn't a person in the room he trusted. The only person in the world he did trust was locked up in his apartment far from this danger.

"You won't even face me like a man!" Bruno screamed. "You get these bastards out of here and we'll settle this."

"Dax is your son," Mauri said. "You should be proud of what he's accomplished, he can take over an empire like the one we built."

"We! We built it," Bruno said. "You betraying fuck—"

"Betraying?" Mauri asked. "You slept with my wife for half a decade!"

Dax hadn't been sure Mauri knew that before Ivy brought it up, apparently, he had.

"You forgave that!" Bruno said. "That was years ago!"

"I caught you together, I had no idea that it had gone on for as long as it had. I let you walk away from here alive because of our history and now you do this? You come in here and threaten me in my home! Kill me, yes, you can do that, but it will change nothing. My assets are still bequeathed to Brad and Dax, a bullet will not change that."

"Please," Carina said. "Everybody calm down, someone will get hurt!"

Mauri had been happy to have Bruno at his side as long as Mauri was still running things, but the betrayal of Bruno and Winnie had come out. That had changed things for Mauri. He wouldn't give the reins of all he had built to the man who had stolen his wife.

"Is that why you wanted to take Ivy out?" Dax asked, seeing his chance to get answers. "You found a wife you couldn't fuck?"

Bruno whipped around but kept the gun waving in Mauri's direction. "I could fuck your wife if I wanted to, she's a horny little bitch who likes it rough. I'd fuck that tight pussy, and she'd never come back to your bed!"

Storming over, Dax was ready to finish this; Mauri was shouting, and security had no idea how to act. Until a few weeks ago, Mauri and Bruno had been on the same team. It wasn't so long ago Dax was a part of that team too.

The gun came toward him in an arc and Bruno fired off a round. The bullet went wide, giving plenty of room to duck it. Dipping down, he thrust his arm up to grab Bruno's wrist and twist it down to free the gun from his grip. The gun fell, but Dax caught it in his lower hand and immediately backed away, bringing the weapon up to aim at the others in the room.

"Well done, Dax!" Mauri said with beaming pride.

Dax wasn't interested in his pride anymore, and he proved that by aiming the gun at him.

"You all out of here," Dax said to the security men. "This isn't your fight and take those two with you."

Security did as they were told, taking the two men Dax had hit out of the room with them. Dax had worked with many of them and didn't want to see them sacrificed for the good of the two scumbag men who remained. The drawing room door closed.

Dax waved the gun at the bedroom door. "Go and lock it," he said.

It was unlikely there was anyone in there, certainly anyone who would take a bullet for Mauri, but he didn't want any surprises.

Mauri went over to the door and turned the key in the lock, then he about-faced to saunter back to his place behind his armchair.

"You," Dax said to Carina. "Get up and go stand by Mauri."

"No," Mauri said. "She's not welcome at my side. She has been feeding Bruno information."

Dax glared at Carina, who hovered in front of the fireplace. "He called me," Carina said. "When we were at the beach house, I was so surprised and—"

"And you thought you'd get in on the action," Dax said. "Why not claim the bounty for yourself?"

"She's no killer," Bruno said. "And I wanted to see Ivy go slow, the wait was worth it. I knew she was living in fear never knowing who to trust or when the bullet would come… I went to Vegas, we were gonna get together, and that fucking fuckwit of a boyfriend got in the way."

"Saul died trying to protect you from the man who wanted Ivy dead," Dax said to Carina.

He wasn't hurt or disappointed for himself, he had nothing invested in the strangers. But Ivy would be hurt to hear the woman she'd been trying to trust was in cahoots with Bruno.

"What are you going to do now, boy?" Mauri asked.

"Now it's time to tell a few truths. I'm not coming back," Dax said to Mauri. "I will never willingly work for you. Kidnap me, hold me at gunpoint, I won't do it."

"You would if Ivy was at the end of that gun," Mauri said.

"No," Dax said. "I'd do exactly what I just did, and I'd turn the tables on you. I'll let you walk away from this today but only because your days are numbered, old man. Brad and Trystan can have your empire, they don't want me to be anywhere near it and for once the three of us agree on that."

"So much for the experiment," Bruno said to Mauri. "You were so sure that he would come through for you, Mauri. So sure, that picking him up at that shitty club when he was a squirt of a kid was going to benefit us all, now look at where we've ended up."

The triangle of men scrutinized each other, each waiting for the other to act. All of them were the alpha types who liked to be in control, but Dax was the only one with a weapon, Bruno's weapon. Mauri would have a weapon somewhere in this room, but he wasn't revealing its location, yet.

"Tell me why you put the bounty on Ivy," Dax asked Bruno.

He grumbled but did respond. "Because she's a bitch who took everything away from us! Look at this shit! We're ready to kill each other because of her!"

"Not because of her," Dax said.

"If you had stayed, done what you were told, Mauri would've let us run the show. But I fucked up, my reputation is in the shitter because you had to fall for that cheap piece of ass. Taking her out meant you had no reason not to come and work for Mauri… I was doing you a favor!"

"You're jealous I listened to her instead of you," Dax said. "That's it?"

"She deserves it," Bruno growled. "No stinking bitch is gonna ruin me. I should've kicked you out of that beach house, taken over, trained that bitch to sit, heel, and beg. You were weak, but I could've done it. She'd have done fucking tricks for me if I'd been in charge."

Bruno's wounded pride? That was the reason he'd almost lost Ivy. "You were left alone out there because you were trusted," Mauri said. "You were the two men in the world I trusted more than any other… You let me down, Dax."

"I don't give a fuck about disappointing you," Dax said. "The only thing I'd do differently if I did it all again would be to get Ivy out of there the first chance I got."

"You're a fucking asshole," Bruno said.

"You're gonna call it off. The bounty, it's done," Dax said to Bruno. "Get out your phone and call Benny, you tell him to call off the hunters."

"They want their money, and I can give it to them!" Bruno exclaimed. "I made a mint off this family. Using some of that dough to blast a hole in your fucking happiness is worth it. No kid of mine will be a mushy fucking lovesick pup. You need to be angry, bitter, out to hate the world, then you'll fucking know what it is to be respected."

"I'm not interested in being your kid," Dax said. "Take out your cell and call it off, or I'll put a bullet between your eyes right now."

Bruno's lips squeezed together; he didn't like to be given orders. Dax would guess he'd like losing his life less. Bruno reached into his pocket and took out his phone. Punching in a phone number, he lifted the phone to his ear.

"Put it on speakerphone," Dax said. Again, Bruno grumbled something, but lowered the phone and did as he was told. "You tell him it's over, that Ivy isn't to be touched."

The four of them listened to the ringing until Benny picked up. "Bruno? What the fuck is going on?" The guy sounded panicked; his panted words were rushed. "Ravager was here, him and that big fuck he hangs with, they were looking for you... they know about—"

"I know," Bruno said. "Call it off."

"What?"

"The bounty, it's over, send out word, the girl isn't to be touched."

"Are you...? Are you sure?" Benny asked. "You were sure about—"

"Yes, I'm fucking sure," Bruno said. "Don't question me you little fuck, just do it."

"Okay, boss, whatever you say."

"Happy now?" Bruno asked Dax.

"One more thing," Dax said before Bruno hung up.

"Who...? Who is that?" Benny stuttered.

"It's Ravager," Dax said. "You tell anyone who thinks about trying to collect anyway that they'll have to face me."

"Oh... okay," Benny said.

"You tell them the money train isn't capable of delivering," Dax said.

"What the fuck are you talking about?" Bruno asked probably ready to go on another rant about how much money he had.

"Where Ivy's safety is concerned, I'm not gonna take any chances," Dax said and squeezed the trigger.

The kick didn't move him, he kept his eyes trained on Bruno whose stunned expression froze. Carina wailed and dashed across the room. The phone clattered to the floor before Bruno's body followed and the blood seeping from his head spread on the floor. Carina threw herself down on Bruno and began to sob, but Dax turned his attention to Mauri, uninterested in her dramatic display.

"You're gonna make sure no one comes near Ivy again. You're going to leave us the fuck alone. If I so much as see Trystan or Brad again, they'll hit the deck just as fast, understand?"

Mauri nodded, his jaw slack and his eyes wide, he obviously hadn't expected Dax to shoot the threat to Ivy because of their relationship. Dax didn't care about blood; it hadn't done him any favors. Ivy was his family, his future, and that was all he needed.

Carina lifted herself from Bruno. "Why? Why did you do this? Why did you hurt him?"

"You're a sucker for it," Dax said. "He didn't love you. He heard you were back in town and could give him information. You handed it out because you thought it would gain you his approval. Have some self-respect. Don't ever come near me or Ivy again, we're not interested, you had your chance and it's done."

With one last look at Mauri, Dax went to the door and moved through the house. Numbness took over the adrenaline. When he'd walked out of the mansion after the midnight meeting, he'd thought he'd never be back. His purpose then was to hunt Ivy down. Now he knew exactly where she was and getting to her was all the purpose he needed. This chapter of his life was finished.

FORTY

IVY WANTED TO DO what Dax had told her, but as the minutes ticked by, she began to think up all sorts of terrifying scenarios. He might need her, he might need back-up, and she couldn't sit here doing nothing. So, when she finally couldn't take it anymore, Ivy whipped up her jacket and keys and began to head for the front door.

Just before she got there, it opened. Running into the entryway she was so relieved to see her husband nudging the door closed. But when he closed his eyes and rested back against it, relief became concern.

"Dax?" she asked. Dropping the items in her hands, she rushed to him and began to run her hands all over him. No blood or injuries. The lump she discovered in the front of his jeans made her lift the edge of his tee-shirt. When she identified what it was, she gasped and stumbled back. "Where did you get the gun from?"

"From the man I shot with it," he said, taking the weapon out of his waistband. "It's okay. I'll get rid of it. I just didn't want to leave it at the scene. I didn't trust those bastards not to set me up."

His hand came to the back of her head. He pulled her forward for a kiss, then shoved her aside to go into the bedroom where he began to strip his clothes off.

"Grab whatever you need," he said. "We're getting out of here."

"In a hurry?" she asked. "Who did you shoot?"

"Don't worry about it," he said, throwing the gun onto the bed. "I had to take care of it. We won't have to worry about bounty hunters anymore."

He'd told her it would take time for that information to get out even after it was called off by the source.

"Are we going on the run?"

"They're not going to call the cops, I know too much," Dax said, moving into the bathroom. "I've told you before that Mauri doesn't want anyone looking too closely. The Starks get rid of bodies all the time. It's no big deal."

Ivy followed him and watched him turn on the shower then retrieve a towel from the top shelf above the mirror. "Did you see Carina? Did she say what... what happened to Saul?"

"She was feeding Bruno information," he said, hanging the towel over the corner of the shower screen, then stopping to take her hands. "Saul died trying to protect her. Bruno showed up at his place, I guess he and Carina were going to hook up."

"Saul thought he was keeping her safe," Ivy muttered. "She told me she didn't see who had done it."

"I doubt she called the police about it either."

"Why would she come back to Mauri's?"

"Mauri can't have known she and Bruno were communicating again. Mauri is the best person to go to if you're in trouble. Either Bruno sent her there to set Mauri up for something, or Bruno dumped her and took off, so she went there because she had no other choice."

"Where is she now?"

"I don't care." he shrugged. "I left her there and told her not to contact us again."

Ivy wanted Dax to have a mother he could be secure with. If Carina had so easily succumbed to Bruno's coercion, she wasn't a reliable person or one with integrity. They knew all they needed to know about his past. It was Dax's decision to cut his mother out, so she would support that.

He kissed her again then went into the shower to wash off the exploits of the day. Dax could do no wrong as far as she was concerned. He acted in the best interest of their relationship. His actions taught her just how much he valued her and their marriage. She trusted Dax to do what was necessary, he didn't take pleasure in the suffering of others. If someone needed to be extinguished, it was through necessity not depravity.

"So where are we going now?" Ivy called over the drum of the shower spray.

"Back to North Carolina," he replied. "We have friends there, a life."

"But they know how to find us there!"

"If they wanted to find us, they would. Mauri doesn't have much time and Brad isn't interested in us being a part of his future."

Going over to the shower, she slid back the stall door to look at him. "It was Bruno, wasn't it?"

He'd referred to everyone else. If Dax was going to kill Trystan, he would've done it already. Bruno was the only one left.

"Come here," he said.

Reaching forward, Dax took hold of her wrist and pulled her into the spray with him.

The cotton of her dress clung to her as it absorbed the moisture falling on them. But when he cupped her face and angled her head up to join their mouths, she forgot about her clothes. The negativity that had plagued them circled the drain beneath them.

Dax peeled down the straps of her dress and stepped back to draw them down her arms to expose her breasts. Locked in place with the wet fabric tight around her elbows, she couldn't maneuver, shaking and wriggling didn't free her. When he pushed her back against the wet tile and crouched to bring his mouth level with her chest, she could only experience the sensation of his tongue swirling around her tight, wet peak.

Without the ability to touch him, he took advantage of touching her, cupping, and kneading her breasts until the humidity of the space made her throat tighten.

"Dax," she said.

His body went lower and with it went her dress. Pulling it down, he freed her arms then stripped it away from her hips and dropped it behind him in a sloppy heap, saturated with water. He didn't waste his time removing her panties with any finesse. The frail lace tore away with a single yank and then with the rough fabric still coiled in his fingers, Dax pressed his hands to her and used his thumbs to part the folds between her legs.

"I'm starved," he said, delving his tongue into her.

He squeezed her clit between his lips and rubbed the tip of his tongue up and down. The rhythm of the motion increased. Her hands splayed on the tile, the clack of her wedding and engagement rings against it fed into the frenzy of sensations consuming her. His skillful mouth worked on her. The heat of the shower brought sweat to her skin while it was cleaned in the cascade of fresh, clean steam.

Her breathing grew shallow. "Dax," she said again.

He sprung to his feet, hooking his arms under her knees in the process. Before he was at full height, he was sliding into her. His thick shaft forced its way into the tunnel reserved for his pleasure.

Sliding out, he came back in and kept pumping until climax was inevitable. Hissing out her orgasm, Ivy coiled her fingers into his hair and made him look at her.

"I love you," she said. "Goddamn it, Dax, I fucking love you."

Maybe it was all they'd been through, or the knowledge he'd killed to protect her life, but her love for him came pouring out in a long scream. Her body spasmed into another crescendo of pleasure, and he forged his way in deep to fill her.

Dax lowered her onto her feet.

With the shower still battering each of their shoulders she rested her hands on his chest. "I'm never going to make you sorry," she said. "You picked me. You gave up everything. I won't forget that."

"I won't forget the risk you took," he said. "You didn't have to marry me; you could've run for your life."

"You are my life," Ivy said. "We're going to pack up here, and we're going home, to where we belong."

"Next to you," he said. "That's where I belong."

"You don't have to fight anymore. You won. We both did."

"Well…" he said, taking her hair in his fists behind each of her shoulders like bunches. "Fighting for our lives is done, now we can just fight for fun."

She grinned and rose to her tiptoes to kiss him. "At least until we have some little fighters running around."

"You're hung up on this kid thing, aren't you?"

"Family is important to you. It's time you started one of your own and got it right this time. Maybe we can help each other find what neither of us had growing up."

"What was the thing in your backpack Mauri mentioned at the party? You never told me what it was. Did you check inside, is it there?"

"Yes," she smiled. "And it wasn't something for me, it was something for you and our little fighters."

"What is it?"

"My grandfather's pocket watch. I adored him; he gave it to me before he died. He gave me my morals, taught me why it was important to live right. I didn't get why it was so important back then, but I looked after it like it was the most important thing in the world. When he was sick and came to stay with us, my mother tried to pawn it, but he would never let her. When it came to me, I looked after it, took it from place to place all my life. It's the only possession I valued because it could never be replaced. Carrying that piece of him with me kept me honest."

"And you want me to have it?" Dax asked, stroking his fingertips down her spine to the dimples above her ass.

"Yeah, I do."

"Why give it away now? If it's the only thing you've ever owned that you love—"

"But it's not anymore," she said. "You're the only thing I own now that can never be replaced. I value you more than anything else on this earth. Giving it to you is giving you a part of me."

"I want more than a part," he said, pinning her to the wall. "I want all of you, and I'll fight every day until I have it."

"Oh, Master," Ivy said, sliding her hands up to the back of his neck. "Every inch of me is yours; you own all of me."

"Good," he said, lowering for a kiss. "Get used to it, because I am where you belong."

Thank you for reading this tale!
If you can, please take the time to review.

~

Ask your local library for more Scarlett Finn novels!

~

For all things Scarlett Finn
check out:

www.scarlettfinn.com

RISQUÉ

BOOK THREE

OUT NOW!